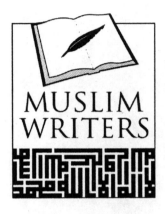

MUSLIM
WRITERS

Also by Jamilah Kolocotronis

Echoes Series: Echoes (Book 1)
Echoes Series: Rebounding (Book 2)
Innocent People
Islamic Jihad

Echoes

Book One of the *Echoes* Series

by

Jamilah Kolocotronis

Muslim Writers Publishing

Tempe, Arizona

Published by Muslim Writers Publishing
P.O. Box 27362
Tempe, Arizona. 85285
USA
www.MuslimWritersPublishing.com

Library of Congress Catalog Control Number: 2006927349

ISBN 978-0-9767861-9-2
ISBN 0-9767861-9-1

Book cover designed by Zoltan Rac-Sabo
Interior design by A.P. Fuchs

Printed in the United States of America

Echoes

Table of Contents

Prologue

When Joshua Adams was thirteen years old he wrote this note:

Dear Mom,

By the time you find this i will be dead.

i'm sorry for my bad grades. i'm to dumb too do good in skool.

i'm sorry for pushing you, to. i hope i didn't hurt you.

You can be happy now. You don't have to werry about me eny more.

your son,
joshua

His mother never saw it. Instead of killing himself Joshua fell asleep. When he woke up the next day he tore up the note and went to meet his girlfriend at the movies.

Evelyn: My Wild Child

*"A child is a certain worry and
and an uncertain joy."*
- Swedish proverb

I should have known something was wrong when he first told me about the divorce. At the time, I just chalked it up to Joshua being Joshua.

The marriage didn't get off to the best start, after all. He had been dating Heather for two years when she turned up pregnant. He was eighteen, she was seventeen. She's a nice girl, from a nice family, but they were so young. Her parents went ballistic, of course, and I wondered if Joshua had married her just to save his own neck. He swore to me, though, that he loved her and he would work hard to make it last.

That should have been my first clue. Joshua never worked hard at anything, except maybe getting into trouble.

He was a beautiful baby—dark curls framing his little round face, and a little dimple in his chin. I hadn't wanted another boy—the first two wore me out—but when I held him in my hospital room for the first time he looked at me, right into my eyes. He stared at me for, I don't know, it must have been thirty seconds. Then, of course, he started searching for his food. And, for a little while, I thought that having three boys would be just right.

We tried to do everything right, starting with a good Christian name. He was christened Joshua Michael Adams on his fourth Sunday of life. Now that I think of it, he cried terribly at his christening. I know babies cry, but Joshua screamed so loudly that my poor Aunt Martha, his chosen godmother, had to cover her ears. Reverend Franklin just smiled tightly and quickly finished the job. Maybe Joshua was trying to tell us something.

I stopped being surprised by Joshua long ago. Sam hadn't wanted another child. I did. We talked about it, and finally agreed to wait until we could afford a house, but Joshua wouldn't wait. Sam wasn't pleased, but I thought he would learn to love the baby. I was ecstatic. I spent seven months dreaming about all the fun I would have with my beautiful little girl.

My water broke, and I went into full-fledged labor a month ahead of schedule. The baby was breech, so I ended up needing a Caesarean. When he finally emerged, healthy and strong, and not too small, I was too relieved to be disappointed about not finally getting my daughter.

I loved my third son from the day he was born, just as I loved my first two. I worried about him because of his early arrival. I fretted over him and held him tight. I sang to him and gazed at him while he slept. I refused to feed him cereal until he was four months old, in spite of my mother-in-law's constant nagging, and I continued to breastfeed him until he was five months old. I dressed him in cute little outfits and I smiled proudly when the ladies at church remarked at what a sweet-looking baby he was. I never once complained when he woke me up in the middle of the night, every night. I was a good mother.

But it wasn't easy to concentrate on my new baby. I had other problems. Even after Joshua was born, Sam remained cool toward the baby. I tried to make him love our new son but he was convinced I had deceived him by having another child without his permission. And Joshua was not an easy baby to love. In those first few months he had it all. It started with colic and cradle cap, followed by a bad case of diaper rash, and then a screaming ear infection. I held him and rocked him, ignoring Sam and his needs.

Joshua was three months old when Sam went to his ten-year high school reunion. I had thought about going, and then begged off at the last minute. I still had almost twenty pounds of "baby fat" and perpetual circles under my eyes (Joshua didn't sleep through the night until he was a year old) and I didn't feel like getting all dressed up to try to impress a bunch of strangers, so I told him to go alone. Big mistake. Cynthia was there. Cynthia, his first love, the girl he'd passed notes to in eighth grade, the woman who had broken his heart about a month before we met. Cynthia, who wasn't married, didn't have children, and still wore a size 5. When Joshua was five months old, Sam and Cynthia walked off into the sunset together, leaving me with two small boys, a screaming infant, and a body which looked like it belonged to somebody's grandmother.

During those early months, I saw the pediatrician more often than I saw my own husband (although much of that had to do with Cynthia). On the night Sam left, I was pacing the floor with

Joshua and his stuffy nose. I didn't notice Sam was gone until sometime the next afternoon, when I found his note on the kitchen table.

I still remember the moment I found that note. Joshua was sleeping, finally, and I went to the kitchen to see what I could do about dinner. The chicken was in the oven when I sat down at the table to relax with a cup of coffee. I saw the note. I sat at the table and I read that note, over and over again. I was still sitting there at that kitchen table, reading that note, when Joshua woke up and started screaming. I let him scream. The chicken burned before I finally remembered to turn off the oven. We all went to bed hungry that night.

I didn't know what I would do. Sam and I had been married for nine years. I had given up everything to be his wife and the mother of his children. I drifted through the next few days, letting Brad and Chris fend for themselves. After those first few days I guess Joshua got used to being ignored, because he finally stopped screaming.

I decided to take charge of my financial survival. Four days after Sam left I dropped the boys off at my parents' house. Then I went back to the insurance firm, where I had worked as a secretary before Sam turned my head, and begged them to give me my old job back. I worked hard, went back to school, earned some promotions, and ended up making a good salary. Enough to get along without Sam.

I survived, but life wasn't easy. About a month after Sam walked out my mother was diagnosed with breast cancer. I know that wasn't Sam's fault, but I have always associated the two events in my mind. Mom struggled for nearly four years before she finally lost her battle. After she died, my father just disappeared into nothing. Six months later his housekeeper found his lifeless body in his recliner, where he had gone to take a nap.

Sam was gone, and my parents were gone. I was alone.

(I do have one brother, Rob. He flew in for the funerals. And once, about ten years ago, he stopped by to see me when he was in Chicago on business. The rest of the time he has been too busy with his life on the west coast to remember he has a sister.)

I had a good job, and I had my inheritance. When Joshua was eight we finally moved out of that little apartment and into my dream house in Lincoln Square. I love the high ceilings and hardwood floors. My house has been my pride, and my sanctuary, for the past fifteen years. But, strange as it sounds, sometimes I sit in the quiet of my beautiful house and think about how I'd rather be living in that little apartment with Sam. And, of course, I wish I still had Mom and Dad.

Sam married Cynthia a day after the divorce became final. At first he contacted the boys once or twice a year. Once, he did stop by with Christmas presents—but he couldn't be bothered to stay and watch the boys open them. He had to get back to Cynthia. After a few years, we hardly heard from him at all. The last time he came to see his boys was a few days before Joshua turned eight. We were still living in the apartment. He screamed at me again before he left, and then he was gone for good. I still missed him, but life was simpler without him.

In those first few years, without Sam, raising Joshua was already a struggle. Once Joshua started walking he was unstoppable. He broke my mother's heirloom vase and nearly poisoned himself with some pills before he turned two. On the day he turned three, he fell down the stairs in our building and needed twenty stitches in his forehead. A few months later, he broke his arm trying to jump from the kitchen counter. When he was four, he started using swear words he had learned from some neighborhood boys. When he was five, he stole a pocketful of candy from the corner store. And he was always trying to bring filthy creatures into the apartment.

He became a little easier to manage after he started school. I received the calls from his teachers, of course, telling me he wouldn't sit still or hadn't done his homework. But he didn't get into any fights until fourth grade. And, that time, the other kid deserved it. It was some snotty-nosed fifth grader who called my son names. Just because he didn't have a father. The principal called me in and told me to control my son. I wanted to tell her to control her mouth. Of course, Joshua was suspended for two days while the other kid, whose father was a police officer, was bandaged and kissed and given a lollipop. I probably should have talked with Joshua about how fighting was not the correct way to solve his problems, but I was angry. And I didn't know, then, that this fight would be the first of many.

While Joshua was starting to give me nightmares, my two older boys, Brad and Chris, were a mother's dream. They brought home good grades, helped around the house, and received stars from their teachers rather than notes from the principal. I don't know why Joshua couldn't be like them. There was just always something about Joshua.

No matter what Joshua had done before, everything became much worse after he hit puberty. That's when he started skipping school, and kissing girls out on the football field. By the time he was fourteen, he was hanging out with a crowd that drank and smoked pot. By the time he was sixteen, he was sneaking out almost every night, and coming home drunk or stoned sometime the next morning. We fought often. He was selfish and irresponsible, and had a violent temper. He had conflicts with almost all of his teachers. I don't know how he finished high school. Somehow, he did manage to graduate. I guess they just wanted to be rid of him.

He had never talked about college, and I'm sure he wouldn't have been able to handle it. I don't think any college would have accepted him. It didn't matter, because a month after he finished high school, Heather told him she was pregnant. She never did graduate.

In spite of the circumstances, Joshua and Heather started out with high hopes. Joshua, who had never held a job in his life, managed to get a position flipping hamburgers. He stopped drinking so much and quit smoking pot. For the first couple years of their marriage, he stayed home with Heather and stopped looking at other girls.

When little Michael was born, Joshua was ecstatic. "He's beautiful, Mom. He is so beautiful," he said as he held his newborn son in the hospital room. "I can't believe that he's mine."

Michael was a beautiful baby, just as Joshua had been. He

looked like Joshua, though he had Heather's little turned-up nose. I hoped he wouldn't turn out to be like Joshua.

After Michael's birth, I began to see a different side of Joshua. One moment in particular stands out in my mind. Michael was a few months old. Heather and I were chatting away over dinner about Michael's progress and how to get rid of those extra pounds. Suddenly Joshua, who had been very quiet, started to cry. I hadn't seen him cry since he was five.

"What is it, Joshua?" Heather asked. "What's wrong?"

"Nothing. I was just thinking about it. I'm a father. I'm somebody's father. And I'm not sure that I can do it."

"Sure you can, Babe. We'll do it together." She rubbed his shoulders and gave him a kiss on the cheek.

But he kept shaking his head, tears running down his face. "I don't know, Baby. I don't know if I can do it."

I sat there, not saying anything. The truth is, in spite of the recent changes in his behavior, I didn't know if he could do it, either. Over the next few years my doubts increased. When Michael was almost one, Joshua just upped and quit his hamburger flipping job.

"It's too boring," he said. He kept the next job, driving a delivery truck, for another year before leaving. Then he worked in a warehouse until he became tired of that, too. At the time of the divorce, he was calling people at dinnertime to sell them aluminum siding or a new phone plan.

He did try. For a couple of years, while Michael was little and around the time Jeremy was born, he worked hard and came home every night. He drove a decent car, cut his hair, and stopped wearing jeans all the time. He had even started talking about taking some college classes. But when Heather told him she was pregnant again, for the third time in four years, Joshua got real quiet. I think Heather was mostly alone during those months.

Little Jennifer was another beautiful baby. She had curly hair, blonde like Heather's, and a sweet smile. They are all beautiful when they're newborn. The trouble is what comes next.

Joshua was at work when Jennifer was born, and he didn't

bother coming to the hospital until the next day. I drove Heather home with the new baby. Joshua was out with his friends.

After five years of marriage, they had three children and thousands of dollars in credit card debt. Jennifer was six months old when Joshua came to my house and told me he had left Heather for the last time. I thought of Sam.

"Is there another woman?"

"No, nothing like that."

"What, then?"

"It just won't work. I can't do it."

"You can't do it? Joshua, you're talking about your family. Those are your children. Do you think it's easy on Heather? She's practically raising those children by herself as it is now."

"Then she should be able to manage without me."

"Joshua!"

He held up his hand. "Cut me some slack, Mom. No more lectures. I'm out of here."

"Out? What do you mean? Where are you going?"

"I'll see you later, Mom." He gave me an awkward kiss on the cheek and walked out, slamming the door behind him. I wouldn't see him again for over six months.

I called Heather a few minutes after Joshua left, but she hung up on me. I think she blamed me for giving birth to the man who was walking out on her and their three small children.

I put down the phone, sat at the kitchen table and wept.

❧

I don't see Heather again for three months. Actually, Michael sees me first. I've stopped for a few groceries on the way home. I'm nearly finished when I hear his voice.

"Gramma! Look, Mommy, it's Gramma!"

I'm reading the list of ingredients on a can of soup when I hear his sweet voice. I look up. "Oh, Michael. How nice to see you. Hello, Heather."

Heather smiles tightly. "Hello, Evie."

"How are you?"

"Oh, we're getting by okay. Your son didn't leave us with much, and my family won't talk to me because I was stupid enough to have three kids with him, but we're getting by."

"Gramma, I can read now."

"That's wonderful, Michael."

"Yes, he's a smart boy. And he doesn't need a father who will walk out on him. We're getting by just fine."

"Heather, don't speak that way in front of the children." As soon as I say it, I wish I hadn't.

"Excuse me? I have to watch what I say, that's what you're telling me? Well, then, who's been feeding these kids for the last three months? Can you tell me that? And who had to get up with Jenny while she was teething?" She's getting louder. "Who takes care of these kids every day and night? Your son," she spits these words, "left us and never looked back. I haven't had as much as a call or a check from him in three months. He didn't bother to show up or even send a card for Michael's birthday. And you think you can tell me how to speak? Excuse me." She turns and walks away, with Jeremy crying and Michael trailing behind, casting me a backward glance.

A few people have stopped to listen. They're leaving now, with a story to pass around at the dinner table. Don't they have enough to worry about in their own lives?

She's right, of course. My son, the bum, did walk out on his wife and children. She's been on her own, and I know that's not easy. I know she's right.

Which is why I'm so angry. What right does she have to criticize my family even though—especially though—she's right?

I wander through the back of the store for several minutes, until I'm certain Heather is gone. I don't want to risk another run-in. Those poor children.

When I do finally go to check out, the cashier gives me a dirty look. God only knows what Heather told her about my bum of a son and me.

After I get home and put away the groceries, I call the bum on his cell phone. I haven't talked to him since the day he left Heather. He hasn't called, and I've been too upset to call him.

Now I am angry, and he needs to be told. He answers after the third ring. I'm glad I didn't get that ridiculous message again.

"Hi, Mom."

"Joshua, you haven't called or come by in three months. What in the world are you up to this time?"

"Just getting my head together. So what's up?"

"Getting your head together? Joshua, I saw Heather and your children at the grocery store today."

"Oh yeah? How are they?"

"Do you care? Heather told me that in three months you haven't been by to see them once. And you're 'getting your head together'? How can you do that?"

"It's not that easy, Mom. You don't know how tough things are."

"Tough, huh? Taking care of yourself, thinking only about yourself. That's tough all right. What's so tough about seeing your own children?"

"You know it's not the kids, Mom. It's Heather. She is such a . . . well, you know. I just couldn't take it anymore. Just a little while longer and I'll be free."

"You'll be free. But what about her? What are the custody arrangements? What about child support?"

"I guess I'll have to pay child support one of these days, but they'll have to take it out of my paycheck, and right now I'm not working so it doesn't matter. And I've already decided that I'm not going to try to see the kids. Heather will do a good job. They're probably better off without me. Anyway, right now I need to be free. No strings attached."

I'm screaming now. "What do you mean, no strings attached? Those are your children. Heather was your wife for five years. Are you telling you're just going to walk away from everyone?"

After a moment he says quietly, "Yeah, I guess so."

"Then I don't have anything more to say to you." After I hang up on him I put a check in the mail. That should help Heather a little. I hope she doesn't return it.

It's been almost four months since I hung up on Joshua. Heather kept the checks—I've been sending a little every couple of weeks—and she called me this afternoon while I was doing my Saturday cleaning.

"Hi, Evie."

"Heather, how are you? How are the children?"

"Listen, I need a favor. I'm going to apply for a new job and my regular sitter can't help out. Could I drop the kids off at your house for a little while?"

I take a deep breath. I don't want to sound too excited. "Yes, Heather, I'd love that."

"It'll only be for an hour or two."

"Don't worry. I can keep them for as long as you need."

"Okay. Thanks."

Twenty minutes later the doorbell rings. Heather is out in the car. Michael and Jeremy are standing there on the porch. Michael is carrying Jennifer, and Jeremy has her diaper bag. When she sees me, Heather waves and drives away.

I watch Heather's car for a moment, and then turn to the children. "Michael, Jeremy, come on in. Oh, you boys have grown so much. And look at little Jennifer." I take the baby from Michael. She fusses. "It's okay, Jennifer. It's Gramma." Michael and Jeremy are still standing there, shyly watching me handle the baby. "Come on, boys. I put some cookies in the oven when your mommy called. Let's go see if they're done yet."

I gently push the tops of a couple of cookies. "Not yet. What do you think we should do while we wait for those cookies?"

Michael finally talks to me. "I brought some books, Gramma. Remember, I always told you I would read to you. And now I can read, all by myself. My summer school teacher says I'm the best reader in the class. Do you want to hear me read, Gramma?"

I started reading to Michael before he could walk. When he was three, he started saying he wanted to read to me. He is growing up so quickly.

"That's a wonderful idea. I would love to hear you read."

He takes out a book from the diaper bag, and we sit together on the couch. Jeremy sits close to Michael and Jennifer begs to go down. I was careful to babyproof the family room before they came, so she is free to explore.

We check the cookies after the first book. They're done. After the second book, they're cool enough to eat. Michael quickly grabs one. Jeremy stares at the plate.

"Go ahead, Jeremy. They're chocolate chip, your favorite."

He slowly reaches for a cookie. When the cookie is in his hand, he almost smiles. Almost.

Michael is nearly finished with the third book when the doorbell rings. "Hold on, Michael. Let's see who that is."

It's Heather. She's wearing short shorts and a tank top. I wonder what kind of job she went to apply for. I decide it's better not to say anything.

"Thanks for watching them. Let's go, kids."

Jeremy runs for his mother. Jennifer stops her babbling and toddles toward the door. Michael closes his book and walks slowly toward Heather.

"Why don't you come in for a minute? Michael has been reading to me. He is such a smart boy."

"Thanks, but we really have to go."

"Heather." She looks at me with a hard expression. I had better be careful this time. "It was so nice seeing the children again. Why don't you all come over for dinner tomorrow night?" What I don't say is, *Why can't things be the way they used to be?*

She looks at the floor. Michael looks up at her. "Please, Mom."

"Oh, I guess we could. Now let's get going, kids."

As I walk with Heather out to her car, she turns to me and almost smiles. Almost.

☙

I wake up early the next morning with a sense of purpose. Heather has always loved my spaghetti. I served spaghetti the first time Joshua brought her here for dinner. After a while, I made a tradition of having spaghetti on Sunday nights. It has been a long time since our last spaghetti Sunday.

Some people say they can make a good spaghetti sauce in a flash, but my sauce needs hours of simmering. I'm cutting the onions when the doorbell rings. I quickly rinse my hands. My eyes are a little moist from the onions.

Usually I peek outside before opening the door. There has been a rash of home break-ins lately, and you just can't be too careful. But I'm in a good mood, thinking about my spaghetti and seeing the children, so I just grab the doorknob and swing it open.

There on my doorstep stands a bearded man, wearing a long white robe. Maybe he was on his way to a nativity play and got lost. Except this is July. He must be a religious fanatic collecting donations. I didn't know they went door to door these days. He's probably not dangerous, but you never know. I close the door a little. I just need to get rid of him. I'll try to be polite.

"Can I help you?"

He takes off his sunglasses. "Hi Mom," he says quietly.

I look into his eyes. It is Joshua. Underneath the beard and the Biblical-era clothing is my son, fruit of my womb.

"Joshua? What in the world has happened to you? Where have you been? Why are you dressed like that?"

"Can I come in?"

I hope my next-door neighbors didn't see him. There are all kinds of people living in this area now, but the Meyers next door are still very traditional. They've lived in their place for over forty years, and they're always complaining about the changes in the neighborhood and the number of foreigners in the city. What if they see this strange looking man on my doorstep? What if they see me ask him inside?

"Mom?"

He is my son. "Yes, Joshua, get in here before someone sees you standing there looking like that!" I pull his arm, forcing him inside, and quickly shut the door.

"Joshua, what have you done with yourself? You couldn't afford a razor?"

He smirks. "I missed you too, Mom."

The same old Joshua. "So, where have you been? Jennifer is walking now, in case you care."

This is where he usually loses his temper and walks away. He's been good at that since he was two. After he leaves, I can get back to my spaghetti sauce.

But he doesn't scream at me this time. He closes his eyes and stands there, silently, for several minutes. His lips are moving, without sound. Did he learn a mantra to help himself deal with me? Should I ignore him, or should I wait? Is there another surprise coming, something to go along with his get-up?

When he does speak again, his speech is slow and deliberate. "Mom, I didn't come to fight this time. Could you give me a chance?"

"I'm all ears."

"I had to leave. I just needed some space. Every day it was the same thing. Going to work, coming home to a noisy, dirty house, trying to pay the bills. I didn't expect my life to end up that way."

"No one does, Joshua. It's called growing up."

"Let me finish."

"Go ahead," I sigh.

"After I left Heather, I moved in with some friends who rent a house over near Devon. I met one of the guys at my warehouse job, and we stayed in touch. Anyway, they're Muslims. I didn't think too much about it at first. I mean, it was weird because they wouldn't go drinking with me, and they spent a lot of time praying. But they were good guys, and they let me stay there for free until I got another job, so I figured, what the hell.

"After I was there a while, I started to tell them about how I was feeling. Lost. That's what it was. Nothing made sense anymore. One day when they asked me to go to the mosque with them, I decided to tag along. I went that day, and I kept on going."

I don't want to hear what he's going to say next.

"After I went to the mosque that first time, I read a book they gave me. And I talked with a lot of different people. I told them my story, how I was feeling. They helped me. And they taught me. And they welcomed me. And, well, I didn't feel lost anymore.

"So, about six weeks ago, I became a Muslim."

Hundreds of thoughts run through my head. Finally, I just say, "Why?"

"It's incredible. All of my life, people have treated me like I'm some kind of freak. But the people at the mosque accept me for who I am. They listen. For the first time in my life I feel like I belong."

His words are like a slap in the face. I snap, "You belong? You 'finally feel' like you belong? While you turn your back on me, on Heather, on your children, on your brothers? You belong to your family, not some damn foreigners."

"I knew you wouldn't understand."

"What's there to understand, Joshua? You haven't changed. You're all dressed up like a nomad, but I know who you are. And you'll never change."

"Never mind, Mom. I'm sorry I bothered you. I just thought you should know that I'll be leaving in a few days. For Pakistan."

Pakistan? Why is he doing this to me? I take a deep breath. Remember, this is Joshua. Other boys his age are making their marks on the world. Matt Pierson, who used to play ball with Joshua, owns a successful business. Kurt Baker, that cute little redhead, just landed a job on Wall Street. But not Joshua Adams. He has to be the one who walks out on his family, joins a cult, and goes to Pakistan.

"I know I've given you a rough time, Mom. I'll try to make it better."

"How? By running off to Pakistan? Instead of facing your responsibilities right here? Tell me, how is that 'making it better'?"

"It's just something that I have to do. I can't explain it right now. You wouldn't understand. I need to go."

"Then go. Try to be back before Michael graduates from high school."

"I don't want to leave it like this."

"There is no other way to leave it. Either you stay here and act like a man, or you keep running away, chasing your fantasies."

"I have to go."

"Then go. And don't come back until you're ready to be a man. Then we'll talk."

We're still standing by the front door. I firmly guide him out. He's gone too far this time.

He turns around. "I love you, Mom."

The door slams on his statement. For a moment, I reconsider. I could open the door, ask him to come in, and get to the bottom of this mess. No, I have been trying to understand that boy all of his life. I have made sacrifice after sacrifice for him. All he has ever given me is a headache. No. Let him go.

I go back to my onions. They're diced so small no one will be able to see them. The tears run freely. These damn onions.

❧

The spaghetti is ready to serve and Heather and the children should be here soon. Should I tell her about the bum?

I can just pretend. He'll be gone in Pakistan for who-knows-how-long and she won't even notice the difference. Unless he does something stupid and gets himself blown up. Then I'll probably have to tell her.

He is my son. Why do I hate him so much? Is it from all these years of trouble, or just his latest stunt? I don't know, but even the sight of him today made my blood boil. And what's all this business about 'being lost' and 'belonging'? I have stood by that boy through every problem he has ever gotten himself into. And he goes out and latches on to the first bunch of strangers who feed him a line. I wonder how long this Moslem thing will last.

I know I shouldn't, but sometimes I think it would have been better if Joshua had never been born. I would have gone to that reunion with Sam and we would have raised our two sons together. I wouldn't have had to worry about drugs or teen pregnancy or weird religions. My life would have been so much easier.

At least, there are the children. Heather's mother thinks it is scandalous, having three children so close together, especially in a marriage that was shaky from the beginning. In principle, I must agree with her, but I love those children, all three of them. That's the only thing Joshua has ever done right. Helping Heather conceive those three beautiful children.

I need to fix my relationship with Heather. Mostly because I need to see my grandchildren. But I miss Heather, too. I remember the first time I met her. She was fifteen and giggly, and she had a big red pimple right on the tip of her nose. After dinner she helped me do the dishes and I knew she would be good daughter-in-law material. But they were so young. She's only twenty-two now, and she should be enjoying herself.

I'm lost in thought when the doorbell rings. I've decided not to say anything for now. I put on a smile and open the door.

"Gramma! I brought some more books."

"That's wonderful, Michael. Come on in."

"Hi, Evie." Heather is lugging Jennifer in her right arm, and Jeremy is clinging to her left leg. The diaper bag is sliding down her left arm.

"Hi, Heather. I'm glad you came. Let me help you with that diaper bag."

She smiles briefly. "Oh, the house smells wonderful. I've missed your spaghetti. You should bottle your sauce. It's better than anything on the grocery shelf."

"Thank you, but I'll stick to insurance." *I've missed you. I'm so glad you're back.* "Okay, Michael, I think we have time for one book, and then we'll eat."

❧

It was a wonderful evening. Heather and I talked and laughed, just like old times. I may have lost a son, but at least I've regained a daughter.

It's been almost two weeks since I last saw Joshua. I suppose he is in Pakistan now. There was a bombing in Karachi a few days ago. I hope he wasn't there.

I'm just settling in for a few hours of mindless television when the phone rings. "Hello?"

"Hi, Mom. What's up?"

"Brad, how are you? I was wondering why you haven't called lately."

"I know. The baby got sick, and Beth's just started back to work. You know how it is sometimes."

"Yes, I remember. Is everything okay now?"

"Yes, we're fine. Beth misses the baby during the day but she's glad to be back at work. You should see him. A couple of days ago he actually laughed out loud. It was great."

"Oh, I need to see him. How about tomorrow night?"

"Sure, come on over. Just don't expect any home cooking. Beth is frazzled these days. So how is the rest of the family? What about my prodigal brother? Have you heard from him?"

I haven't told anyone yet because I am still trying to work it out in my own mind. Brad is a good place to start.

"I heard from him all right. He showed up here a couple of weeks ago."

"How is he? Is everything okay?"

"Brad, your brother showed up on my front porch wearing a long robe and a beard."

"What? Mom, you're joking."

"No, I'm not, that's the problem. He came over here and told me all about how he was feeling lost, until he went to live with some Moslems, over on Devon."

"Moslems?"

"It gets worse. He says he's one of them now. And you'll never guess where he is."

"I don't know. Timbuktu?"

"Pakistan."

"What the hell is he doing in Pakistan? Did he sign up with one of those terrorist groups?"

"I certainly hope not, but you never know. It would be just like Joshua to go blow himself up in front of some embassy."

"Have you told Chris yet? He's going to freak."

"He's called a couple of times since Joshua came by, but I

didn't know what to say. You know how Chris is. When Heather became pregnant, Chris wouldn't talk to either of them for nearly two months. I don't know how he'll react this time."

Brad chuckles. "I think we're going to have our own little holy war. Don't worry, Mom. I'll talk to Chris. I mean, after all the things Joshua has done we shouldn't be that surprised. I just hope he didn't get himself mixed up with terrorists."

"And that is all too possible, knowing Joshua."

We wrap up the conversation on a more mundane note, talking about Beth's job at the hospital and Kyle's attempts to roll over. I'm glad Brad will be the one to talk to Chris.

How can two boys from the same family be so different? Joshua's teen years could have landed us all on one of those daytime talk shows. But, when Chris was fourteen, he found Jesus. I'm not a religious person, and sometimes I get tired of hearing Chris go on and on about his faith, but it certainly helped keep him out of trouble. I didn't have to worry about Chris coming home drunk or getting a girl pregnant. He went to a nice little Bible college and married a sweet girl he met there. Melinda is a stay-at-home mom. They have an adorable little girl and another one on the way. Chris teaches at the Bible college now. While he's training nice, clean-cut students to become missionaries, his brother is growing a scruffy beard and probably learning how to take hostages.

I know Brad will stay out of the holy wars. Beth and he go to church once in while, but they don't take it too seriously. He's more worried about landing that promotion in the engineering firm. I'm sure he'll get it. He's one of the best.

I try to lose myself in a silly hit sitcom, but I'm thinking about my boys. It must be tomorrow morning in Pakistan. Joshua's lesson for the day is probably something like Anthrax 101. Meanwhile, Brad is talking to Chris about their infidel brother. I can just imagine that conversation.

I don't have to imagine for long. The sitcom is almost over when the phone rings.

"Hi, Chris."

"Hi, Mom. Brad just called."

"He told you?"

"Mom, why didn't you stop him?"

"What was I supposed to do? Take away his robe? Tie him down and shave off his beard?"

"I'm serious. You should have talked to him. At least, you could have called me. We should have kept him away from those Moslems until we talked some sense into him."

"Chris, you have known Joshua all his life. Since when has anybody been able to talk any sense into that boy? You couldn't even talk him out of climbing up on the roof when he was nine."

"We have to try. This time it won't be just a broken leg. This is his soul we're talking about."

The holy wars have begun. "Okay, Chris, calm down. Before you condemn your brother to eternal damnation, stop and think. Joshua has always been a wild child. For God's sake, he started drinking when he was thirteen. And you're saying this is worse?"

"Yes, Mom, definitely worse. Before, no matter what he did, he still had a chance to repent. But now, now he's completely turned his back on God. He has rejected Christ. There is nothing worse."

I don't want to get into a theological discussion. Besides, my favorite reality show is about to start. "First of all, Chris, he'll probably give it up, just like he's given up everything else in his life—even his own children. And when he comes back, in a month or two or three, if he is still a Moslem, you can come over and stay up all night talking with him."

"I just hope it's not too late."

"I don't know, Chris. Sometimes I'm amazed Joshua has even survived this long with all the stunts he's pulled. We'll have to see what happens when he comes back."

"Remember, Mom, this is very serious."

"I know it is, Chris, but I'm missing my show. Kiss Melinda and Ruthie for me. I'll talk to you later."

"Okay," he sighs. "I love you, Mom. Talk to you later."

Tomorrow I'm sure he'll ask one of the older professors for advice, and gather pamphlets designed to save Joshua's soul. He'll probably keep poor Melinda up all night, fretting over his damned brother.

I haven't seen Joshua for almost six months. During this time I have been able to renew my relationship with Heather and the children. She comes over for dinner a couple of times a week and we talk on the phone in between times. She has a waitress job which pays well, and with my help she's been able to meet her expenses and even start paying off some of those debts. Best of all, I can see the children whenever I want.

We had a wonderful Christmas together. Brad and Chris came over with their families, and Heather brought the children. We all sat in front of the fireplace and talked and ate while the children played with their new toys. Brad got that promotion. I am so proud of him. Melinda is due in another month. They say it's a boy this time. I don't know what Joshua did for Christmas in Pakistan. I suppose Moslems celebrate Christmas. Doesn't everyone?

Last Christmas, I didn't know the divorce was coming. They came to my house with the children, and we all opened presents, and ate. They seemed happy enough. It wasn't until later when I thought about Joshua's behavior that day. He stayed mostly to himself. While we were all eating and laughing, he was sitting in a corner and brooding. He walked out on them less than a month later. Last Christmas, I couldn't have imagined the changes one year could bring.

I received a letter from him on New Year's Eve. He wrote a little about his life in Pakistan—how much he enjoys it there, and all the new friends he's been meeting. He said he's spending most of his time learning Arabic. He didn't say anything about learning how to build bombs. He closed by saying he'll be flying back here in another month, and ended with a P.S.—"Mom, I'm ready to be a man."

Two days ago I received another short letter, letting me know his flight number and arrival time. He'll come home tomorrow.

I wonder if he actually is ready, this time. I doubt it. He

doesn't seem to have given up on this idea about being a Moslem. If anything, he sounds more committed to it than he was before. Is he ready? Am I ready to find out?

I have been going back and forth on this in my mind. I want to see him, to see if he is serious and ready to grow up, but I don't want to deal with any more of his foolishness. I still haven't decided about going to the airport, but I have decided it's time to have a talk with Heather.

During all these months with Heather, neither one of us has even mentioned Joshua. It's as if he really had never been born. But the fantasy ends tomorrow, and we will have to stop pretending. He'll be back.

I wait until we're chatting over coffee. Michael is playing computer games, and Jeremy and Jennifer are watching a video.

"You know, Heather, I'm very happy we're friends again. I missed you."

"Yeah, I guess I missed you, too. I've never been that close to my own mom, you know. And you're great with the kids."

"There is something I have to tell you. Do you remember that first night you started coming over again, our spaghetti Sunday?"

"Yeah, I remember. What about it?"

"Something happened earlier that day. I think you need to know. First, can you promise not to be angry?"

She giggles. "Angry? Of course I won't be angry. How bad can it be?"

"Joshua stopped by that morning." At the mention of his name, her smile disappears. "I hadn't seen him for months. He was different."

"What, was he wearing a suit and tie?"

"No. Not Joshua. He was wearing a long white robe, the kind they wear in Christmas pageants, and he had let his beard grow out."

"What? Has he gone completely nuts?"

"I don't know, Heather. He told me he's become a Moslem, and he was planning to leave soon for Pakistan."

"Pakistan? Pakistan? He couldn't come to see his own kids,

but he could go to Pakistan? What is he now, a terrorist?"

Her face is getting red. Even thinking about Joshua is difficult. I know, because I remember those few times when Sam walked back into our lives.

"I hope not. He's been in Pakistan for the last six months, and he's coming home tomorrow. He wrote to me a couple of weeks ago, asking me to pick him up from the airport."

"What?" she screeches. "He just floats in and out as he pleases, joins a terrorist group and expects to be welcomed back with open arms?"

"I haven't decided if I'm going to the airport or not."

She is quiet for a moment. Her teeth are clenched. When she looks at me, her glare is piercing. "Look, Evie, these last few months have been nice. But if you go to meet that, that terrorist at the airport, then you can just forget about seeing me and the kids."

I'm tempted to tell her to settle down, but I don't want to make that mistake again. We've built a truce, and a budding friendship, these past months, and I'm not going to jeopardize it. I shake my head. "No, Heather. I will never choose that bum over you and the children."

Late at night, while lying in bed, I think about it. My son, fruit of my womb, versus my ex-daughter-in-law, mother of my grandchildren. It's no contest. When he flies into O'Hare tomorrow, he can call a cab.

❧

I'm at work when his plane arrives. I don't think he'll call me at the office, but somehow I know he's back.

The first trace I see of Joshua is the bright yellow note stuck to my front door. I hope he didn't stand there in his get-up. What will the Meyers say?

"Hi Mom," he wrote. "I got in okay. I'm staying with the guys at the house. Talk to you later. Love, Joshua."

The last time I saw him, he said he loved me. He has signed every letter and note with love. When he was twelve he screamed that he hated me while he shoving me into a wall. I thought he stopped loving me when he was eleven. Has he changed?

Heather calls a few minutes after I get in. I tell her about the note.

"Do you think he could have changed?"

"Even if he did, it's too late. Can we just stop talking about him?"

"Sure Heather." I have to remember how I felt about Sam. It has taken so many years for the pain to stop. "How's our little princess today?"

"She's beautiful. This morning she said 'Michael.' Actually, what she said was 'Miko,' but that's close enough."

After I hang up, I think again about the bargain I've made. At least Heather and I can still talk. When Sam left, his mother completely disowned us. Not so much as a card on the boys' birthdays. I hear she died a few years ago. I hope she suffered.

~

Joshua calls in the morning. I'm reading the Saturday Tribune and eating a croissant when the phone rings.

"Hi, Mom. How are you?"

He really is back. His voice sounds older. He has a slight accent, too, just a tinge of something.

"Hello, Joshua. I see you made it back okay."

"Yes, I had a good trip. Is it okay if I come over? I'd like to see you."

Who will I see? Will it be the Joshua in torn jeans and a T-shirt, or the one in the long white robe? Do I want to see him at all?

"Mom? Are you still there?"

"Oh, yes, Joshua. Yes, come on over."

"In about an hour?"

"I'll be here."

I have an hour to get mentally prepared for the return of the prodigal son. I have so many questions, but I don't know which ones to ask. Most of all, what I want to know is, who are you now?

Chris will be disappointed if I don't call him, but this time I need to talk to Joshua alone. There will still be time, I think, for Chris to try to save his soul.

I'm deep in thought when the doorbell rings. I reach for the doorknob, pausing briefly. I wonder which Joshua is standing on the other side of the door.

When I see him, I'm not really surprised, just disappointed. He still has the beard, which is longer now. Instead of the robe, he's wearing a brown tunic with matching, baggy pants. He also has some kind of round cap perched on his head, white with green embroidery. If we were passing on the street I wouldn't recognize him, except for those eyes.

He's thin, too. Thinner than usual. I wonder if he had enough to eat while he was over there.

"Hi, Mom. How are you?"

He sounds so casual, as if we just saw each other yesterday, as if he has been just around the corner, not in a strange land halfway around the world.

"Oh, I'm okay, I guess. Would you like to come in?"

"Sure."

He's my son, and yet he's a stranger. I want to go beyond the polite banter of conventional conversation, but not too far.

"Did you have a nice flight?"

"It was okay. I'm glad to be back."

You are? What does that mean?

"So, how was Pakistan?"

He smiles. I suddenly realize that I haven't seen him smile in a very long time. I cannot even remember how many years it has been. He has been sullen for so long, I had come to not expect anything else.

"It was great. It's hard to explain, but things are different over there. Life seems more real."

"More real?"

"I don't know how to say it. The people I met were so simple, and so kind. They didn't know me but they invited me to share their meals. We sat on the floor and ate from one large platter. We prayed together, standing shoulder to shoulder. We called each other brother."

"You ate on the floor? That doesn't sound very pleasant. And you already have two brothers here in Chicago."

"I knew you wouldn't understand. But, anyway, it was great."

"What are you going to do now? Another trip halfway around the world?"

"No. While I was in Pakistan I decided that it's time for me to get serious. I'm going to get a good job and a nice place to live. I need to settle down."

My mouth opens wide, but for a moment I'm mute. Is this Joshua? Is he actually standing there, with his beard and baggy clothes, talking about getting "serious"? Could he have really changed?

"That sounds wonderful. It's all I have wanted from you all these years. Why now, though? Have you finally decided to give up on this silly idea about being a Moslem?"

"Actually, Mom, it's Muslim, with a 'u', not Moslem. No, I would never give it up. It's the best thing that's ever happened to me. I need to get serious because I'm going to get custody of my kids."

"You're what?" I feel weak.

"I'm going to get a good job, find a nice place to live, learn how to be a better Muslim, and get custody of my kids."

"Since when do you care about your children? You weren't even there when Jennifer was born. You walked out on them without as much as a backward glance. Just a few months ago you were bragging about how relieved you were to be free of them. What is this about, Joshua?"

He doesn't shout back at me, as he usually would. Instead, he takes a deep breath and looks me straight in the eye—just as he did on the day he was born. "You're right, Mom. I've been a bum. When I walked out, I didn't know what I wanted. But now I've found it. I've found Islam. I'm a Muslim now, and I have to take care of my kids."

"Why not just send them a check? That would be new."

"I will, as soon as I get a job. Believe me, Mom, I'm not

proud of the person I used to be. But I'm different now. I'm a Muslim. And I have to get custody of my kids so I can teach them how to be Muslims, too."

There's nothing left for me to say. I stare at him.

"Mom? What is it?"

"You said you want to make them Moslems too?"

"Yes Mom. That's what I plan to do."

"Oh, Joshua." I fall into a nearby chair, bury my face in my hands, and begin quietly sobbing.

Joshua sits on the arm of the chair and rubs my back. He hasn't touched me since he was eleven—except for the times when he shoved me. He sits and rubs my back for a long time. Then his touch is gone and I hear the front door softly close.

I continue to weep. This is all wrong. Today should be the happiest day of my life, the day when Joshua finally grows up. But it's all backwards. He wasn't supposed to go to Pakistan. He wasn't supposed to become a Moslem, or Muslim, or whatever. And the children.

How could he think of doing that to his children? It's bad enough he wants to ruin his own life. Now he wants to take those children away from Heather, away from their very lives. Does he think he's going turn them into little Moslem robots, or miniature terrorists?

No, Joshua hasn't changed. He still thinks only of himself.

ॐ

I fall asleep in the chair, exhausted by Joshua once again. I don't remember any dreams, but when I wake up I have a plan of action.

Heather and the children are supposed to be here in an hour. I'm not ready to see her right now. Not yet. I call.

"Heather? I can't get together with you today. Can we make it tomorrow?"

"I guess. Is anything wrong?"

"Oh, I might be coming down with something. I'm just so tired, and I have a headache. I should be feeling better by tomorrow."

"This doesn't have anything to do with Joshua, does it?"

"Oh, no. Not at all. So I'll see you and the children tomorrow then?"

"Sure. See you then."

That's taken care of. Now I have to call Brad.

The phone rings several times before he picks up. "Brad, I am so glad you're home."

"Mom? Is anything wrong?"

"Yes. Your brother is back."

He chuckles. "How is the family infidel?"

"This is not the time for jokes. I need you to come over. Tonight."

"I don't know, Mom. Beth and I were looking forward to a quiet night at home. The baby's sleeping through the night now, so we finally have a little time to ourselves. Know what I mean?"

"Yes Brad, wink, wink. I just need you for an hour or so. I'm going to call Chris, too."

"Oh, a family meeting."

"The most important one we've ever had."

"The first one, too."

"Maybe if we had done this sooner your brother wouldn't have turned out the way he did. Just give me an hour or so. You'll still have plenty of time to spend with Beth."

"Uh, okay. I'll see what I can do."

"I'll expect to see you in an hour."

I'm sorry to break up Brad's romantic plans with Beth, but this is an emergency. Now for Chris.

"Chris, your damned brother is back."

"What?"

"Joshua. He came over today. And I need you to come over. I have something important to discuss with you. I've already called Brad."

"Is he still a Moslem?"

"He is. And it gets worse. Come over as soon as you can."

"Is he there now?"

"No. You can talk to him later, but first we need to think of a plan."

"I told you this meant trouble."

"I know you did. Now get over here."

Whatever I do, I have to stop Joshua from getting to those children.

Joshua: "Finding Myself"

"Let chaos storm!
Let cloud shapes swarm!
I wait for form."
- Robert Frost

Part One

She would deny it, but sometimes I think that my mother never really loved me. It wasn't my fault at first. It was Sam's fault. Sam, the man who never came around often enough or stayed around long enough for me to call him Dad.

Later, it was my fault. But I didn't mean to push her away. I don't know what I meant. At least when I got into trouble she stopped ignoring me.

As I drive away from her house, I keep thinking about her reaction just now. I figured that she might not be too happy about it, but I didn't think she'd get so upset. They are my kids, after all. She's the one who's been telling me to take responsibility for them. I know she wouldn't change her mind about that.

Being a Muslim is a big part of it, I know. She probably thought that I would come back from Pakistan and leave Islam, just like I've left everything else. She doesn't understand. This is different.

I have to get custody of those kids. Heather takes care of them and all, and she's really a pretty good mother, but she can't teach them to be Muslims. They need Islam just as much as I do. What if Michael gets into all the stuff I got into? Man, I don't know what I would do then.

When I get back to the house, I'll talk to Mahmoud. Maybe he can get me a job back at the warehouse. It's not like I was fired or anything. It just wasn't my thing. This time I won't quit. I have to think about my kids.

I guess I shouldn't have left them like that. Heather just got to me for the last time. Always complaining, always telling me what to do. I couldn't take it any more.

On the morning I left, she started in on me again, when I was still half asleep. It was the same old thing. I didn't earn enough money. I didn't give her enough attention. I didn't help her out with the kids. I didn't do anything when I came home except watch TV and drink beer. I was a bum.

I had enough. Finally, I had enough of her. By the time I got out of bed, I was yelling back. When she wouldn't shut up, I started throwing things. I didn't hit her, I've never hit her, but I sure wanted to. I got dressed, grabbed some of my stuff, and slammed the door behind me. I knew I was never coming back.

But I had nowhere to go. I stopped by my mother's house, but she started hassling me, too. I should have known that she wouldn't take me in. And I could forget about Chris. Brad might have let me stay with him, for a day or two, but he would have told me to go back to Heather. The only person I knew who wouldn't give me a hard time was Mahmoud.

I first hooked up with Mahmoud a while back, when we were working together at the warehouse. We were a good team. After a while, we started hanging out after work, too. He wouldn't go out with me to get a beer. But sometimes we went to play some b-ball or pool.

After a while, I got tired of being hassled by the boss at the warehouse job, so I quit. But I kept hanging out with Mahmoud. Sometimes we went to the house he shared with a couple of other guys. We'd order some pizza and play video games until early morning. And, once in a while, we'd talk. The guys knew I was having trouble at home. So when I finally left Heather for good, I knew I could go to Mahmoud.

They were cool about letting me stay with them. I wasn't feeling too good about my life right then, so I stopped going to work and just hung around the house. But they didn't mess with me like Heather and my mom. Once in a while, I still went out for a beer. I could tell Mahmoud didn't like it, but he didn't rag on me. All the guys gave me the space I needed so I could figure things out on my own.

The first time they asked me to go to the mosque with them, I laughed out loud. I never cared much about religion of any sort before, and, anyway, I was too messed up for a place like that. But they kept asking, every few days I guess. No pressure, they said. They just wanted me to come with them. Every time I said no, they shrugged and went ahead without me. One day, when I was starting to feel a little better about myself, I got to figuring that I owed them something. So I went.

I've been to church a few times. It was okay, but I couldn't relate. The seats were hard, and we had to keep sitting and standing and I thought that the sermon would never end.

The first time I went to the mosque, I thought that it wasn't much different than going to church. Most of the time, we all sat on the floor, which was hard. The sermon was long. And when I watched them pray, it seemed like they just kept standing up and sitting down again.

It's what happened afterward that was different. Some of the other guys in the mosque came over and started talking to me. They shook my hand and patted me on the back. They called me brother.

When we got back to the house, Mahmoud gave me a book to read. I've never been much for reading, but he had already done so much for me, so I figured I might as well.

This book talked about God as the creator of the universe. I had never really thought about God before. When Michael was born, whole and beautiful, I did wonder, just for a second, who had made him. I knew Heather and I couldn't have come up with something that good all on our own. While I was reading, I started thinking about that again. And other things, too, that never quite made sense to me. And what I read made sense.

The best thing I liked about Islam, at first, was being called brother. The guys at the mosque didn't seem to see how screwed up I was. They acted like there was something good in me.

The other thing was the rules. One day I asked Mahmoud what I would have to do if I became a Muslim. First thing, he said, I'd have to give up the beer. And I'd have to pray. Not just pray, but do it five times every day. And a few other things, like not fooling around with girls and keeping myself clean. At first I thought it sounded like too much of a hassle. But then I got to thinking about it. I had been a mess for so long, I figured that the rules might help me. My way sure hadn't worked.

So, one Friday after the prayers, I sat in front of the leader of the mosque—they called him the imam—and said that I would worship One God and recognize Muhammad as God's prophet. I figured that Allah had to be the one who made Michael. And since Muhammad had taught all those rules that would help me straighten out my life I figured he must be a prophet.

It was good. The guys in the mosque all came around me and started hugging me. I didn't even know guys could go around hugging each other. But it was cool.

Things were okay for a week or so. Then I started getting restless again. I got to missing the taste of beer, and I was getting tired of praying all the time. One night I talked to Mahmoud about it. Mostly he just listened. When I was finished, he patted me on the shoulder. "Don't worry, Joshua. I can help you. You'll be okay." He and the other guys spent more time with me after that. Then, a couple of days later, he told me that he was going to send me to Pakistan to stay with his uncle, Abdul-Qadir, for a few months. I could learn Islam better over there, he said, and it would help me get away from my old life.

That sounded great. What I needed was a fresh start. But Mahmoud wasn't a rich guy. Months later, I got to wondering who had paid for my ticket. I never did find out.

I got to admit, when I first left for Pakistan, I wasn't so sure about this whole Muslim thing. It seemed to be okay, but I didn't know if it was for me. I figured that if I didn't like what I saw in Pakistan, I could always change my mind.

I'll never forget the first time I saw Abdul-Qadir. He's a little guy, thin and a few inches shorter than me. His clothes were old and faded. I'm thinking, this is the guy who's supposed to take care of me?

We rode in a strange three-wheeled contraption he called a taxi from the Karachi airport, and I'm looking around the whole time. Lots of little shops. Kids playing on the sidewalks. We pulled up to his house, a little place not even half as big as my mother's. And there were kids all over the place. I laughed when he told me they were all his. I thought that he was joking.

It was dinnertime, so his wife brought out a huge platter of rice and meat. I'm thinking, man, even I can't eat that much. Then she brought this little bowl full of water, and I just looked at it. Abdul-Qadir smiled and showed me how to wash my hands in that little bowl. Then he called his two older sons over and they motioned for me to eat. I finally figured out that we were all supposed to eat from that plate. No wonder it was so big.

There weren't any forks or spoons, and I really wanted one. I'd seen Mahmoud and the guys eat with their hands, but I had never tried it. So I grabbed a handful of rice, and dropped about half of it before getting it to my mouth. Abdul-Qadir and the two boys didn't say anything. But this little guy, he couldn't have been older than six, came over and showed me how to hold the rice with just three fingers so I wouldn't drop any of it. It was kind of embarrassing, but at least Abdul-Qadir didn't laugh at me. He just kept on eating, and smiling, and telling me to eat more.

After dinner we went to the mosque to pray. I had spent some time at the mosque in Chicago, so I knew what to do. This mosque was different, though. It was beautiful, really, but in a simple way. Besides that, all these people were standing around speaking Urdu, and I didn't know what the hell they were saying. They just talked to Abdul-Qadir, nodded at me, and smiled. At least the prayer was the same. The imam read verses from the Qur'an, a few of which I knew, and when he bowed down or knelt we followed him. Just like in Chicago.

When the prayer was over, the imam gave a talk. Most of it was in Urdu, with some Arabic, I think. I was trying to listen, hoping that I could figure out what he was saying. But it had been a long day, so I started nodding off. I ended up leaning against a wall and pretending to listen, while closing my eyes for a little rest. Nobody seemed to mind. They knew that I had just come. By the time he was finished, we had to pray again, the last prayer of the day. After that prayer, we finally went back to Abdul-Qadir's house.

I was dead tired. I had never flown before, and all during the trip I couldn't relax. Besides, the night before I left, I was too excited to sleep. I was looking forward to crawling into a nice soft bed.

Abdul-Qadir brought me this thin mattress, all rolled up. I couldn't believe that he expected me to sleep on that. But his two oldest sons, Ahmed and Ibrahim, went and got their own thin mattresses out, so I figured that it was all they had. I was so tired, by the time I laid down it didn't matter what I was sleeping on. I passed out, and didn't wake up again until early morning.

We had to get up before sunrise to go to the mosque for the first prayer of the day. Man, I never used to roll out of bed until sometime around noon. Even after I became a Muslim, I almost never made the morning prayer. It was too hard. But Abdul-Qadir made me get up while it was still dark. I had to make ablutions, too, and that water was cold. Abdul-Qadir's house didn't have hot running water. That sure woke me up.

On the way to the mosque, I heard two new sounds outside. One was the call to prayer, blaring through the neighborhood over a microphone from the mosque. The other was the crowing of roosters. They didn't seem to mind getting up so early.

After the prayer, the imam gave another talk. This time I tried harder to stay awake and listen. I still didn't understand too much, but I was picking up a few words. And I liked listening to his voice. It was gentle, but strong. I started feeling anxious to learn the language so I could figure out what he was saying.

After a breakfast of bread and scrambled eggs, Abdul-Qadir took me back to the mosque for my first lesson in Qur'an. That first morning, I really wanted to go back to sleep, but I figured that I had better just do what Abdul-Qadir told me. He was so nice, I couldn't get mad at him.

It took me about a week to get used to living there. After two weeks, I was able to get up on my own in the morning. After a month, I could hold a simple conversation in Urdu.

It turned out that I was pretty good at learning languages. Back when I was in school, I didn't think I could learn anything. Some of my teachers even told me how dumb I was. They passed me on anyway, though, probably just to get rid of me.

After a couple of months, Abdul-Qadir had me helping him out at the store after my classes. By then my Urdu was good enough that he could leave me alone sometimes to run the store. No one had ever trusted me that much before.

While I was at the store, I picked up a shadow, named Nuruddin. That little kid, the one who showed me how to eat with my hand, followed me everywhere I went. At first he laughed when I tried to speak Urdu. After a while, though, I knew more than he did, and I think that he started to respect me. No one has ever respected me before. Except maybe Michael. The way Nuruddin looked at me, sometimes, he reminded me of Michael. And I started to remember how much I really did love that kid.

Abdul-Qadir has eight kids, three boys and five girls. They don't have much—I think Jennifer has more toys than all of those kids put together. But I think they are happy. You could see it in their eyes. They have their father, working for a living during the day, and playing and praying with them at night. The little ones would run and hug him the minute he walked into the house. And the older ones would smile and sit close to him and listen to what he said. All eight of them, you could see how much they love him. And he loves them.

Abdul-Qadir is the man who taught me what it means to be a father, and what it means to be a man.

I was only supposed to be there for six months, and it was over way too soon. When it was time to go back, I didn't really want to leave. I felt more at home in Pakistan than I had ever felt in Chicago. Not everyone was as good as Abdul-Qadir and his wife, but I met a lot of good people. And they all made me feel better about everything in my life, better than I had ever felt before.

On my last night there, Abdul-Qadir and I stayed up late, drinking tea and talking. I wanted to tell him how I felt.

"Thank you for everything. Thank you for being a father to me." Tears ran down my cheeks, and for the first time in my life, I wasn't ashamed. I had only cried once since I was ten. And when I was five, I learned that I wasn't supposed to let anyone see me cry.

He called me by the Arabic name he had given me soon after I came. "You're a good boy, Isa. Remember what's important, and work for it. Don't lose your focus. Rely on your faith."

"I guess my kids are what's important."

"Yes, they are. You have to focus on doing what's right for

your kids. First you turn to Allah, and ask Allah to help you take care of your children. If you're sincere, Allah will help you in all things."

I am sincere, Abdul-Qadir. I just wish you were here to help me get through this right now.

"Mahmoud. Are you home?" I call as I walk into the house.

I pace through the empty rooms, looking for Mahmoud, Ismail, or Tariq. No one's home. What can I do? What should I do? I have to get started and I don't know how long they'll be gone. I can't wait.

It's almost time for the afternoon prayer. I walk on over to the mosque, hoping that Mahmoud or one of the other guys will be there. I do find about twenty other brothers, but none of my roommates. I'm thinking so hard, so fast, that I don't concentrate on the prayer. I have to do something to help me get my kids.

I know this feeling. I'm about to burst. Before, when I felt this way, I went out for a beer. I've had about eight months without that numbness, and it feels pretty good. Don't want to go back to that. I'll take a walk instead.

Small shops line the sidewalk. Most are owned by Muslims. I walk down the street, peeking into the windows, looking for something to take the edge off. Maybe a plate of hot curry will do it. I step into a restaurant on the corner.

I eat the curry, so hot that it burns all the way down, thinking all the time about how to help my kids. It isn't until I go to pay that I see the "Help Wanted" sign.

I try not to sound anxious. "Assalaamu alaikum, brother. Are you hiring?"

"Walaikum assalam. Yes, I need somebody to help out in the kitchen. Wash dishes, bus tables, mop the floor, things like that."

I have always hated any kind of kitchen work. Some of the earliest fights between my mother and me started because I refused to do the dishes. After Michael was born, Heather asked me to help her out. At first, I'd just sit down and watch TV instead. Later, when she was pregnant with Jennifer, I'd walk out and get a beer.

"I can do it. Please, brother, I need a job."

He looks me over, and smiles. "You're a Muslim?"

"Yes. I converted about eight months ago. And I really need a job."

"You need to come in early and stay late. You can eat for free, but no sitting around. You have to work hard, keep the place clean, make customers happy to be here."

"I can do it. Give me a chance."

"What is your name?"

I'm tired of being Joshua. "My name is Isa."

"Okay, Brother Isa. Be here tomorrow morning at ten. And get a good night's sleep because you're really going to work."

I offer my hand. "Thank you, brother. May Allah bless you. Thank you."

When I walk out, I realize that the restlessness is gone. And I did it without a beer. Just a little hot curry and someone who will give me a chance.

As I walk into the house, I hear voices speaking Urdu, and laughing. Mahmoud and Ismail are home.

"Assalaamu alaikum. Thanks, man, for letting me use your car." I toss the keys to Ismail.

"Did you talk to your mom?"

"Yeah, I talked to her. And she ended up crying, really crying. I don't get it. All these years she wanted me to take responsibility. And now?"

"Now you told her you're going to raise your kids as Muslims, didn't you?" says Mahmoud.

"Well, yeah. And I am, just as soon as I get to be with them again. It's not like she goes to church every week. Why would she care?"

"This is your country, man. You have to know how people think. Islam scares them. I'll bet your mom thought you were in one of those so-called terrorist camps while you were in Pakistan."

"Yeah, that sounds like my mom. Anyway, I am on my way to getting those kids. I got a job today."

"Already? That's great, Joshua. Where?"

"At a restaurant down the street. Karachi Kitchen. You

know, washing dishes, things like that."

"Good. I know that brother. Fawad. You'll like working there."

Ismail smiles. "Man, I never saw you wash dishes in all the time you've been here."

"I know. But this is for my kids."

"Okay," says Mahmoud, "this sink is full of dirty dishes. Why don't you start practicing?"

And I do. It's the least I can do for the guys who have helped me get my life together.

A couple of hours later, I call Heather.

"Hi, Heather. It's Joshua. I need you to let me see the kids."

First she curses me out. Then she lays it on the line. "There are only two ways you are ever going to see those kids again. Either you come back to us or you're going to have to take me to court." Then she hangs up.

I guess I'll be going to court.

❧

The work is hard, but I keep thinking about the kids. Every day I miss them more. I can't believe how stupid I was, just walking out on them like that.

I worked for Fawad for three days before he knew I could speak Urdu. At first I pretended not to know, and after a while I got so caught up in the work that it didn't matter. But one day he was talking to Khalid, the cook, about some customers who had come in earlier, and I jumped into the conversation.

Fawad and Khalid stopped what they were doing.

"What's the matter? Don't you think that a white guy can speak Urdu, too?"

They laughed, and we all got back to work. After that I was one of them.

I've been working here for almost two weeks now. I'll be getting my first paycheck tomorrow. Part of it will go to pay Mahmoud some rent, but I'm going to save most of it. In the old days, I spent my checks as soon as I got them. I can't afford to live like that again.

I'm almost finished cleaning up from the lunch crowd when I see them walk in. They go over to the front counter, where Fawad is. They don't see me.

"Excuse me. We're looking for our brother. Joshua. I think he lives somewhere around here."

"Sorry," says Fawad, "I don't know any Joshua."

I put the last clean pot aside and walk out to meet them. "It's my Christian name. Remember? The one you're going to put on my paycheck. Hi, guys, how you doing?"

I wish I had a camera to get that expression on their faces. I trimmed my beard after I got back from Pakistan, but it's still longer than anything they've ever seen. I'm covered with a white apron, which is spotted with stains, and under that I'm wearing some clothes Abdul-Qadir got for me in Karachi. They just stand there, staring at me.

I speak to Fawad in Urdu. "Could I take a break? These are my brothers, and we have some unfinished business to discuss."

He replies, also in Urdu. "Go ahead, Brother Isa. Take a half hour. Sit down over there, and I'll bring you some tea."

"Thank you."

My brothers look even more surprised. They didn't know that their good-for-nothing kid brother could learn anything. They look wary, too. They probably think I was making plans to tie them up and hold them hostage.

"Let's go over there and talk. I've got about thirty minutes. Fawad said he'll bring us tea."

They're quiet until we sit down. Then Brad turns to me and whispers angrily, "What the hell are you thinking of?"

I have to stay calm. "Right now I'm thinking about having tea with my brothers."

"You know what I mean. You have screwed up so many times I lost count, but this last year or so takes the cake. You leave Heather and the kids, become a Moslem, go to Pakistan, then turn up and tell Mom you're going to take the kids away from Heather and make them Moslems, too. As I said, what the hell are you thinking?"

I'm a little boy again, being yelled at for my latest goof up. I'm glad he hasn't raised his voice yet. I don't want Fawad and Khalid to know too much about "Joshua" and all his problems.

Chris is still sitting there, quiet for now. I'd better say something before he starts his sermon.

"You're right. I've been screwed up for most of my life. I was so screwed up that I left my three beautiful kids. But I became a Muslim, and I went to Pakistan, and I'm not so screwed up as I used to be. I'm going to take care of my kids. I shouldn't have left them, and now I'm going to make it right."

"Make it right?" I knew Chris couldn't stay quiet for long. "What are you doing to make it right? You need to shave off that beard, get out of this place, and come back to the church. That's the only way you can begin to get right again."

I knew it was coming, sooner or later, and I've been trying to work on my argument. My mind is blank now, though, so I'll have to wing it. "Chris, you found Jesus. You have a faith that gives you strength. So do I. But my faith is different than yours. Live with it."

Chris is sputtering, red-faced, so Brad takes over again. "Listen, Joshua, I don't know what kind of game you're playing this time. I sure didn't think you'd take it this far. The beard, the clothes, even the language. How long will it be this time before you get tired of it and go on to something else?"

I guess I'll always be a loser to them. I try to make them get it. "This time it's for good. When I was in Pakistan, I learned what life really is. It's not in that big office you go to every day, and it's not at the Bible college. Not for me, anyway. Life is being with people. And life is learning, each day, how to be obedient to Allah."

At the mention of "Allah," Chris jumps up. Brad has to grab him by the shoulder and pull him back to his seat. "Take it easy, man."

"Take it easy? My little brother is worshipping a false god, and you tell me to take it easy? And now he wants to drag Michael, Jeremy, and Jennifer with him. I won't let you do it, Joshua. You can go ahead and ruin your own life, if you're that determined. But don't you dare mess with those kids."

"They're my kids." From the corner of my eye I see Fawad coming over with a tray of hot tea, steam rising from the cups. I look at him and shake my head. Tempers are hot enough. We don't need the tea. "They're my kids. And I have to do what I think is right for them. I never had a father, remember? You had him for almost eight years, Brad, but I never had a father. Now I'm ready to be a father to my kids."

Chris is calmer now, but still tense. "What kind of father looks like that? What kind of father worships 'Allah'?" He spits out the name of my Creator. "Your kids don't need you, not the way you are now."

I want to punch him. I've been able to beat him up since I was ten. But Fawad and Khalid are watching and, besides, I've changed, haven't I?

"Just leave. I don't want to see you right now, either of you. Go, please."

"Listen to reason, Joshua. Don't throw everything away."

"I don't have anything more to say to you, Brad. Just go." My teeth are clenched. I lower my head so they won't see the pain in my eyes.

Brad throws his business card on the table. "Give me a call if you change your mind. Let's go, Chris."

After the door closes, Fawad comes over. "Is everything okay?"

"I still have some time left on my break, don't I?"

"Sure you do. Take as much time as you need."

I go outside, looking around to make sure Brad and Chris are really gone. Then I walk around to the alley, next to the dumpster, and slam my fist into the brick wall. It hurts, but it feels good. A few more times, until my knuckles are bleeding. And I cry. I have to cry, a little. In a few more minutes, I'll go bandage my hand and get back to work.

Late at night, I think about it. This isn't Pakistan. Now I have to deal with my brothers and my mother and Heather. I'm not ready, yet, for all their crap.

The best thing, for now, is to just forget about them. They're never going to understand me. I need to stay focused on getting my kids. Worrying about what they think will get me off track.

Part Two

I've been working at Karachi Kitchen for more than three months now. I just moved into my own apartment last week. It has two bedrooms, so I'll have enough room for the kids when they come. For the last couple of months, I've also been asking around about lawyers. I can't afford much, but I finally found a Muslim brother, Zakariya, who will represent me for almost nothing. In another month, I'll have enough for a decent used car. I'm almost ready.

I haven't sent any child support yet, and that kind of bothers me. But I'm trying so hard just to get myself stable first. I want to save every penny I can. As soon as I get the kids, I'll give them everything they need.

I have to convince a judge that I'll be a good parent, even though I'm the one who left them. I have a job, an apartment, and a lawyer. The guys at the house think I need something else, too.

It was about a month ago. We were sitting around talking late at night, just Ismail, Tariq and me. Mahmoud was on the phone, talking to his family. When he was finished, he came in and made his announcement.

"It's official. I leave at the end of the month, insha Allah."

"For real? You're going to go and marry a girl you've never met just because your mother likes her?"

"Why not, Tariq? And I have met her. We used to go to school together when we were young, before my family came to America. Our mothers have been friends for many years. And if my mother likes her, I know she must be good."

"Be careful, Mahmoud," I say. "I've been there before. It won't take long before you start feeling tied down."

"But your life was different then. You weren't a Muslim, and neither was your wife. You married her because you had to, and you were always under pressure. I'm marrying Halima because I want to, and it's the right time for me start a family of my own.

Maybe you'll try it again someday with a Muslim girl. You'll see how different it is."

"Hey, that's a good idea," says Ismail. "Why don't you get married?"

"What?"

"Get married. Then, when you go to court to get your kids, the judge will see a nice, two-parent home. It will help."

"Sure it will. Anyway, I can't marry someone just to help me get my kids back."

"Aw man," says Tariq, "don't you miss it sometimes? Having a woman to come home to?"

"I don't know. Those last couple of years with Heather weren't much fun."

"That was Heather, man. That was then. What about now?"

"Maybe someday, after I get the kids back. I can't even think about it right now."

"Why not?"

I had to get to bed soon. "Okay, Ismail, you go and find a woman for me. If you can do that, I'll think about getting married again." All I wanted was for the guys to leave me alone.

"You've got it, brother."

I was too busy working and looking for an apartment to give it another thought. But a couple weeks later, while I was in my room writing a letter to Abdul-Qadir, Ismail came in.

"Assalaamu alaikum, man. I've got good news for you."

"You're going to give me a million bucks?"

"Better than that. I've found a woman for you."

"You're joking."

"I'm for real, man. There's this dude I know who has a sister. They both became Muslims in the last few years. She's living with him and taking classes at Northeastern. He's been looking for a good brother for her, and I told him you're the man."

"What? Ismail, you're crazy." I threw my pen at him.

"I'm doing you a favor, man. She's a nice girl—at least that's what her brother told me. You'll be so grateful you'll be naming all your kids after me."

"So what do you want me to do?"

"You said if I found you a woman you'd think about it. Man, you're a Muslim now. You've got to keep your promises."

I should have remembered I was talking to Ismail. "Okay, so what should I do? Call her up and ask her out?"

"No, man, that's not how you do it with a Muslim girl. What it is, I'll talk to her brother and set up a time for the two of you to meet. Then you'll go see her and talk to her, with her brother and me as chaperones. You don't get to go out with her until after the wedding."

What have I gotten myself into, I thought. "Okay, go ahead and arrange a meeting. How bad can it be?" I'll meet her, we'll have nothing in common, and Ismail can go bother someone else.

I'll see her tonight. Ismail arranged for us to meet them at the restaurant. When I left work today, Fawad winked. "You're going to meet your wife tonight, eh?"

"Nothing like that. I'm just doing this as a favor to Ismail. She'll probably take one look at me and run screaming down the street."

"We'll see," he said, and winked again.

I'm about to head out to meet her when there's a knock at the door. It's Ismail.

"Yo man, what's wrong with you?"

"What's the problem, dude?"

"The way you're dressed. You've got to impress the girl. Blue jeans? I didn't know you wore those any more. Dress up a little. Do you have a suit?"

"Are you kidding? I haven't worn one of those since my mother stopped buying my clothes. I don't want to impress her, anyway. This was your idea."

He's looking through my closet. "Here, wear this. You got it in Pakistan?"

It's a dark blue tunic with matching pants, one of my best Pakistani suits. "Yeah. I only wear that on special days."

"This could be your special day, brother. Put it on."

"Well, you've got to get out of my room then." He is going to owe me big for this one. I close the door and change.

While we walk to the restaurant, Ismail continues to coach me. "Just remember, be yourself. Smile a lot—girls like that. Be sure not to stare—Muslim girls don't like that."

"What makes you such an expert?"

He just winks and opens the restaurant door. She's here.

I see her. That must be her. I hope that's her. She's sitting at a corner table, wearing a long green dress. Her scarf is a pattern of flowers, and matches her dress. As we walk toward her, she looks up briefly, and then lowers her eyes.

The man sitting next to her stands to greet us. He's a few inches taller than I am, and has broad shoulders and a full black beard. "Assalaamu alaikum. I'm Umar, and this is my sister, Aisha."

"Walaikum assalaam. My name is Isa." I shake hands with Umar, and glance at Aisha. Her eyes are still lowered, but she smiles.

"First of all," says Umar, "I need to know more about you. Ismail tells me you were married before, and have children."

He's going to interview me. I am going to get Ismail for this. "Yeah, that's right. I guess I can tell you that I did some stupid things when I was younger. I got Heather—that's my ex-wife—I got her pregnant, and we got married. We had, we have, three children. Michael, Jeremy, and Jennifer. I'm trying to get custody of them."

"Why didn't you get custody when you first divorced?"

"Like I said, I was stupid. I walked out on them. It wasn't until I became a Muslim, not really until I went to Pakistan that I realized what I had done."

"Have you ever thought about reconciling with your ex-wife?"

"No. That whole marriage was a big mistake. We were young."

"But you did have three children together."

"Yeah, we did."

"And what are you doing now?"

I'm sweating. I didn't know it would be like this. "I have a job here at this restaurant. I'm trying to get myself set right, so I can get my kids back."

"And you want to marry my sister because that will look good to the judge."

"No, not at all." I laugh nervously. "Look, this was Ismail's idea. If you don't like me, then we can just all go back home and forget about it."

"Take it easy, Brother Isa. I just need to know what kind of man you are. Aisha is my only sister, and she's very special to me."

I can tell. She is special. "Yeah, sure. Is there anything else you want to know?"

"What are your plans for the future?"

"Just to get my kids. After that, I don't know."

"What about college?"

"I haven't really thought about it."

"Aisha is almost finished with her undergraduate degree in elementary education. She would need a husband who is educated, also."

"Brother Umar, school and I never got along very well. I just barely graduated from high school. I did find out in Pakistan that I'm pretty good at learning languages, but that's about it."

"Did you like living in Pakistan?" It's Aisha who speaks, not Umar. Her voice is soft and light.

"Yes, yes I did. It was, well, it was good. The people actually cared about me. Especially Abdul-Qadir. I stayed with him while I was studying."

"What did you study?" I'm glad she's asking the questions.

"Qur'an, and Arabic. Like I said, I'm good with languages. So I picked it up pretty easily."

"Do you speak Arabic?"

"Some, but I'm still learning. I do speak Urdu. Um, can I ask you a question?"

Umar nods. "Go ahead."

"Are you going to be a teacher?"

"Yes. I love children. I plan to graduate at the end of next year, insha Allah. I can't wait to have my own classroom." As she talks she continues to lower her eyes. I try to lower mine, but she is so pretty.

"That's great. Um, how did you become a Muslim?"

"Umar is the one who taught me about Islam. He came to Chicago first, and while he was here, he converted. When he came back to Moline—that's where we're from—he told me a little about Islam, and I wanted to learn more. We convinced our parents to let me study here. I took Shahadah two years ago, soon after I came to Chicago."

"You're the only girl?"

"Yes. Besides me, there's Umar, and our thirteen-year-old brother, Marcus, who lives back in Moline with our parents."

Umar interrupts. "Tell me, Brother Isa. Why did you convert to Islam? What did you see that made you want to become a Muslim?"

This is the toughest question yet. I still have a hard time putting it into words. "Well, it started with Mahmoud. After I left my family, I didn't know where to go. Mahmoud let me stay with him and the guys. And I saw how they acted. It was different than anything I'd ever seen before. Especially the way they accepted me. No one ever did that before." Umar raises his eyebrows. "My father left us when I was a baby, and I think my mom always blamed me for it. Anyway, she always thought that I was a major loser, and I usually was. But Mahmoud and the guys were good to me and they didn't try to hassle me. So when they asked me to go with them to the masjid, I went. And I liked the way everything in Islam works so well. I just felt like I belonged. Then Mahmoud sent me to Pakistan, where I studied Arabic and Qur'an, and learned how to be a better Muslim. I stayed with a brother named Abdul-Qadir. He's the one who taught me the things I should have learned from my father."

"Do you pray regularly? What about your fasting?"

"Yes, I pray. I try to go to the masjid, but I don't always make it. Fasting was rough last Ramadan, but I got through it. I think it helped that I was in Pakistan. And everyone tells me it'll get better."

"I have to tell you, Brother Isa, that I have some major concerns about your interest in my sister, especially because of

54

your previous marriage and the children. But I do like your honesty. I'll go home, talk with Aisha, and let you know. Aisha is the most important person in the world to me and I would never let anyone hurt her."

"Yeah, of course. I understand."

We spend a few awkward minutes eating the appetizers Fawad has brought over before Ismail and I excuse ourselves.

I shake hands with Umar, knowing that I'll probably never see him again. "It was nice meeting you. Assalaamu alaikum."

"Walaikum assalaam," both Umar and Aisha reply.

When we get outside Ismail starts up again. "Good job, man. See, I was right. I'm always right about these things. You two were made for each other."

"What are you talking about? Umar hates me, and I don't blame him. He would never let me near his sister again. And Aisha is nice, very nice, but she's going to college. What do I have to offer her?"

"See, you like her. I knew it."

"It doesn't matter. I'll never see her again." I'm surprised at how that thought makes me feel.

I wouldn't have minded getting to know Aisha better, but I need to concentrate on getting my kids back. After a couple of days, I've almost forgotten her. Once in a while, though, while I'm washing dishes or clearing a table, I think about her smile.

I work hard the next week, even putting in a few hours overtime. At the end of the week I'm exhausted. I'm stretched out on the couch, almost asleep, when there's a knock at the door.

"Assalaamu alaikum, Brother Isa." It's Umar. I recognize his deep voice.

"Walaikum assalaam. Come on in." I lead him to the couch, picking up dirty socks and a banana peel on my way. "Have a seat. Can I get you something? Water, or some tea maybe?"

"No, I'm fine. Come sit down. We need to talk." He sits down and leans forward, looking me straight in the eye. "I'm going to be blunt with you, Isa, but first I have to ask you a question. How do you feel about my sister?"

Should I say what I feel? I may never get another chance. "Honestly, Brother Umar, I like her. She's beautiful. But I know I don't have a chance with her. She's too special. And I'm just, well, just a guy with an ex-wife, three kids, and a dead-end job."

He shakes his head. "If it were just up to me, you wouldn't have a chance. I don't think you're good enough for her. But," I wait as he takes a long sigh, "Aisha likes you, too. She says she sees something in you. Something more than the man you just described. She told me she sees someone who could be special."

Maybe I'm dreaming. I've never been special, especially not to someone like Aisha. I reach into my sleeve and pinch my left arm.

"As I said, I don't think you're good enough. But Aisha wants to get to know you. We've talked about it all week, and I want my sister to be happy. So, we've reached a compromise."

"Which is?"

"I will allow you six months to get to know one another. During that time you can meet once or twice a week, always in my presence. Also, during that time, I will be conducting a thorough background check. I will be talking to everyone who has ever known you—even your first grade teacher, if that's what it takes. If even one thing you've told me doesn't check out, you will be history.

"At the end of six months, if Aisha is attracted to you, and if you feel the same, I'll take you to meet our parents. Then you will ask our father for his permission. If he agrees, you will marry her."

My head is spinning. A week ago, I was practically cursing Ismail for trying to fix me up. Now I might have the chance to marry this beautiful Muslim girl. If I can pass the tests.

"I should point out that you don't have any say in these conditions. No negotiations. Only a simple yes or no."

My smile should be answer enough, but he's still looking at me, waiting. I clear my throat. "Yeah, uh, yes, I'd like that."

"Good. Aisha will be pleased. I will call you tomorrow about your next meeting with her. At that time I will also need contact information for all your family members. Including your ex-wife.

For the background check."

I have the feeling that he's trying to scare me. But I'm lost in my dreams of what might be. When I come back to reality, Umar is still there, looking at me.

"I, uh, I'm sorry. Are you sure I can't get you anything?"

"No, I'm fine. I need to get back. Aisha is waiting for me. You can wait for my call. Assalaamu alaikum."

"Walaikum assalaam."

After he leaves, I make ablutions, say my evening prayers, and stretch out on the couch. My dreams are filled with Aisha's smile.

I see her again three days later. She's waiting for me at the restaurant. With Umar, of course. When she sees me, she smiles.

"Assalaamu alaikum. Thank you."

"Walaikum assalaam. Thank you for what?"

"For giving me a chance. Would you like to take a walk?"

We both look at Umar.

"That sounds okay, but I'll have to go too. Where do you want to walk?"

"Around the neighborhood. Just to walk and talk."

"Let's go, then." We leave the restaurant, with Umar between us. It's going to be hard to talk to her that way but it's the best we can do, for now.

She's petite, much smaller than Umar. I'm a few inches taller than her, I think.

"Um, Aisha, Umar said you see something in me. No one has ever said that before. What is it, that you see in me, I mean?"

"I don't know. Part of it is your honesty, I guess. You haven't tried to feed me a line. I just want to get to know you better."

"Where should we start?"

"What about your family? You mentioned your father. What about your mother? Do you have brothers and sisters?"

I tell her about the last time I saw my mother, many months ago, and the last time I talked with my brothers. "They've never seen anything in me but trouble. That's why I haven't talked to them for so long."

"But you need to. We can't just cut off ties with our families. I'm sure you know that. You say they don't understand you, but have you ever tried understanding them?"

"There's not much to understand. My mom hates me for making Sam leave, Brad can't stand me because I'm not successful the way he is, and Chris has condemned me to hell. What can I do?"

"You should try to see things through their eyes. Do you think they still love you?"

"I don't know. Maybe, somewhere deep down. I really don't know."

"I think they do. And I think you love them, too. Otherwise, their words and attitudes wouldn't bother you so much. Think about contacting them again. I mean it."

When she puts it that way, everything sounds so simple. It's never felt that simple to me. "I'll think about it. What about you? What kind of family do you have?"

She tells me about her father, a high school principal in the Quad Cities area, and her mother, a registered nurse. "They've always been strict with me, especially since I was the only girl. But they've always supported me, too."

"Even when you became a Muslim?"

"Yes, even then. Of course, Umar became a Muslim first, so he helped them get used to the idea. My parents are devout Christians, but they respect all of their children and trust us to make the right decisions. Even if we're not Christians like they are, they realize that we still worship God and try to live godly lives. That's all they need from us."

She tells me more about growing up in Moline. The family lives in a brick house on a quiet, tree-lined street. When she was young, she loved to bike and rollerblade up and down the street. She always liked school and always got good grades. She loves to read and never cared for "girly" things like dolls and gossiping. She was an honor roll student in high school and she's attending Northeastern Illinois University on a full scholarship.

Chicago is less than 200 miles from Moline, but my

childhood was a million miles from hers. I wonder if we'll be able to bridge the gap.

We've walked about three blocks. There's an ice cream shop across the street. "Do you like ice cream?"

"I love ice cream. Especially mint chocolate chip. Actually, I like anything with chocolate."

"Sounds good to me. Let's go."

I dated Heather for two years before we got married, but we never had a normal courtship. She was hot. I had a long list of conquests before her, and she was just another good-looking girl. At first I liked some things about her, like her giggle. But that got old after a while. We never talked about important things. We never even went for ice cream.

The next day, while I'm washing dishes, I remember what Aisha said about trying to understand my family. She's right, I do love them. And I guess they love me, too. But why do they treat me the way they do? Why are they so angry? Maybe Aisha will be able to tell me. I can't wait to see her again.

❦

The next time I see her, I find out that her favorite color is red. She loves animals, and she had to leave a calico cat named Frisky back home in Moline. When she was five, she got spanked for lying to her mother, so she learned to never lie again. When she was fourteen, she sneaked into an R-rated movie, but Umar found out and told their father. She was grounded for a month.

I just listen. I like listening to her. She'd probably like to know more about me, but I don't want to tell her that when I was five I learned how to shoplift and when I was fourteen I started smoking weed. Maybe later.

We do talk about my family again.

"Have you thought any more about what I said? About keeping in contact with your family?"

"I think about it a lot. But I don't know how to do it. If I visit them, or call, they'll just tell me all over again what a major disappointment I am. You're right, I think. They probably do love me. But why do they treat me like that?"

"That's how they express their love."

"Huh?"

"Okay, when my dad gets a difficult student sent to his office, he has to be firm. If you ask the kid, he'll probably say Dr. Evans yelled at him and Dr. Evans hates him. But I know Dad really cares about his students. He has to discipline them. And sometimes he does yell, if he thinks that's the only way they can hear him. Some of his students have come back to him, many years later, and thanked him for being so strict. Once they get out in the world, and have children of their own, they understand."

"Yeah, I had a principal like that. But I don't know if he really cared about me, or just felt like yelling. Anyway, what does that have to do with my family?"

"Every family establishes its own pattern of communication. In your family, the way they communicated with you was to rebuke you. They probably didn't feel comfortable showing their affection, so they exhibited their concern in other ways."

"You know, I can hardly understand what you're saying. How can a smart girl like you ever be interested in a bum like me?"

She looks at me. For the first time, I see her eyes. They're dark and round. "You are not a bum. Don't keep thinking about yourself that way. We become what we expect to become. If you expect to always be a bum, then we might as well not even bother seeing each other again."

Now I'm really confused. "What?"

"Isa, you have many good qualities. You're honest and caring. And you're smart. I know you're good at learning languages, and I'm sure you can learn many other things, too. Any teacher who told you otherwise should have been fired. But you won't stop being a 'bum,' as you call it, until you stop thinking of yourself as a bum."

"Would you help me?"

She smiles. "Yes, I'd like that."

"By the way, my family calls me Joshua. But I like Isa better."

"Then I'm pleased to meet you, Joshua. My family calls me Angela."

I would like to ask what they call Umar, but he still scares me a little. While we talk, he plays the part of the quiet chaperone. But I know he's watching me closely. He hasn't said anything about the background check. I wonder if he's talked to my family yet.

We see each other every few days, and each time I learn something new about her. Often, I also learn something new about myself.

One day, after we've been seeing each other for about two months, she hands me a magazine of some sort. "What's this?"

"It's a college catalog. You still have time to enroll and register for fall classes."

"College? I told you, I barely made it through high school. You're the smart one."

"Stop that, Isa. Give it a try, at least. You might be surprised."

"What do I have to do?"

"Fill out some forms, to start with. Then they'll ask you to take placement tests, to see if you need extra classes in math or composition. After that, they'll tell you what classes to take."

"You left out the part about taking the classes."

"Yes, of course that's part of it."

"Can't you just accept it, Aisha, that I'll never amount to anything? I don't know, maybe you should think about another guy. I'll never be good enough for you."

"Stop saying that!" Her soft voice is lost in a yell. "I am so sick of hearing you put yourself down. 'Oh, poor Joshua, he never could amount to anything, you know.' I fell for it, at first. But now I know it's just a lame excuse for never trying."

Umar is smiling. He must know this side of her. I sure didn't. "What's going on? Why are you ragging on me?"

"Because I'm tired of your great, big, pity, party. Poor Joshua, his father left him and nobody ever understood him. Poor Joshua, my foot! You have got to start getting over yourself."

No one says anything for several minutes. She's quiet, but when I glance over I see a tear run down her cheek. She really means it.

"Okay," I say finally, "I'll give it a try. If it means that much to you."

"It does," she says softly. "Thank you."

Three weeks later, I'm enrolled at Wilbur Wright College. Based on the advice of a counselor, I sign up for freshman composition and college math. Aisha would have liked for me to take more classes, but my budget won't allow it. Anyway, two classes will be enough to see if I really can do it.

She keeps talking about how I should get in touch with my family, and I finally decide that she's right. I'm still not ready for a confrontation, though. I write them each a note.

I tell my mother that I have a good job and I'm signed up for college classes. That should give her a nice shock. I also tell her that I'm still determined to get custody of my kids. Most importantly, I tell her that I'm still a Muslim. I don't tell her about Aisha. Not yet.

First, I have to see how this all turns out.

The note I send to Brad is almost the same. I tell him, too, that I haven't thrown anything away, except for the pain and the craziness of my youth.

It's harder for me to write to Chris. I start many times, but end up throwing the paper in the trash. Finally I write, "There is no God but Allah, the One God, and Muhammad is his messenger. This is what I believe, what I will always believe." I include the same news that I put in the other two letters, but end by saying, "In Islam, I have finally found peace."

Two days after I send the letters, the imam delivers a sermon about keeping ties with family members. Finally I can listen without guilt.

❧

Except that I'm still guilty. I haven't seen my kids in almost two years. My lawyer has tried to get me some visitation rights, without going to court, but Heather won't allow it. I did walk out on them.

After sending the letters, I think even more about my kids. I could write to them, but Heather wouldn't allow that, either. Suddenly I'm aching for them. I remember holding Michael in my arms. I can hear his laughter. I can see Jeremy's little round face. I can't picture Jennifer at all, and that hurts the most.

I start driving by the old apartment in the evening after I get off from work. Heather might have moved by now. She could even have remarried. Each time I stop for a while, looking at the window on the second floor. They could still be there.

I've been driving by, off and on, for about a month. Finally, one day, I see a dark-haired boy in the distance. Could that be Michael? He's so tall. Behind him is a little round-faced boy who's holding the hand of a beautiful little girl. Their mother is yelling at them all to hurry up and get home.

I stop so suddenly that I almost get hit from behind. The other driver honks his horn and Heather looks in my direction. I don't want her to see me. I keep on driving down the street, with just a glance as I go past the children I left behind.

I'm starting to feel like my life is out of control again. The last time I felt this way was when Heather told me she was pregnant with Jennifer. We already had too many unpaid bills and I didn't see how we could afford another kid. Until I saw Jennifer today, I had never thought of her as my little girl. I do have a daughter. And it might be too late for me to know her.

There are just too many things going on at once. I'm trying to work hard at my job and save money. But I also spend half of my time thinking about Aisha. And I have to take those stupid college classes.

I'm only doing it because of Aisha. I still don't think I'll be any good at college. But it means so much to her, and she's starting to mean so much to me.

I'm going to get Ismail. There I was, just working at my job and focusing on my kids, when he had to go and complicate things. And I still don't know how it's all going to turn out. We have three months to go. Will she change her mind when she sees that I really am just a bum? Or will it be her father who throws me out on my ear?

I'm feeling restless again. I won't see Aisha for two more

days. I can't get to my kids. The college classes start tomorrow. I'm way past drinking beer to help me through things, but I don't think hot curry will help this time, either.

There's only one person I can talk to. It should be early morning in Karachi right now.

One of the boys answers.

"Assalaamu alaikum. This is Isa, from America. Is this Ibrahim?"

"Oh, assalaamu alaikum, Isa. Yes, I am Ibrahim. How are you?"

"I'm okay. Are you still playing football?"

"Yes, my team is in the city finals. Would you like to talk to my father?"

"Yes, please. It was nice to talk to you."

It's another minute or two before Abdul-Qadir gets to the phone. I can hear all of the kids in the background. I wonder what little Nuruddin is doing now.

"Assalaamu alaikum, Isa. How are you? Is everything okay?"

"Walaikum assalaam. I need to talk." I tell him about everything. About how much I miss my kids. About my relationship with Aisha. About how worried I am over taking those college classes.

"You're going to college? That's very good."

"But Abdul-Qadir, I can't go. I'm no good at school."

"You were very good at school when you were here."

"But that was Karachi, not America. I was lousy at school in America."

"Lousy? No, don't say that. Maybe when you were young. You're older now, and you know much more. You'll be fine."

We talk a while longer, about his business and his children. Nuruddin is laughing and shouting in the background. "Hello, Uncle Isa."

I suddenly remember how much this must be costing me. "It's been very good talking to you, Abdul-Qadir, but I have to go."

"You'll be fine. Don't worry. I trust in your ability. And I'll be looking for a wedding invitation in a few months."

"You would come?"

"If I can, insha Allah. I would like to be there for you, my son."

You are here for me.

Aisha is right. All my life I've been cursing myself because of Sam. Sam left because of me, my mother used to say when she was mad. And I believed her. I wasn't good enough for Sam. And I wasn't good enough for my mother.

But Allah brought me to Abdul-Qadir, who is ten times the man Sam ever was. And Abdul-Qadir loves me and believes in me. I thank Allah for Abdul-Qadir.

I'm not quite so edgy now, but I do have trouble sitting still. I stop by the house. Mahmoud and his wife live in the suburbs, but Ismail and Tariq are still here. They're playing a video game when I walk in. I still have a key.

"Assalaamu alaikum, dudes. What's up?"

"Hold on," says Tariq. "I'm about to kill Ismail."

"Whatever, man! I'm gonna whup you."

I hang around until they're done. Ismail wins. "Yeah, dawg!"

"Whatever," says Tariq. "So what's up, Isa?"

"Nothing. I just felt like chilling."

"You ready to hit the books, man?"

"Dude, I don't know what's up with that. I can't do school again."

"Don't worry, man," says Ismail. "You'll be aight."

We go out for pizza and come back for more video games. I can't stay too late, though. I've got to get ready for tomorrow.

I go to bed early, but I don't sleep well. I've got to go to those classes. The teachers will probably laugh me right out of the classroom.

❧

My classes are every Tuesday and Thursday morning. Fawad let me change my schedule to fit them in. My first class is Composition.

I didn't have much trouble getting to the college. It's only a few miles from my apartment. I felt a little strange, though, looking for the classroom. I sure wasn't going to ask anyone.

I finally find it about ten minutes before class is supposed to start. Some people are already in the room. I find a seat in the back. A few others straggle in after me. Most of them are younger than me, all pimply faced and long-legged. Man, did I ever look like that?

After a few minutes, a man comes in, puts some papers and a book on the table at the front of the room, and clears his throat. The teenagers in the front stop talking. "Good morning. I'm Mr. Walker. I'll be your instructor for this course."

He looks nice. He must be about Brad's age.

"First of all, I'd like you each to introduce yourself. Say your name and something else you'd like us to know about you."

Oh great. I thought I was going to be able to sit back here and be invisible. The teenagers go first. They talk mostly about their summer jobs. One of them just got out of braces. One of them giggles, like Heather.

It's my turn. "I'm Joshua Adams, and I don't really want to be here."

Did I say that? Oh well. Aisha says she likes my honesty.

"All right, Mr. Adams. We'll see what we can do about that."

I hate when teachers talk like that. My junior high principal did that. "Now, Joshua, why do we think we were sent to the office today?" Great.

"How many of you like to write?" Just a few people raise their hands. Mr. Walker nods. "The rest of you might be surprised. By the end of this semester I'm willing to bet that most of you will be raising your hands. Even you, Mr. Joshua Adams."

Good. I've been in class for ten minutes and already he has it in for me.

He starts talking about different kinds of writing, and why writing is important. I stay awake, but it's hard to pay attention. The class is almost over when he gives us an assignment.

"For next time, I want you to write an essay about yourself. Feel free to express yourself any way you wish. This is just an exercise, to help you become more comfortable with writing. Any questions?"

The giggly teen raises her hand. "Can we write about anything?"

"Anything at all. Try not to confess to any crimes, though. That would put me in a sticky situation." He smiles. What a lame joke. "If there are no other questions, you are free to go. I'll see you on Thursday."

Well, that's over. Just one more class. At least he didn't laugh at me—not yet, anyway.

I'm almost out the door when Mr. Walker calls out, "I'm looking forward to your essay, Mr. Adams."

❧

Math class was okay. I wasn't that bad in math, back when I was in high school. I just hated doing the homework. The teacher, Mrs. Collins, is okay, too. We have to do twenty problems for Thursday, but I think it's the same stuff I learned before. It shouldn't be too hard.

I get back to the restaurant toward the end of the lunch rush. When the customers are gone and everything is cleaned up, Fawad calls me over.

"Let's sit down, Isa. We have a few minutes."

We each fill up a plate.

"How were your classes?"

"They were okay. I guess they went better than I thought they would."

"That's good. I have a problem, and I was wondering if you would be interested in helping me with it."

After everything Fawad has done for me, I couldn't possibly say no. "Sure, whatever you need."

"As you know, running a restaurant is a lot of work. You've been around here long enough to see everything I have to do—ordering supplies, paying bills, making work schedules, keeping up with repairs, all that. And, of course, I always have to make sure my customers are happy.

"The problem is, my wife and children hardly ever get to see me. My wife has been complaining a lot lately about me not being home. And when I do get home, I'm usually too tired to enjoy being with her and the children. I would like to be home more, to spend time with them and be a family."

"What can I do? Do you want me to work longer hours?"

"Not exactly. You're a smart young man, I can see that. Now that you're taking college classes, I think you may be ready for something more than washing dishes. What would you think about becoming my assistant?"

He must be kidding. I laugh. "Sure, I could do that. No, I'm better off as a dishwasher."

"I mean it, Isa. You really could do that. Of course, you would need some training, but that wouldn't be a problem. As long as I can tell my wife that I'm working on cutting back, she'll be happy. I think after a few months you could be ready to run this place and give me a little free time."

"If you think I could do it."

"I know you could. You helped Abdul-Qadir with his store back in Karachi, didn't you?"

"Sure, but that was different."

"You can do it. Starting tomorrow, I want you to wash dishes part time. The rest of the time, you'll be my trainee. There will be a raise too, of course."

"Okay. Thank you."

"Once I can stay home more, my wife will be thanking you. Just keep working hard on those college courses. You'll be surprised at how far you can go."

I can't wait to tell Aisha. I wonder if she's one of those women who likes to say "I told you so."

We meet the next evening at the restaurant, as usual. We go for our usual walk—with Umar between us. There are times when I want to hold her hand. Sometimes I would like to grab her and kiss her. But I have to follow Islam. No touching unless, until, we're married.

We walk in silence. I want to see how long she can wait.

Not long. "Do you have anything to tell me?"

"Oh, I don't know. Khalid came up with a new dish

yesterday. I think the customers are going to like it. Ismail is still bugging me, but I think it's his job. We have three more months before I face your father. Anything else?"

"Oh, come on, Isa, you know. How were your classes?"

"Classes? Oh, yeah, I forgot."

"What? You didn't forget to go, did you?"

It's like a slap in the face. I stop where I am, and she turns around. "I'm sorry. I didn't mean it. It's just, well, the way you were talking. You were playing with me, weren't you?"

"I was. I don't feel like playing anymore."

"I'm sorry."

"You really thought I would forget to go? Is that how you think of me?"

"No, no, I'm sorry. That's not it. It's just, well, the way you talk sometimes, I never know."

"You don't trust me."

She's silent.

I turn back toward my apartment. "It was nice meeting you, Sister Aisha. Good luck with your life."

I don't glance back to see her standing there, in the neon light of our ice cream shop, alone with Umar.

Part Three

It's a good thing I came home early. I haven't done my homework. Aisha won't care anymore about me or my studies, but I have something to prove to myself.

I do the math first. I still remember most of the formulas from high school, and the calculator does a lot of the work, anyway. The twenty problems are quickly out of the way.

Now I have to think about Mr. Walker's essay. Write about myself. Where do I start? Where do I stop?

I decide to start with the day I became a Muslim. I tell about my life in Pakistan, and how much I miss Abdul-Qadir. I write about the time my mother cried, and how I felt when Fawad gave me the job. I don't write about Aisha. I don't want to think about her. She thinks she is so superior to me.

I do write about my kids. Especially about how much I want to be with them. And I write about seeing them, driving past, and not being able to stop and hug them.

Once I start writing, it's hard to stop. The words come from somewhere inside of me. I write them down as quickly as I can. My life and feelings are turned into ink.

I finish, finally, with the moment when Fawad asked me to become his assistant. I started my training today. I think I can do it, insha Allah.

❧

I turned in my essay last Thursday. Mr. Walker asked each of us to read a paragraph to the class. I decided to read about the day I saw my kids, but couldn't stop. Everyone was quiet, even the giggly teenager.

Today after class, Mr. Walker asks me to stay for a moment. I know I'm not in trouble, because I've been doing all my work. He pulls out my paper from his briefcase.

"I wanted to talk to you about this essay, Mr. Adams."

"What's wrong with it?"

"Not very much, really. You need to work a little on your spelling and grammar, but you did an excellent job of communicating your feelings. I thought you didn't like writing."

"I didn't, not back when Miss Stevens taught it in ninth grade."

"Well, it looks like both you and your writing have matured a great deal since then. Has anyone ever said you have a talent for language?"

Many people have. But I think of Aisha. I try to picture her smile, but it looks more like a sneer now. "Someone did, once."

"You wrote in your essay about your time in Pakistan. You were studying languages there?"

"Yes, I went to learn Arabic. I also learned to speak Urdu."

"Well, Mr. Adams, I think you have a definite talent. Keep up the good work."

She really didn't think I could do it. What would she say now?

I fall into a pattern of school, work, and training. Life is almost normal, except that I don't have my kids, and I don't have Aisha.

I've been going to school for two months when Ramadan starts. I'm a little worried about fasting and going to school. Fasting isn't easy for me, and I need more energy to concentrate on my studies. But I need to keep going to school, and I must fast. I can't drop out of either one.

Fawad changes the hours of operation during Ramadan. He stays open during the lunch hour for our non-Muslim customers. Then he closes the restaurant in the early afternoon and opens it again about an hour after sunset. That's when our Muslim customers come in to celebrate another day of fasting. During Ramadan, the restaurant stays open until nearly midnight.

When I'm not working or going to school, I spend my extra time in the masjid. I go there every night for the special night prayers. After the prayers, I stay late, reading the Qur'an and praying on my own. This is my second Ramadan, but I feel that it's my most important one. I have to decide what direction I'm going in. Next year at this time will I still be in school? Will I have my kids with me? Will I have found someone to take Aisha's place in my life?

I spend the last few days of Ramadan living at the masjid. This gives me extra time to pray, and think. I can see, now, how I messed up my life. I'm still not completely sure how to fix it, but I think I'm getting there.

I've bought a new Pakistani suit for Eid. On Eid day, I go to the prayer with Ismail and Tariq. Ismail never asks about Aisha. I guess Umar told him.

At the end of the prayer, we hug each other in happiness at the end of Ramadan. It was a good month. Now it's time to take what I've learned and use it during the rest of the year.

Thousands of us are standing outside after the prayer, too happy to leave. There's talking and laughing all around. Then, through the noise, I hear a woman's voice calling my name.

Aisha.

She comes running toward me, with Umar nowhere in sight. I want to hug her, but I have to hold back. She runs up, and nearly hugs me.

"I'm sorry, Isa. I'm so sorry. I've missed you so much. Can you forgive me?"

Three months is long enough to be angry. I smile. "Yes, I forgive you."

I want so much to hold her and kiss her. I think I would have, if Umar hadn't appeared.

"Assalaamu alaikum, Isa. Eid mubarak."

"Eid kareem." We shake hands.

"I heard about your promotion. Congratulations."

"Alhamdulillah. Fawad has a lot of trust in me, and I'm grateful for everything he's taught me."

"Your classes are going well?"

"I'm getting A's in both of them so far. My composition instructor has been mentoring me. I'm finally starting to like school."

"That's good, very good. So, it's been six months. What do you think?"

Now it's my turn. "I don't know. She is a little bossy. And she can be distrustful, which is not very good for a relationship."

"Yes, I agree." He smiles. "So?"

"So I guess I'll have to marry her so she won't go hurting the feelings of some other poor guy."

"And you, Aisha?"

She looks into my eyes. "Yes, I want to marry you."

Ismail comes up from behind me. "I knew it. Didn't I tell you? Man, I knew it all along."

Part Four

It's Thanksgiving Day. I'm in her parents' living room. We've just arrived, and I've just shaken hands with her father, Dr. Evans. He looks like Umar, but older. He's heavier, and his black hair and beard are streaked with white.

"It's nice to meet you, Joshua. Have a seat." His voice is deep and imposing.

"Thank you, Dr. Evans. It's very nice to meet you, too." My throat is dry.

"Angela, can you come here and help me with these pies?" Aisha's mother pokes her head through the kitchen door. "Welcome to our home, Joshua. If you would excuse me, I'm trying to get this dinner together. Angela?"

"Yes, Mom." She walks slowly toward the kitchen, glancing back at me, and her father.

"Good. We'll have some time to talk. You know Tony, of course." So that's Umar's other name. I still haven't felt comfortable enough to ask him. "And this is our youngest son, Marcus."

I shake hands with Marcus. He's at that awkward age. Too tall to be a kid, but still young.

"Did you have a nice trip? I was worried about the snow they've been predicting."

"Yes sir, it was a good trip. We didn't run into any snow, though it may come later tonight, I've heard."

"It's been getting cold, too."

"Yes sir, it has. They say it may be a rough winter this year."

"Yes, that's what I've heard, also."

The topic of weather has been exhausted. In the background, I hear a television, with sounds of a football game. Aisha and her mother are making noises in the kitchen. But in the living room, where we sit, there is silence.

A calico cat jumps on to the couch and comes over to sit on my lap. "This must be Frisky." I stroke her head and neck.

"Yes, that's her. Do you like animals?"

"Yes, I do. Very much." I have always liked animals, but my mother would never let me have a pet. Dogs sometimes found me and begged for my attention, but she would shoo them away. Once I brought home a black and white kitten, but she made me take it back. When I tried to collect live bugs she had a fit.

"That's good. Frisky seems to like you, too." She purrs and rubs her head against my hand.

"Um, Dr. Evans, Aisha, I mean Angela, tells me that you're a principal."

"Yes, for over twenty years now. A lot of things have changed since I first started. But I like it. I like to think I'm making a difference."

"I'm sure you are. It's good. To make a difference, I mean."

"And Angela told us you're the assistant manager at a restaurant."

"Yes sir. I've been working there for almost a year now. It's a good place. I have a good boss."

"Is that your career plan? To work in the restaurant business?"

"Um, I'm not sure yet. I've been taking some college classes, trying to see what I should do. People tell me that I'm good with language. I'm just not sure yet."

"Angela will be a teacher soon."

"Yes, sir, she's told me. She's very smart."

"Yes, she is."

A brief exchange, and we're quiet again. Mr. Walker told me that I'm good at expressing my feelings. Why can't I do it now?

"Listen, Joshua, Tony has told me why you've come here. Why don't you go ahead?"

Tony? Oh yeah, he means Umar. Since Eid day, Umar has been friendly toward me. He's on my side now. Or maybe he always was.

"Well sir, Aisha, I mean Angela, and I have been getting to know one another. It was all very proper, sir. Umar, I mean Tony, was always with us. That's the way it is in Islam. Anyway, we've been getting to know each other, and, well, sir, if it's all right with you, I would like your permission to marry her." There, I've said it. Now what?

He leans back in his chair and takes a deep breath. "Angela is my only daughter, you know. It won't be easy for me to have another man in her life."

He stops there, and says nothing else for several minutes. Was that his answer? What did he mean?

Finally he continues. "Joshua, I need to know a little more about you. Tony told me all about his part. He did the background check, and he's satisfied with what he's found, but I still have some questions, if you don't mind."

"Oh, no sir, not at all."

"First of all, about your ex-wife and your children. Tony tells me she was pregnant when you married her."

"Yes sir. As I told Tony, I was pretty stupid when I was younger. I did some things I'm not proud of. That was one of them. But I've been trying very hard to change."

"Yes, so I see. And what about your children? How is your relationship with them now?"

"One of the stupidest things I ever did was to walk out on them. I didn't try to get custody when the divorce went through because I was feeling, well, trapped. I didn't know, then, how precious they were to me. That began to change while I was in Pakistan."

"Yes, that's another thing I wanted to ask you about. What is it you did in Pakistan?"

"I stayed with a family, and studied Arabic and Qur'an at a small school near their home. The man I stayed with, Abdul-Qadir, is the one who showed me how important it is to be a father."

"I have to ask you this. Did you get involved in any terrorist organizations while you were there?"

"No sir. I went to the mosque to pray, went to school, and helped Abdul-Qadir in his store. That's all."

"Okay. I hope you're telling me the truth, because I don't want to see your name up on the news. You didn't finish telling me about your children."

"Well, sir, Heather, my ex-wife, won't let me see them. I have a lawyer, and he's filed for a new custody hearing. It should be soon, in a few months, I think. I miss my children very much. That's why I have a two-bedroom apartment, so they'll have a place to stay when they come to live with me. I know now that I shouldn't have left them like that. Like I said, I was stupid."

"And now? How are you now?"

"I'm not perfect, but I don't think I'll ever be that stupid again. Angela and Tony have taught me some things, and I have a lot of friends who have helped me. Mostly, Islam has shown me what is right."

"Well, Joshua, Christianity does that, too. Didn't you go to church when you were a boy?"

"No sir, not very often. I do have a brother who teaches at a Bible college, though. He was always the religious one in the family."

He smiles. "I see. I still have a couple more questions. What about race? Have Angela and you thought about the difficulties you two may face in an interracial marriage?"

"No sir, I haven't. And Angela has never said anything about it. In Islam, we don't pay much attention to race or color. Abdul-Qadir is like a father to me, and he's darker than you are."

He chuckles. "Is that so? Well, that may be fine when you're with Muslims, then. But this isn't a Muslim society, it's a racist one. How will you handle the attitudes of some of the people you meet in this society? People who aren't so tolerant?"

I think of my mother. She has African-American friends from work, but I'm not sure she'd be happy if she knew who I am hoping to marry. "Yes sir, I am aware of that. But I think that Angela and I can handle it, whatever people try to say or do."

He nods. "Okay. Then I have one more question for you. Do you really care for my daughter?"

"Yes sir, I do."

"Are you aware that she's not perfect? Are you willing to accept her faults?"

I guess Umar didn't tell him about our three months apart. "Yes sir, no one is perfect. But Aisha, Angela, is beautiful."

"Yes, I know. And would you stay with her, in every kind of circumstance? We don't have divorces in this family, and I sure don't want to start with my daughter."

"Dr. Evans, I was a different man when I married Heather. You're around teenagers every day, so maybe you won't be shocked when I tell you that my relationship with Heather was mostly physical. But I've changed. I'm a Muslim now and Islam has given me a new direction. I know what I've done wrong and I'm determined to avoid the mistakes of my past. My relationship with Angela is different, too. I haven't even touched her. I love her for who she is. She's bright, energetic, and caring. She's beautiful."

"Yes, she is." He leans back, closes his eyes, and sits that way, silently, for a long time. I squirm, and Frisky jumps off my lap. I am literally sitting on the edge of my seat. What does he think? What will he say?

It feels like hours before he opens his eyes again. He leans forward and looks me in the eye. "You're right, Joshua. I deal with young people almost every day and I'm often required to make decisions which will affect their futures in some way. But none of those decisions has ever involved my daughter, my family. I have been sitting here wrestling with my emotions. Tony and Angela have had six months to get to know you, but I never set eyes on you until you walked into my house not thirty minutes ago. Should I give you permission to marry my Angela based on what you have said in the past thirty minutes?" He stops, and shakes his head. "At the same time, we've got a big dinner coming. In less than an hour, this living room will be crammed full with Angela's grandparents, aunts, uncles, cousins. I'm afraid, if I withhold my decision, it will ruin the dinner for all of us. And Mrs. Evans would certainly not be happy about that.

"Twenty years of being a principal has made me a pretty good judge of character, especially when I'm dealing with young men like you. Any principal who can't tell when someone is lying won't last long. I know you're being honest with me."

He leans back in his recliner again and looks up at the ceiling. His voice is soft and low, as if he's talking to himself. "I keep thinking back to when Angela was a little girl. She always wanted her daddy. When she was afraid, I would hold her. When she was happy, she would run and hug me. She has always been my girl."

His voice gets louder. "I think you are a good man, Joshua. You've made some mistakes in your life, but it seems to me that you've learned from them. I do believe you care for my daughter, and I know she cares for you, too. I'm not a poor man, but if I give my consent I'll be handing over my greatest treasure."

Another long pause. He leans forward and looks at me, wordlessly. I wait, holding my breath.

"Yes, you may marry her." He offers me his hand. He has a firm grip.

Aisha bursts from the kitchen and runs to her father. "Thank you, Daddy." She hugs him tightly.

I turn to Umar and Marcus. "Thank you for everything, brother."

"Just take good care of my sister."

"I will, Insha Allah. You know, Marcus, I've never had a little brother before."

He just grins.

It seems like only a few minutes later when the doorbell rings.

"I'll get it," says Aisha. She opens the door and calls out, "Grandma, Grandpa. Guess what. I'm getting married!"

Her grandparents are still standing on the front porch. They look stunned. Umar goes to their rescue. "Hi, Grandma and Grandpa. Come on in." After hugs from Aisha, Umar, and Marcus, the grandparents look around.

"So," says Grandpa, "who's the lucky man?"

"He's right here. This is Joshua."

They look at me. No, they stare. Grandpa raises his eyebrows. "You're marrying a white boy?"

"He's white? Oh, you know what, I didn't notice. I guess he is."

They shake their heads. "Don't get smart with us, little girl," says Grandma. "You're still not too big for me to take you over my knee."

"I'm sorry, Grandma." She hugs her. "Anyway, just talk to

him a little. You'll see how special he is."

This scene repeats itself several times as Aisha's other relatives arrive. I'm introduced to five aunts, four uncles, and I-don't-know-how-many cousins.

When I have a quiet moment, I whisper to Umar, "You sure have a lot of people in your family."

"This isn't all of them. Aunt Laura couldn't get in from California and my cousin Jerome is stationed overseas. You'll meet them later."

My mother has one brother who lives in L.A. I've seen him once or twice. Her parents died when I was young. Of course, I never knew any of Sam's family. It's a long way from Chicago to Moline.

❧

The rest of Thanksgiving was a blur. I tried to learn the names of the relatives. I answered questions about my parents, my past, and my future plans. One of Aisha's cousins was especially curious about my time in Pakistan. Aunt Vivien kept asking about my ex-wife. I often heard Aisha's laughter above the commotion.

At night, before I went to sleep on the spare bed in Umar's room, I thought about the day. I'm getting married again. I hope I can do it right this time. How could I live with myself if I ever hurt Aisha?

Umar and I walk into the kitchen soon after making the morning prayer together in his room. Their mother is already up and fixing breakfast.

"Good morning, Mrs. Evans. How are you?"

"I'm fine. How are you, Joshua? Did you sleep well?"

"Yes, thank you."

She's trying to flip pancakes while stirring the scrambled eggs and setting up the coffee maker.

"Can I help you? I know my way around a kitchen."

"Okay, why don't you take over the pancakes?"

"Sure. Um, I didn't get much of a chance to talk to you

yesterday, Mrs. Evans, but I just want you to know how special Angela is to me. I'm very grateful to you and your husband for allowing me to marry her."

"That's very nice, Joshua. And you can call me Sharon. I guess we'll be family soon. Angela's told me that Muslims usually have short engagements."

"Yes, that's right. We're not allowed to date or, anything, so it's better if we get married sooner."

"I understand. I was hoping for a garden wedding in May, but I guess we'll have to settle for December. What about your family? What do they think about all this?"

"Well, Mrs. Evans, they don't know yet. I guess Tony told you that I never really got to know my father. He left when I was a baby, and I only saw him a few times while I was growing up. I haven't talked to my mother for a few months. She and I don't exactly see eye to eye."

"That's a shame. Angela's family is so close. I was hoping your family would be like that, too. In fact, all day yesterday I was thinking about how much they must miss not having you there for Thanksgiving. Why is there a problem between your mother and you?"

"Well, I'm sure you've heard that I was a little wild when I was young. I've made a lot of mistakes. That didn't help. But even when I started trying to get my life on track, she didn't much like the idea of my being a Muslim."

"In a way, I can't blame her. It was a little hard for me, too, first with Tony and then Angela. I kept wondering if I had done something wrong. But then I realized that we had raised them to be thinking adults, and they were just doing what we had taught them. They were looking at the world through their own eyes, and the best way they could figure it all out was through Islam. Each of us has to find his or her own way. I guess your mother just hasn't reached that point yet, where she can understand. Try to be patient with her. She is your mother."

I guess she's right. Now I know why Aisha is so special.

The pancakes are almost done when Dr. Evans walks in. He looks at me, standing there in front of the stove with a spatula in my hand. "Oh, so you cook, too?"

"Well, sir, I have been working in a restaurant."

"Good, good. They smell delicious. Did you have a good sleep?"

"Yes sir."

"I didn't. I was awake most of the night thinking about my little girl. But, time passes, doesn't it?"

"Yes, Jim, it does. I guess we're going to have to get used to it. Now you know how my father felt when you married his little girl."

"But this is different, Sharon."

"How is it different?"

"I don't know. It just is. I don't mind telling you, Joshua, that I still have some reservations about you marrying my daughter. I like you, don't get me wrong, but a father has the right to worry. I'm glad you can cook, though. That's a good sign. A man who can cook won't expect his wife to wait on him."

"Do you cook, Dr. Evans?"

Mrs. Evans laughs. Dr. Evans looks at her. "I do, son. Just not here in the kitchen. I like to do my cooking outside, on the grill. When you come here in the summer, I'll fix you up a nice plate of ribs, or whatever it is Muslims eat. We have a big barbecue here every year in the middle of July. Everyone we know comes to the house just for a plate of my chicken and ribs. The secret is in the marinade, by the way. Now that's cooking."

Aisha is the last to come in for breakfast. "Good morning, Daddy." She kisses him on the cheek. "Assalaamu alaikum, Isa." She glances at me, and smiles.

"Angela, why are you wearing that scarf? I thought you told us you only wore that when you went outside the house."

"Because, Daddy, I have to wear it in front of Joshua, for now. Until we're married, that is."

"Okay, family, breakfast is ready. Marcus, could you go get the plates? Joshua, bring those pancakes over to the table. Angela, go fix some coffee for your father. Tony, can you get the biscuits out of the oven and set them over here? We'll have a nice breakfast, and then we can talk about the wedding."

"The wedding? So soon? What's the rush?" Dr. Evans glares at me. "You said you didn't touch my daughter." I almost drop the pancakes.

"He didn't do anything, Jim. Settle down. Have your coffee first, and then we'll talk about it."

We start to eat, but the mood has changed.

Dr. Evans picks up his mug and drinks his coffee in just a few gulps. Then he slams the mug down on the table, spilling most of whatever was left. "Okay, I've had my coffee. Now will you tell me what is going on?"

"Relax, dear. Your blood pressure. It's nothing, really. Joshua is telling the truth. He hasn't done anything to Angela. But Muslims like to have short engagements because they don't date the way other American kids do. Angela and I were talking about it last night, after you went to bed. They are young, after all."

"All right, then. I just don't want history to repeat itself." He glares at me again. "Angela, could you get me another cup of coffee?"

❧

After the dishes are cleared, Aisha and her mother tell us their plans for the wedding. They must have stayed up pretty late figuring it all out.

"Okay, Jim, are you ready? Because we're going to start talking about the wedding now and I want you to be involved."

"Go ahead."

"First of all, Angela and I were talking about the date. We decided the best time would be the last week of December. That way they can get married before their schools start up again. And Angela has to be back for her student teaching right away in January. Of course, we'll have to hope the weather cooperates. You never know, that time of year.

"Now, since Angela has a lot of family members here in Moline, and you have such a small family, Joshua, we thought it would be only right to have the wedding here. Is that okay with you?"

"Yes, Mrs. Evans, of course. As far as I know, it's traditional to get married in the girl's hometown."

"Oh good. That will be perfect, then. Now, one of the most important things is where in Moline to have the wedding. Angela won't get married in a church, but I don't think our family will want to go over to the mosque. What do you think about renting a hall here in town?"

"Are you asking me?"

"Yes, you and Joshua, of course."

"No church wedding? I've often thought about the day when I would walk my Angela down the aisle at our church."

"She's right, Dad. A Muslim shouldn't get married in a church. That's just the way it is."

"If you say so, Tony. Can I still walk her down the aisle in the hall, then?"

"I've been to a few Muslim weddings, and people do it different ways. If you really want to walk her down the aisle, I'm sure it can be done."

"Good. I'm glad to see I'm not completely left out of things."

"Don't worry, Daddy. You'll always be an important part of my life."

It's decided that Mrs. Evans will take care of renting the hall. Aunt Vivien and Aunt Debra will be in charge of the food. Uncle Paul will be the photographer.

"Now what about the invitations, Joshua? Do you want us to include both of your parents' names or your mother only?"

"My mother only. Sam was never a father to me."

"And how many people do you think you'll be inviting?"

"Well, there's my mother, Brad and his wife, the guys I used to live with, and Fawad. I hope Brad will come, but I don't think Chris will. That's it. Except for Abdul-Qadir, but I'm not sure he can make it all the way from Pakistan."

"Go ahead and invite him. I'm sure he'll appreciate it. So, that makes, oh, about ten or so from your side. And we'll have well over a hundred from Angela's side, what with family and her friends from high school and all. It's a little lopsided, I know, but I guess that's the way it is."

"Mom, what about the decorations? Can we get Aunt Arlene to do them?"

"Yes, that's a good idea. Arlene has a special knack for that."

"Okay, so we've talked about the hall, the ceremony, the food, the invitations, the decorations. Anything else?"

I never knew getting married could be so complicated. Heather and I just went down to the courthouse one day. Our mothers were too embarrassed to make a big fuss. Besides, her father refused to pay for a wedding.

"My dress! Do you think Grandma and Aunt Helen would help me with it? Maybe they could make one for me."

"But Angela, we have only a month to get ready. That's not much notice."

"I'll go talk to them today."

Aisha and her mother continue talking about details surrounding the special day. Dr. Evans, Umar, Marcus, and I sit and listen for a while, until we get bored. I did the hard part yesterday when I asked for her father's permission. Now it's their show.

❧

The rest of the weekend is uneventful. Aisha and her mother are gone most of the time, arranging for the hall and other details.

I don't think Dr. Evans likes me yet. I've tried to talk with him, but our conversations never get past the weather or the bowl games. He's still so formal. I think my past bothers him more than he's said. It's taken me a long time to realize that even though I've changed, I can't run away from the consequences of who I used to be.

I have started getting to know Umar better. After their father said yes, he seemed to accept me. He still doesn't talk much, but he's more relaxed around me now.

When we're ready to leave on Sunday, Dr. Evans shakes my hand. "I could say it's been nice to meet you, but the fact is you're not just a stranger any more. You'll be a part of my life from now on. I hope we can get to know each other better."

"Yes, sir, I do too."

"Have a good trip back. Drive carefully, Tony."

"Don't worry, Dad. I'll call you when we get in."

Aisha and Umar kiss their parents, and we're off.

We've driven several miles when Umar speaks again. "You know, Isa, you've forgotten another part of the wedding plans."

"What's that?"

"The dowry. You must give something to Aisha at the time of your marriage. That's one of the teachings of Islam."

"Yes, I remember hearing about that. So what should I give her?"

"I'll leave that for Aisha and you to decide."

She speaks up from the back seat. "What I'd like, more than anything, is for you to have a college diploma."

"That's it? What about jewelry, or money, or something?"

"Okay. How about a college diploma and a wedding ring?"

"That's all?"

"That's enough."

"It will take me a few years, you know."

"That's okay. I can wait. As long as you agree to keep going to school until you graduate."

I turn to Umar. "What do you think?"

"If that's what my sister wants, it's fine with me."

"Okay, Aisha. If that's what you really want, that will be your dowry."

She falls asleep on the way back. Umar and I talk a little. I don't really know anything about him, except that he's Aisha's very protective older brother.

He became a Muslim when he was twenty. "I was in college when they were making all the fuss about that book, by Salman Rushdie. Do you remember? It was nearly ten years ago now."

I laugh. "Ten years ago? Sorry, but I wasn't too interested in things like that back then. Back in those days, I was stoned half the time."

Umar shakes his head. I've said too much. "I'm sorry. You were saying?"

"It's a good thing you weren't that frank in front of my

father, Isa. Are you sure you're ready to marry my sister?"

Why did I say something so stupid? "It's just something I did when I was in high school. With my friends. But I have new friends now. Better friends. I hope you're still one of them."

"I am. But you have to get over your past. I thought you were beyond that now."

"I thought so too. Anyway, I want to hear your story."

"Okay. While you were busy getting high, the rest of the country was making a big fuss about a book. This man, Salman Rushdie, had written some things against Islam, even though he came from a Muslim family. Muslims all over the world had been calling for his execution. When I was in college, his book came out in paperback, and he went on a tour here in the U.S. Of course, his book became a best seller here. I read it. I wasn't impressed. Then I decided to read the Qur'an. I wanted to know what it was that made all those Muslims get so upset.

"When I first picked up the Qur'an, I started out looking for the mistakes. Every book ever written by man is bound to have some mistakes. But I couldn't find any in the Qur'an, and I knew it had to have been written by God. What I found in the Qur'an was a rational and comprehensive approach to life. I considered myself to be a Muslim for about six months before I actually met other Muslims, and made Shahadah."

"That's the opposite of me. I met Muslims first. I didn't start reading the Qur'an until I went to Pakistan."

"Every one of us has his or her own way. What's important is that we all reach the same place."

Umar also tells me that he graduated from Northeastern with a degree in psychology. For the last few years, he's been working with a Chicago youth organization, helping kids in the city get their lives together. He's thinking about going back to school to get his Masters in Social Work. He's twenty-eight, the same age as Chris.

"Have you ever thought about getting married?"

"Not since I became a Muslim. There was one girl. I thought about marrying her. But we were young. It did not end well." He's quiet for the next several miles. I have the feeling that there's a lot more to the story. But I'm not going to ask.

He continues where he left off. "After I made Shahadah, I decided to concentrate on my faith and my studies. For the past few years, Aisha has been the main focus of my life, outside of my work. But I guess you're going to put me out of a job. As long as you're done with all your foolishness, that is."

"I am. For me, the Qur'an has been a life preserver, pulling me out of all that mess. It's just once in a while, you know. I'm still learning."

"We're all still learning. That never ends."

On Monday morning, I go to the campus to register for the next semester. I've decided to take four classes this time. I sign up for Biology, Composition II, U.S. History, and Spanish. My Arabic studies are going well, and I'd like to try another language. Mr. Walker will be my composition instructor again.

My new class schedule will keep me even busier, especially with my new responsibilities at work. But it will also get me closer to fulfilling my promise to Aisha.

After registering for classes, I have a few other important errands to run. My first stop is the building downtown where Brad works. I haven't made an appointment, but I hope I can catch him.

The secretary stops me in the outer office. "May I help you?"

"Yes, please. I'd like to see Brad Adams."

She's staring at me. Oh yeah. I'm wearing Pakistani clothes. I'm so used to dressing this way that I don't even think about it most of the time.

"May I have your name, please?"

"Yes. I'm Joshua Adams, Brad's brother."

Her eyebrows shoot up. Brad's going to be the talk of the break room. She picks up a phone, speaks in whispers, nods a few times, and turns back to me. "Would you please have a seat, Mr. Adams? Brad will be right out."

I wait for ten minutes, thumbing through business magazines, before Brad appears.

"Thank you, Carol. I'll talk to him."

"Hi Brad."

"Joshua, what are you doing here dressed like that?"

"I knew you'd be happy to see me."

"Come on in to my office."

I follow him through a long maze of offices and cubicles. Finally we reach Brad's private office. It's not large, but it's comfortable. I guess he got that promotion.

"Sit down," he says, closing the door. "What are you doing here?"

"I just wanted to see my big brother. Oh, and I have some news."

"Another trip to a terrorist camp?"

"Terrorist camp? Oh, you mean when I went to Pakistan. Sorry to disappoint you, but I didn't meet any terrorists there."

"Okay, whatever. I'm busy, Joshua. What is it?"

"I wanted to let you know that I'm doing well. I'm going to college, getting A's even. I've been promoted to assistant manager at the restaurant. Oh, and I'm going to get married. I'd like for you to come, and Beth."

"Married, huh? Who's the poor girl this time? Someone you met in Pakistan?"

"No, she's an American. African-American, technically speaking. Very nice. She's studying to be a teacher. Her name is Aisha."

"Really. So I guess she's a Muslim, too. Does Mom know?"

"Not yet. I'm debating whether to go see her or just send another letter."

"Oh, the letters. Chris went berserk over what you wrote in his."

"I figured he might. I'm not sure I'll invite him to the wedding."

"It might be better not to. He probably wouldn't come, anyway."

"By the way, the bride isn't pregnant this time. She's a nice

Muslim girl."

"Which means?"

"I haven't even kissed her yet."

"Really! Joshua, you have changed. You must be serious this time. So when's the date?"

"We're not sure yet. Her mother is still looking for a hall. Sometime in late December. I just came back from Moline, where her parents live. I had to ask for her father's permission."

"That's different. Boy, you sure didn't ask Heather's father for any permission. I thought he was going to kill you."

"Me too." That was so long ago. "Brad, how are my kids?"

"They're good. Michael is getting so tall. He's into sports now. Especially soccer. Jeremy is still shy, but he's doing real well in school. And Jennifer is such a sweet little girl."

"I saw them once, a few months ago. I was driving by the apartment. They didn't see me. We should be having a custody hearing soon."

"I've heard. I probably shouldn't tell you this, but Mom wants Chris and me to come in and testify on Heather's behalf."

"That doesn't surprise me. Will you?"

"I thought I would, until you showed up here today. You're different—even with that beard and those clothes. I don't know what it is. You're calmer, I guess. And older. You're just different."

"So you'll come for the wedding?"

"Sure I will. I've never been to Moline before."

"Are you still living in the same place?"

"No, the condo wasn't a good place to raise a family. We bought a house in Evanston a few months ago. It's bigger, and there's a backyard for Kyle."

"He must be getting big."

"He is. And he runs everywhere now."

"I'd like to see him. So what's your new address?"

"Here." He writes it on the back of a business card. "I'll look forward to getting the invitation."

"Good. I'm glad to hear it. I guess I'd better be going now. I know you have a lot of work to do."

"Yes, always. Let me walk you out."

We shake hands in the outer office. "Thanks for coming by, Joshua. I really am glad to see you. And congratulations on your engagement."

"Thank you, Brad."

"I'll be looking for that invitation."

Aisha was right. They do care. But Brad has always been the easiest one for me to talk to. I used to confide in him when we were growing up. He's the first one I went to after Heather told me she was pregnant. Now if I can just find a way to relate to my mother and Chris.

I'll go ahead and drop by my mother's office. She won't get angry with me there. I run home first to change my clothes. She'll prefer jeans over my Pakistani clothes.

She has a large corner office on the sixth floor. I remember when she got the promotion that came with the office. She was so excited. We all went out to dinner to celebrate.

When I was younger, I felt at home in her workplace. I'd go with her sometimes on weekends, when she had to pick up some work, and occasionally I'd stop by after school. When I got older, though, my life revolved around girls and beer, and I stopped coming. In those days, I think she was glad I didn't come. The people at her office were counting on their fingers when Michael was born, all seven pounds of him, six months after Heather and I got married. But they still brought baby gifts to her house in honor of her first grandchild. I have frustrated and disappointed her over the years, but the people at her office have always been there for her.

They have security guards on the ground floor now. You can't be too careful, I guess. They stop me at the elevators.

"Excuse me, sir; you can't go upstairs without clearance. Your name, please?"

"Joshua Adams. My mother, Evelyn Adams, works here."

"Yes, I know Evie. I don't remember seeing you here before, but you do look a lot like her oldest son. What's his name again?"

"Brad Adams."

"Yes, Brad, that's it. You can go on up, Joshua."

In the elevator I practice what I will say to her. I hope I'm not interrupting an important meeting. It's after lunch. I hope she's in a good mood.

The elevator stops and the doors open. I remember. It's left out of the elevator, then around the corner and four doors down.

As I turn the corner, I see a woman, about my mother's age, who looks vaguely familiar. She looks at me.

"Joshua? Is that you?"

"Yes. Do I know you?"

"I'm Mrs. Allen, don't you remember? You used to come to my office when you were young. You always wanted a peppermint from my candy bowl."

"Yes, Mrs. Allen. I remember you. How are you?"

"I'm fine. I felt so bad when your mother told me about the divorce. What a shame it was for those poor children."

"Yes, I know. It was."

"Well, I'd better get working on this report. Your mother is in her office. You picked a good time. I'll see you later, Joshua."

Peppermint candy. I remember. Maybe that's why I liked coming to my mother's office.

Her door is open. I knock anyway.

"Yes? Come in."

"Hi, Mom. How are you?"

She looks up and puts down the file she was reading. "Joshua? What are you doing here?"

"Can we talk?"

"Yes, come on in. Close that door, will you? Come sit down."

I remember the soft blue chairs. The last time I sat in one of these was a few months before I left Heather. I came to ask for a loan to help pay our bills.

"Did you get my letter?"

"Yes, yes I did. So you're taking college classes. How is that going?"

"It's going well. I like my classes, and I have one really good instructor. I just signed up for more credits next semester."

"That's good, Joshua. I'm glad you're doing that."

"Also, I got a promotion at the restaurant. I'm the assistant manager now."

"Good. That's all I ever wanted from you. Just to be responsible. Are you still a—"

"Yes, I'm still a Muslim. That's what has helped me get my life together. It's the right thing for me."

"You know I don't really like it. But if you're working hard, and going to school, then there must be something good about it."

"And I'm getting married next month."

"Really? Is she a Moslem too?"

"Yes. She's American. African-American, if it makes a difference." She raises her eyebrows, but doesn't say anything. "Her name is Aisha. She's studying elementary education at Northeastern."

"I guess, if she's going to be a teacher, she must be a nice girl."

"She is. Very nice. Her parents live in Moline. Her father's a high school principal and her mother is a nurse. We went there last weekend. I had to ask for her father's permission to marry her."

"Really? You did that? And he said yes?" She's quiet for a moment. "She must be a nice girl."

"Her mother is looking for a hall, and then we'll set the date. I wanted to tell you in person. Of course, we'll be sending you an invitation."

"This girl. Are her parents Moslem too?"

"No, but her older brother is."

"I see. And does she wear one of those, those things on top of her head?"

"Yes, she wears a scarf. She's very modest."

"I don't know, Joshua. Any girl who would marry you must not be too modest."

She's pushing my buttons again. I swallow my irritation. "She's a Muslim girl. We haven't even been alone together yet. When we walk, her brother walks between us. When we sit, her brother sits between us. It's different this time, Mom. She's different. And I'm different."

"Joshua, if you think all this is going to make me change my mind about testifying for Heather at the custody hearing, you'd better think—" She stops, and puts her hand over her mouth.

"That's okay, Mom. I know. Brad told me. And it's what I expected, anyway. No, I'm not trying to make you change your mind. I just wanted to let you know. I'll be sending you an invitation as soon as they're ready."

"Good. I'll think about it. Let me know what date you've settled on, and I'll see if I can make it."

"Okay. Um, before I leave, Mom . . ."

"Yes?"

"Well, I just wanted to tell you that I love you."

She closes her eyes and takes a deep breath. We're silent for a long time. When she opens her eyes again, I can see that they're moist.

"Thank you, Joshua. I love you, too. And I'm glad you're finally getting your life on track." I know what she wants to say next. Will she?

"I just wish you had done it before you brought those three children into the world."

"I know, Mom. I do too."

For a moment, we just look at each other. I see so many things in her eyes—love, anger, sadness—before I turn away.

"Well, I saw Mrs. Allen in the hallway, and she said something about finishing a report. I guess you have to get back to work, too."

"Yes, yes I do. I'm glad you came by, Joshua. I really am."

And then she gets up, walks around her desk, and hugs me. I remember her hugs. I just don't remember the last time I had one.

"I'd better get back to that report," she says, stepping back.

"Thanks, Mom. For everything."

She walks me to the office door. "Be sure to send me an invitation. And maybe you can bring Aisha to the house sometime."

"Sure, Mom. I'll see you later."

"Bye, Joshua."

As I walk toward the elevators, the warmth of her hug stays with me.

I'm feeling good. I've talked to my mother, and for the first time in a long time I came away without feeling angry or tense. Two down, one to go. Chris is going to be the hardest.

I definitely do not want to talk to Chris at work. I'd be badly outnumbered at the Bible college. I wait until I'm sure Chris is at home. On my way to his house, I pick up a six-pack of root beer as a peace offering. During my wild days, he always told me that I should be drinking root beer instead of that other stuff.

I'm sure they haven't moved. The house is close to the college, and Melinda has always been so proud of her herb garden. Besides, Chris doesn't like change.

The lights are on and there's only one car in the driveway. I'm glad he doesn't have company.

I hesitate. I could just go back home.

But this has to be done.

I ring the doorbell. Melinda answers, with a baby on her hip.

"Hi, Melinda. How are you? That can't be Ruthie."

"Oh, hello, Joshua. It's been a long time. No, this is Isaiah. Please, come on in."

The house is small but neat, and nicely decorated. "Chris, your brother is here."

He calls from somewhere in the back of the house. "Hold on, Brad, I'll be right there."

He's walking into the foyer before Melinda can tell him, "Not Brad. Your other brother."

He takes one look at me and crosses his arms. "Joshua, what are you doing here?"

"Oh, Chris. Come in, Joshua. Can I get you anything? Some tea, maybe?"

"No, thank you, Melinda. How are you, Chris? I brought you a peace offering."

"Root beer, huh? Are you finally off the hard stuff?"

"I am. I guess you were right about that."

"And what about everything else?"

"I'm still a Muslim, if that's what you mean. That's not going to change."

"Chris, Joshua, don't just stand there in the foyer. Come on in. Have a seat, Joshua. Make yourself comfortable."

I remove my shoes before walking into their living room.

"You don't have to do that."

"That's okay, Melinda. It's part of my culture now."

Chris frowns. "So you're still away from the church."

"I was never really with the church. I go to the mosque regularly, if that helps."

"Joshua, have you thought this through? Are you really throwing away everything you grew up with?"

"What did I grow up with? We didn't go to church that much when we were kids. Mom was more serious about her work than her faith. Christianity is something you chose later. Like I chose Islam."

"But it's the wrong choice. What can I say to make you understand?"

"There's a verse in the Qur'an that you might be interested in."

"Why would I be interested in the Qur'an?"

"La kum deenu kum wa liya deen. To you your religion, and to me mine. Kind of appropriate for the two of us, don't you think?"

"But what kind of religion do you have? You worship a false god, speak in a strange language, wear odd clothing, and kill innocent people. You call that a religion?"

I take a deep breath. This won't be easy. "Okay, Chris, first of all, we don't worship false gods or idols. I cringed back there in the restaurant when you put down the name of Allah. I nearly punched you for it. Allah is the One God. The God who created the universe, and the same God you worship. Islam is anti-idol, you could say. We do speak Arabic, because the Qur'an was revealed in the Arabic language. But there are Muslims in every part of the world and they speak every language you could imagine. The clothing is a personal choice, though it should be loose and modest. And as far as killing innocent people is concerned, that's just a bunch of crock. If someone says he's killing innocent people in the name of Allah, he's lying. Islam, literally, means 'peace'."

"You said you worship the same God I worship? I don't think so."

"Did the God you worship create the universe? Does He continue to run the universe every second of every day? Is He all-knowing and all-powerful?"

Chris looks surprised. "Yes, He is. Okay, just for the sake of argument, assume we do worship the same God. What about salvation? Don't you worry about your soul?"

"All the time. I'm the one who broke almost every commandment. But we don't call it salvation. We call it mercy. We do our best to please Allah, and Allah either forgives us or not. We need to have faith, and good intentions. For the rest we depend upon the mercy of Allah."

"And the virgin birth? The crucifixion? You're not going to tell me that Jesus was just a prophet, are you?"

"That's exactly what I was going to tell you. We do believe in the virgin birth, as one of Allah's miracles. We also believe that Allah has no sons or daughters. Jesus was a man, one of thousands of prophets, sent by Allah to teach people right from wrong. We don't believe in the crucifixion. We believe Jesus was raised up to the heavens by Allah, and he will return before the Day of Judgment. But, he is a man."

Melinda comes in from the kitchen, carrying a tray. Ruthie toddles and Isaiah crawls behind her. She hands us each a glass of root beer and sets a bowl of pretzels on the coffee table. "But Joshua," she says, "how do you address the problem of original sin? After all, there must be a way to erase the stain upon humanity. If not the crucifixion, then what?"

"Muslims don't believe in original sin. We believe that children, like Ruthie and Isaiah, are pure and innocent. It's only when they get older that they'll be capable of committing sins, and by then they'll know how to make the right choices, hopefully."

Chris takes a sip of root beer, and smiles. "You got the good stuff. So, Joshua, what about the afterlife. Do Muslims believe in heaven and hell?"

"Absolutely."

"Then how do you think you're going to get into heaven? If you don't believe in the redemption through Christ, what then?"

"We get there through the mercy of Allah."

"That's it? So then everyone goes to heaven."

"No. We have to do our part, too. We have to have faith, good deeds, and good intentions. But our faith and good deeds won't get us anywhere without the mercy of Allah."

"And what about people who aren't Muslims? Do you think I will go to hell because I'm a Christian?"

"First of all, that's not for me to judge. Secondly, Allah said in the Qur'an that among the Christians and the Jews are those who worship Him sincerely. Those people will be rewarded. Who they are is not for me, or anyone else, to decide. Allah alone is the judge."

"Okay. I'm glad you're not worried about my soul, but I'm still worried about yours."

We continue talking and questioning for hours. After a while, Melinda excuses herself to put the children to bed. I think she must have gone to sleep, too, because she never returns to the debate.

By the time we're finished, the six-pack is gone. It's 1:00 AM, and my voice is hoarse.

"So I'm not going to convince you, am I, Joshua?"

"No. And I don't think that I'm going to convince you, either."

"Well, then, I guess we'll have to call it a draw. For now."

"To you be your religion and to me be mine."

"For now. But I'm not finished with you yet."

"I didn't think you were. By the way, I'm getting married in about a month."

"Oh? I assume she's a Muslim."

"Yes. Her name is Aisha. She's studying to be a teacher."

"And I assume her father won't be holding a shotgun to your back."

"I don't think Heather's father really owned a shotgun. He

just said that to scare me. And no, he won't. Islamic courtships are much less physical."

"Oh yeah?"

"You've heard that old Beatle's song that Mom likes? I'm looking forward to holding her hand."

He laughs. "I still don't like Islam, but it looks like it's been good for you. At least you're not breaking any more commandments."

"It's been very good for me. Well, I'd better get going. I've got class in the morning."

"Me too." He walks me to the front door. "I'm glad you came by. I still don't agree, but it was good to talk to you."

"And you'll come to the wedding?"

"An Islamic ceremony?"

"Of course."

"We'll see."

"That's all I can ask for, I guess. Come by the restaurant sometime. If you promise not to yell you might finally get some tea."

"Sure Joshua. Good night."

He shuts the door. As soon as I get into my car, I begin replaying the evening's conversation. Neither of us convinced anyone, but at least we bridged the gap.

~

Talking with Chris about all the commandments I've broken reminds me of something else I need to do. I call my doctor's office to schedule a physical. I was a player for so many years. I don't want Aisha to have to pay for my mistakes.

I get the results on a Thursday. Umar comes over a few days later, in the evening after I get off from work. Aisha isn't with him.

"I need to talk with you, Isa." He looks down. I can tell he's uncomfortable. "I've found out about your past relationships, outside of your marriage. All of that happened before you became a Muslim. I know that. But I'm worried about my sister.

I'm sure you know what I mean."

"I know. I already had it checked out, after we came back from Moline. I'm clean."

"I'm glad you did that. That was my biggest concern. But I still have to ask you this. Are you ready to commit to my sister?"

"Yes, I am. Like you said, that was before. Back in those days, girls and beer defined my life. Now, all I want is to be a good Muslim, get custody of my kids, and be a good husband to Aisha. I don't chase after women anymore. Did you know that when Ismail introduced us I didn't even want another woman in my life?"

"No, I didn't, but that sounds like Ismail. So you're sure that is all in the past?"

Isn't that what I just said? "I don't get it. When I first became a Muslim, the brothers told me that I was going to start my life over with a clean slate. I didn't know, then, that I would have all this crap left over from my old life."

"I've always thought of it as echoes. The source is gone, but the effects remain. Each of us has a history. We can't ignore it, but we do have to try to resolve it."

Getting to know Aisha, getting ready to marry her, I still sometimes feel like I'm dreaming. But reality is always there, ready to slap me in the face.

❦

The wedding plans are coming along. Mrs. Evans found a nice hall, and we've set the date for the last Saturday in December. As Mrs. Evans says, we'll just have to hope, and pray, that the weather cooperates.

The invitations have all been sent. Chris will get one, too, though I'm still not sure he'll come.

Aisha tells me that her aunt and grandmother are making her dress. She says it's going to be beautiful.

I called Abdul-Qadir on the night we got back from Moline and told him about the wedding. He congratulated me profusely and said he would try to come.

I really would like him to be there, but I knew it would be hard for him. The trip is expensive, and even visitor's visas can be tough to get these days. I'm not surprised when his package comes two weeks before the wedding. That's Abdul-Qadir. Even though he can't come he still remembered us with a gift.

I open the brown paper wrapping, expecting to find a wrapped present we could open together after the wedding. Instead I find just a plain brown box. My curiosity gets the best of me, and I open it.

Inside the box is a white suit, both jacket and pants. The jacket has a nehru-style collar with gold embroidery stitched around the collar and down the front. He's written a note.

"Assalaamu alaikum, Isa. I'm sorry I will not be able to come for your wedding. The trip would be too costly. I hope you like my gift. This is your wedding suit. Please send me pictures. May Allah bless you and Aisha. May your marriage be blessed with children and happiness. Your brother in Islam, Abdul Qadir."

My brother in Islam. My father in Islam. Thank you, Abdul-Qadir, and may Allah bless you.

Later in the day, Aisha and Umar are coming to the apartment. She wants to see my place, the place where she'll be living soon. I wash the dishes and pick up my dirty socks a few minutes before they come. I'm just straightening the cushions on the couch when I hear the knock at the door.

"Assalaamu alaikum." She walks right in. "Oh, this is nice. I like the living room. It's nice and large."

"Large enough for what?"

"First of all, we're going to need to get some more furniture in here. It's too plain. Also, we will want to have guests over, won't we?"

"I don't know. I never thought about it. Anyway, it's not big enough for all of your family."

"No, I don't think we'll be hosting Thanksgiving dinner until we get a house."

"A house? What's wrong with my apartment?"

"Nothing. It will be fine, for now."

Umar smiles. "You know, Isa, I've heard that bringing a

woman into your life brings many changes."

"Yes, I'm beginning to see that."

Before she leaves, Aisha has decorating ideas for the living room, kitchen, bedroom, and bathroom. "It's all so bare. How can you stand it?"

"It's been fine for me. Anyway, it won't be bare much longer, I guess."

"Umar will help me bring my stuff over here before we go to Moline. That way everything will be ready when we get back. Make sure you leave me some room in the closet. Oh, by the way, my dress is looking great. You're going to love it."

"That's right. You've got that dress. But I don't know what I'll wear for the wedding. I could just throw on a pair of jeans. Or maybe I can find something in my closet that's not too ratty."

"Oh, Isa, you wouldn't wear jeans, would you?"

"No, I guess I won't have to. Abdul-Qadir sent me a wedding suit from Pakistan."

"I knew you were teasing. What does it look like? I want to see it."

"Not until I see your dress."

"Okay. Fair enough. Can you imagine, Isa? Just two more weeks."

Two more weeks of freedom. Two more weeks of loneliness.

❧

Five days before the wedding, Aisha and I go to get our marriage license. It's exciting, knowing that we're so much closer to being married. Of course, Umar comes with us.

In the afternoon, Umar and Aisha bring her things to the apartment. They show up at the door with two large suitcases, four boxes of books, two boxes of stuff and a plant.

"Come on in. I made room in the closet. You can figure out where everything goes."

"Oh, this is just the first load. Could you go back with Umar to get the rest while I get settled in?"

"You're kidding, right?"

"No, the rest of my stuff is back at Umar's place."

"Let's go," says Umar. "I hope you're ready to do some lifting."

Umar and I make eight more trips between the two apartments. We bring a chest of drawers, a desk, two bookcases, a few more plants, and so many boxes that I lose count. Each time we come back to the apartment-that-used-to-be-my-place, we find Aisha happily putting her things into place.

"Are you sure this is all of it?" I say when we return from the eighth trip.

"Of course not."

"What?"

"We still have five days. I couldn't bring everything."

At night, before I go to bed, I look around at the apartment-that-used-to-be-my-place. Her desk, bookcases, and computer sit in a corner of the living room. Her plants grow throughout the apartment. Her clothes are in my closet. Aisha's touch is everywhere. I can't wait until she comes here to join all her things.

❧

Umar and Aisha drive to Moline the next day. Aisha needs to try on her dress, check on last minute details, and, of course, spend extra time with her family. I have three days on my own before I drive there to get ready for the big day.

I'm not scheduled to work until afternoon. Fawad comes in the mornings and works the lunch crowd. I relieve him in the early afternoon so he can go home to his family. I don't mind working late, especially now that Aisha is gone. I don't know how it will be after we're married.

I'm restless again, so I hop in the car and drive by the old apartment. It could be a school day, but the kids are probably off for winter break. They could be there. I decide to park across the street. Maybe, if I stay long enough, I'll be able to catch another glimpse of them.

My thoughts wander to how my life is going to be. Aisha will be at home with me, ending my loneliness. In a couple of months, after the custody hearing, the kids will come to live with me, too. They'll be happy to have a stepmother as good and as beautiful as Aisha. After a while, they'll insist on living with me all the time. We'll have two or three kids of our own, Aisha and I, move to that house in the suburbs, and live together as one big happy family. I wonder how long it will take before Michael feels comfortable enough to call her Mom.

"What the hell are you doing here?"

Lost in my daydream, I didn't see Heather as she walked behind my car and opened the passenger door.

"Answer me. Why are you here?"

"I, um, I just wanted to be here, to be closer to the kids. I guess I hoped I would see them again."

"I knew it. I knew that was you. What are you up to, Joshua? What are you trying to do, kidnap them and take them all to Pakistan or some other godforsaken place? What's your game this time?"

"Nothing, Heather. I just miss the kids."

She sits in the passenger seat and leans over, shouting in my face. "It's about time you started thinking about them. When did you start missing them? When Jennifer started talking, or when Michael made the soccer team? And where's the damn money you're supposed to be sending me for these kids you miss so much?"

"I've made a lot of mistakes, Heather. I'm trying to make it right now."

"I know your lines. You made a lot of mistakes, and one of them was getting mixed up with me. Now that you're all holy you can just walk away from your mistakes and pretend we don't exist."

I'd forgotten how her nose turns up in that cute way. And her long blonde hair is still thick and wavy. She's gotten her figure back, too. When I left, she had at least twenty pounds left over from Jennifer.

"It's not like that, Heather. We were young. We both made mistakes. We're older now, and it's time to move on."

"Except that you moved on without us. You left me and the kids, and started a new life that didn't include us."

"I want the kids in my life. You're the one who won't let me see them."

"Why should I? I don't trust you. You walked out on us. You left the country. You're the one who turned his back on them. Why should I trust you now?"

"I've changed, Heather. I have a good job now. I'm going to college."

"And how many times did I try to make you go to college? How many jobs did you leave while we were married? I told you to keep trying. I tried to help you then. You wouldn't listen. And how do I know you've changed? Just because you act all religious and everything. I know who you are, Joshua. I know you better than anyone else ever will."

Tears start running slowly down her cheeks. "Why couldn't you change then? Why couldn't you stay with us? You don't know how hard it is."

I wish she wouldn't cry. I never liked to see her cry. I reach over and brush a tear from her cheek. Her skin is so soft. I remember.

"Joshua?" She looks into my eyes. I remember that look.

She comes closer. Before I know it, her face is buried in my shoulder and I'm holding her very tight. I stroke her head. I remember how it feels to hold her.

"It's okay, Baby. Don't cry."

She kisses me. I remember her kisses. And I hold her tighter.

"Oh, Heather. Don't cry, Baby. I'm sorry. It's okay, Baby." I'm kissing her face, her neck. She smells so good. I remember the feel of her, the smell of her.

"Oh, Joshua. I've missed you, Babe. I'm so glad you're back." She's pressing against me. She unbuttons my shirt and caresses my chest. She knows I like that. I remember.

"Oh, Heather, Baby." She's so warm, so soft. I feel her body pressing against me. I remember.

I remember her long kisses. I remember her love.

I run my fingers through her long hair. I don't know how

long Aisha's hair is.

I remember Aisha.

Aisha? Aisha. I'm going to marry Aisha. I remember.

I freeze.

She kisses me. "What's wrong, Babe? Don't worry. Everything's okay now, now that you're back."

What am I doing? I have to stop. It feels so good. I remember.

I kiss her again. I remember the sweet kisses.

And I remember Aisha. I remember that I love Aisha.

It feels so good. I don't want to stop. I have to go. I can't do this. I have to go.

I pull away from her. "No, Heather, I can't."

She comes closer. "It's okay, Babe. Don't worry. Everything's okay now." She kisses me.

I want to. I can't. This is wrong.

I push her away. "No, Heather, this is wrong."

She strokes my cheek. "What? Nothing's wrong, Babe. You still love me. I know you do. I can feel it."

I quickly button my shirt.

She looks into my eyes. I remember that look. I look down.

"No, Heather. I love Aisha." I speak the words slowly. They are heavy, and hard to say.

"You what?"

"I love Aisha. I'm going to marry Aisha." The words are a little lighter and easier this time.

For a moment, she just stares. Then she slaps me, hard, and starts screaming. "How dare you, you, you bastard."

"I'm sorry, Heather. I didn't mean to do that. It, uh, it just happened."

"I should have known. You're still the same. I hate you." She pounds my chest with her fists. I grab hold of her wrists.

"I'm sorry. I'm so sorry."

She jerks away from me. "Sorry? You're sorry all right. And I don't want to ever see your sorry face around here again. You will be so sorry you ever messed with me, Joshua. I'll make sure of that."

"But, Heather. I just . . ."

"I'll get you for this." She reaches over and scratches my cheek with her long nails. I flinch. "If you think that hurt, just wait. I'll make your life a living hell for what you've done to me."

"But I didn't, I didn't. You . . ."

"Who do you think they will believe, a no good bum or a single mother who has to work two jobs to raise the kids he left behind?"

"I . . . I . . ."

"I feel sorry for that Aisha. What would she say if she saw you just now?"

There's nothing more to say.

Heather gets out of the car, still screaming. "I can ruin you, Joshua Adams. Remember that."

She slams the car door and runs into the apartment building. I would like to sit here longer and try to figure everything out, but if I stay here, knowing Heather, she'll probably call the police. I drive away, and keep driving aimlessly around the city.

How could I? How could I have done that? All these months I've been so good. I'd left that all in the past. But she was close, and those old feelings came back.

I can blame Satan. But it was me, touching her hair, kissing her face and neck. It was me. And I liked it. I wanted her.

"Damn!" I punch the steering wheel. How could I do that to Aisha? If she had seen me, there would be no wedding. If she knew, she would never forgive me.

It's time for the prayer. But I can't go to the masjid. I feel strange. A few years ago, it would have been no big deal. I messed around with girls all the time. Even, sometimes, while I was still married to Heather. But now I feel low and dirty. I can't face the brothers. And I can't face Allah. I keep driving.

When Umar came to my place the other day, I was irritated with him for doubting me. But he was right. I can't put it all in the past. I'm not ready.

I finally park in the alley behind the restaurant. "Damn, damn, damn! Damn you, Joshua Adams!" I punch the bricks until it stops hurting.

When I walk into work, over an hour late, my face is still red.

"Isa, what's wrong with you? Is something the matter? Something I can help you with? How did you get hurt?"

My cheek. I reach up and touch it. There's blood on my hand. I remember.

I shake my head. I can't talk to him. The shame sits in my stomach and in my throat.

"Getting nervous, eh? The wedding day is almost here."

I nod. "Yes, very nervous."

"I need to get going. My wife is waiting for me. I'll see you tomorrow. Assalaamu alaikum."

I can't say anything. Whatever I try to say, I'll be a hypocrite.

I don't go home after work. I can't be alone. Especially not in that apartment, with Aisha's things all around me. I go to the house instead. Ismail is here.

"Yo, man, assalaamu alaikum. How's the bridegroom?"

I don't answer. I don't know what to say.

"Hey, Isa, is something wrong? What's up, man?"

I shake my head. How can I tell him? Ismail is the only one I could tell, but how can I say what I've done, and what I almost did? I cry instead.

"What is it, man? Talk to me. Are you worried about getting married?"

I can't talk. I don't know what to say.

"Hey, Isa, say something. What's going on, man?"

I shout at him. "Leave me alone!"

He looks stunned. After a moment, he reaches over and pats my shoulder. "Isa, what is it? You can tell me."

"Okay, I'll tell you. I can't marry Aisha."

"What? What are you talking about? You two were made for each other. You're just a little nervous, that's all."

"No. I can't marry her. I cheated on her."

He looks at me, puzzled. "You mean you looked at another girl? Hey, that happens to all of us. No big deal, man."

"No. It was Heather."

"Heather, your ex-wife?"

I nod, and tell him what happened. He listens closely. I can't tell what he's thinking.

"I can't marry Aisha. I can't. She's so good. And I'm just, just a bum."

Ismail doesn't say anything. I disappointed a lot of people today.

"Say something, dude. Kick me out of the house if you want. But say something."

It takes a long time. He just sits there, looking at me, with a weird expression on his face. Finally, he just says, "I don't know what you should do, man. You really messed things up."

"I have to call off the wedding. That's the only thing I can do."

"So you're going to call Aisha and say, 'Sorry, forget about the wedding. I was lonely so I went and made out with my ex-wife'? Umar's going to kill you. I mean it."

"But how can I marry her, after this? And if I don't tell her, it would be like living a lie."

"Why did you do it, man? You don't love Heather. Why did you even start?"

"I don't know, man. She was close, and soft, and I started to remember. We were married for five years, and not all of it was bad."

"So you do love Heather?"

"No. No. I never loved Heather the way I love Aisha. But she's soft, and so good looking. When I touched her it was all so familiar. And I tried to stop. But, well . . ."

"Okay, man, it's time for a father-son talk here."

"Yeah? I'm older than you."

"Just shut up and listen, kid. Now, all this time you've been seeing Aisha, you never laid a hand on her, did you?"

"No, of course not."

"But you wanted to, didn't you?"

"Well, I guess, sure I did."

"And you didn't touch her because . . . ?"

"Because Umar would have killed me."

"So, all this time you've been seeing Aisha, and you never saw her without Umar around, right? And having Umar there helped keep you in check."

"Yeah, sure."

"Because even though she's a Muslim girl, she's still a girl."

"Man, what are you getting at?"

"I'm going to tell you something. If you ain't heard it by now, you ain't been paying attention. The Prophet said that if there are a man and a woman alone together, the third one is . . .?"

"Satan. Yeah, I know about that. But I can't lay it all on him. I made my own choices."

"You sure did. And not very good ones. Man, in the future, just don't put yourself in that kind of place. We get weak sometimes, you know? And if Umar hadn't been around all this time, you sure would have kissed Aisha by now."

"Yeah, I guess you're right. But what should I do?"

"Get married. And don't tell Aisha. Not until you've been married to her for fifty years. Then one day, while you're sitting on the front porch together in your rocking chairs, you can say, 'Oh, by the way, a few days before we got married, I went and made out with my ex-wife.' By then Umar will be too old to kill you."

"But won't I be lying? How can I marry her, knowing what I did?"

"You're not going to do it again, are you?"

"No. No way."

"Because if you do, I'll hold you down while Umar kills you. For now, you need to pray to Allah. He's the one who can forgive you. Fast for the next two days. Read a lot of Qur'an. And stick with me when you're not working. I'll keep you in check until you get to Moline."

"I can't pray. I can't face Allah. I haven't been able to pray since it happened."

"Dude, you got it all backwards. This is the time you need the prayer the most."

"But how can I? What I did was so wrong."

"Man, don't you think Allah already knows what you did? Allah knows everything, dude. You gotta remember that."

"I don't know, man. Before, a few years ago, I fooled around all the time. But I've been trying so hard to be a Muslim. What I did today, it was like I never made Shahadah. I don't think I can face Allah."

"Man, being a Muslim doesn't mean being perfect. It just means that you try."

"You don't get it, Ismail. I'm the same loser I always was. I'm not ready to marry Aisha. I don't know if I'll ever be ready."

"Isa, dude. Listen to me. You messed up. But that doesn't mean you have to throw everything away. A few years ago, you would have messed with a girl, and then gone out to get drunk before you went home to your wife, and it wouldn't have bothered you. Remember, man, I knew you then. Now you just kiss a girl and you can't handle it. You don't even know how much you've changed. Go ahead and wash up, and make up your prayers. It'll help. You'll see."

He's right. Except that it did bother me then. That's why I would go out and get drunk.

This time, I try to wash away the guilt with water, not beer, and go to bow down to Allah.

After I pray I feel a little better, but I'm still ashamed. And I'm worried. "Are you sure I should go through with the wedding? I don't want to hurt Aisha."

"Then marry her, fool. So, are you hungry?"

"Starved. I couldn't eat all day."

"Let's go get some pizza. Remember, you're fasting tomorrow."

"Hey, Ismail, I've been wondering. How do you know so much about women? You're not married yet."

"Man, I got four sisters back home."

As we head out, I make a mental note to myself. Remember prayer. Remember fasting. Remember Qur'an. Remember Allah. Stay far away from Heather.

❧

Ismail helps me get through the next two days. I stay at the house and spend my last single days hanging out with the guys. I guess I won't have much time for that anymore.

I leave on Friday after the prayers. The brothers at the masjid are all around me, congratulating me. I'm just anxious to get on the road.

Because it is a Friday, the traffic heading out of Chicago is pretty heavy. It isn't until I get away from the city that I can relax. I turn on the radio.

". . . snow storm, heading east through Iowa and Illinois. The storm is expected to hit Chicago around 6 PM, and could produce up to a foot of snow in some areas."

It's 3:15 now. I should be there before the storm hits, I think. I increase my speed to 75, just to be sure.

But I forget that the storm is coming from the west. The first hundred miles are no problem, with just a few flurries turning into light snowfall. But I get into trouble near the Dixon exit. Within just a few minutes, I go from a light snowfall into a blizzard.

I've been driving in ice and snow since I was sixteen, and I know I can handle the car. But I can't see more than two feet in front of me. Before getting into the blizzard, I saw lots of trucks on the highway, but now they're hidden by the whiteout. I slow down to 30, and then 20, trying to get closer to Moline while staying out of the path of those trucks.

In a few minutes, I'm down to 15 miles an hour. I still can't see in front of me. But I can't stop. I have a wedding to get to.

I've been driving slowly, struggling to see, when I hear a truck barreling along in the left lane. It's starting to slide in my direction. The driver honks his horn. I have to pull off onto the shoulder and slide into the grass, now covered by snow. The truck misses me. But the car is stuck.

The snow keeps on coming. I still can't see. And now I'm stuck.

I rev my engine. It's no use. The snow is too deep. I don't know how I'm going to get out of here.

It's getting late. And I'm getting hungry. I search the glove compartment for a candy bar, but I think I ate the last one a few days ago. I'm wearing a coat and gloves, but after about 15 minutes it starts to get cold. I think about running the engine for heat, but then I remember all the stories about people who did that and died because their exhaust pipes were clogged with snow. I can't die. I have a wedding to get to.

I wish I still had a cell phone. I never renewed my contract after I got back from Pakistan. I got used to a simpler life there. But now, I really wish I had it. No one knows that I'm stuck.

I have to stay positive. In a few more minutes, the snow will die down. Then I'll be able to get this car back on the road. Soon I'll be in Moline. And tomorrow at this time, I'll be married to Aisha.

But it's getting colder. And it occurs to me that I could die. I could freeze right here in my car. Or I could get hit by another truck. I think it will take a while before I become dehydrated. I'll probably freeze first.

And if I die here, what then? Aisha and her family will start to wonder, I'm sure, if I don't get there in a couple of hours. But how will they find me? Will they call Ismail to see what time I left Chicago? Will they call the highway patrol? They can't come out to look for me themselves.

Am I ready to die? I have thought about death many times, before, but not lately.

My life is just getting started. I'm getting married to a beautiful girl, I'm going to college, and I have lots of friends who help me get through life. I have so much to do, so much to learn.

I have to see my kids again. The last time Michael and Jeremy saw me, I was screaming and cursing at their mother on my way out the door. Is that how they think of me now? Do they think of me at all, or am I just a distant memory, like a dream nearly forgotten upon waking? And Jennifer doesn't even know me.

I could die. It happens. And what then? My kids lose a father they never knew. Aisha loses a fiancé who cheated on her. They would all be better off. All of them. Aisha, my mother, my brothers would miss me for a minute and then they'd move on. Aisha would find somebody better, somebody she could trust.

Is that all my life is? A series of mistakes, with a few bright spots here and there? Have I ever made a difference to anyone?

No, I haven't. Most of the people in my life would be better off without me, and even my closest friends, like Abdul-Qadir, Fawad, and Ismail, would say a short prayer and move on. And why are they close to me, anyway? They're close to me because of what they've done for me. What have I ever done for them?

It's getting colder. I wonder how long it takes. I've heard that you just fall asleep and never wake up. I hope it doesn't hurt.

I could just get it over with. I could get out of the car and step out onto the highway. I'd be sure to get hit. It would be quick and easy. No waiting for the cold to take over my body.

When I was younger, I often thought about suicide. But the imam has said that suicide is the worst of sins. We have to wait on the will of Allah. Even if the waiting is painful. If I step in front of a truck, I will never see my friends again, not even in paradise. The heat of hellfire might be a nice break from all this cold, but it lasts forever.

I'm getting sleepy. Is that it, then? Will I fall asleep and never wake up? The highway patrol will find me, in a day or two. My mother will bury me and everyone will get on with life.

But I could live. I'm not dead yet. If I do come out of this alive, I need to make some changes in my life. Something deeper, more permanent than holding a steady job and owning a car.

If I do live, I'll put a check in the mail for my kids every week. Two years now and they haven't had a cent from their father. I used to spend like crazy, but these days I've been too worried about money to spend it at all, even for my kids. I always meant to send them something, as soon as I had some more money saved up. But I never felt like I had saved enough. If I live, that will be the first thing I have to change.

I'll work hard to be a good husband to Aisha. No more betrayal. I'll treat her as precious as she is.

I'll start helping other people for a change. Brother Bilal just made shahadah at the masjid last week. Maybe he needs help, like I did at first. I'll talk to him and see what he needs.

I'll be true to Islam. When I was kissing Heather, I didn't just forget Aisha, I forgot my faith. I'll pray more, fast more, study more. And I'll try to make my actions fit my beliefs. No more hypocrisy.

If I live, I have to change. If I don't change, there will be no reason for me to keep on living.

It's getting colder. But the snow is easing up a little. I can see maybe fifty yards now. There's not much traffic. The trucks are either stuck, like me, or long gone.

It's almost 7:00. I wonder if Aisha misses me yet. I doubt it. Right now she's probably surrounded by her family and friends, laughing and getting ready for the day ahead.

I can see a little further now. And there are no trucks in sight. Maybe if I get out of the car I can dig myself out of here. I grab an empty Styrofoam food container from the backseat. It might help.

I work for at least 20 minutes, using the food container as a shovel. My wheels are clear, and the snow is a little lighter, but I'm not sure I can make it. I don't want to just spin my wheels and dig myself further in. Now that I think of it, I've been spinning my wheels all my life.

Before getting back in the car, I make sure the tailpipe is clear. If I can't get out, I'm going to run the heat for a while. It is so cold.

I push the accelerator slowly. The car is moving. A few more inches and my front wheels will be on the shoulder. I'm making it. My front wheels are clear. Now for the back wheels. I keep pushing slowly, steadily. And I'm up and out.

I check the highway for traffic. There's no one in sight. I ease on to the highway and continue driving to Moline. I have to take it slow, but at least I'm moving.

By the time I get to Moline, a couple of hours later, my shoulders are aching and my head hurts. But I've made it. I'm not sitting off the highway, dead from hypothermia. I'm here, and I'm alive.

As I pull into town, it hits me. I've gone through a snowstorm to get to Aisha. I never would have done that for Heather. My relationship with Heather was always one of convenience, not love. I'm not proud of that, but I can't change it, either.

I have to make this marriage work.

The hotel is near the highway. I feel so relieved when I finally pull into their parking lot. They held my reservation and my room is ready. I collapse onto the king-size mattress.

For a few minutes, I just want to lie here, flooded by my thoughts. I made it. I'm alive. Now I have to follow through with the promises I made there in the car, surrounded by snow and cold.

After a while, I call the house. I wonder if they've noticed. Umar answers.

"Assalaamu alaikum, Umar. I finally made it."

"Where have you been? We were all worried about you. Aisha was about ready to call the highway patrol."

She noticed. I knew she would. "I got stuck in the blizzard. A truck forced me off the road. Alhamdulillah, I finally got out."

"Alhamdulillah. Hold on. My mom wants to talk to you."

"Joshua? How are you? We were worried."

"I'm okay now. I'm at the hotel. The snow got pretty heavy there for a while, but I made it."

"You must be exhausted. Have you eaten anything?"

I think of my empty glove compartment. "No, not since lunch."

"I have a big pot of beef stew on the stove. I'll send Tony over to bring you some. You need something warm on a cold night like this."

"Thank you, Mrs. Evans. I don't want to bother you."

"It's no bother at all. And you have to stop calling me Mrs. Evans. You can call me Mom or, if you like, Sharon. By this time tomorrow, we'll be family."

"Okay. Well, thanks. I really appreciate it."

"It's no trouble at all. Would you like to talk to Angela? Hold on. She's right here."

"Assalaamu alaikum, Isa. I was so worried about you."

Her voice sounds wonderful. I don't know how I could have forgotten her, even for a moment. "Walaikum assalaam. I'm fine now, now that I hear your voice."

She laughs. "After tomorrow, you can hear my voice any time you want."

"And I'll never get tired of it."

"I miss you."

"And I miss you more." *You have no idea how much.*

"I'll see you tomorrow, insha Allah."

"I'll be there. I can't wait to see your dress."

"Is that all?"

"No. I can't wait to see you."

"Tomorrow, then."

"Tomorrow." I hang up, the sound of her voice still in my head.

Umar brings the stew over about fifteen minutes later. We pray together, and he leaves. I guess he doesn't feel much like talking, which is good because I don't either.

I finish the stew and fall asleep. Thanks to the blizzard, and Mrs. Evans's stew, I sleep very well.

Part Five

I wake up with a mixture of excitement and dread. I'm getting married. I made it to Moline, and Aisha and I are getting married today.

But the guilt of my betrayal stays with me. Is that why I got caught in the blizzard? Was it to prevent me from coming to Moline? Or was it a punishment, and a reminder of my weakness?

After the morning prayer, I grab an envelope and a piece of paper from the desk in the room. I write out a check, and a short note. "Dear Michael, Jeremy, and Jennifer. This is for you. Love, Daddy." I address the envelope to Michael Adams. Of course, I have to make the check out to Heather.

The front desk clerk helps me get it in the mail. One promise kept.

"By the way, sir, don't forget our continental breakfast." She points across the room to an array of doughnuts and bagels.

"Yeah, thanks."

I'm not hungry. That stew filled me up and, besides, I'm too nervous. I just grab a cup of coffee and head back to the room.

There's nothing for me to do. I could watch one of the thirty-eight channels on the TV, but there's probably nothing good on. There's a Bible in the room, but no Qur'an. I wish I had brought mine. From now on, I'll make sure I keep a copy of the Qur'an in my car. I pray some more, then doze a little. The wedding isn't until late afternoon.

I'm awakened by a knock at the door. It's probably the maid. I roll over, ready to sleep again.

"Assalaamu alaikum, Isa. Are you there?"

It's Umar. I jump up and let him in.

Dr. Evans and Marcus follow Umar into the room. "We wondered what you were up to this morning. The women are all in our house, running around and talking up a storm. And here you are, just sleeping."

"Well, Dr. Evans, I guess the women are running things

today."

"That's the truth. By the way, we're going to be family in a few hours. I can't have you calling me Dr. Evans. But, to tell you the truth, I'm not quite comfortable having you call me Jim, or Dad. What do you think we should do about that?"

Umar helps out. "Remember, Dad? A lot of your old students call you Doc."

"I guess that would work. What do you think, Joshua?"

"Sure, Dr. Evans. I mean, Doc. I think that would work just fine."

"Anyway, you're going to be stuck with us, son, until it's time to go to the hall. The women have chased us out of the house." He shakes his head. "Such a fuss. But she's worth it."

"Yes, she is."

"I bet you're getting nervous. I can still remember my wedding day. Couldn't sit still to save my life." He pauses. "But this is your second time, isn't it? I guess it's different for you." He frowns.

"Dr. Evans, um, Doc. I know how much that bothers you. It bothers me, too." *You'll never know how much.* "If I could change things, if I could go back in time, I would have never looked at another girl until I met Angela. I wish that she were my first love, my first wife. But I can't go back and change things. I just have to try, even harder, to show Angela how much I love her, and how important she is to me."

"I know that, Joshua. You've told me how much you care for her, and I believe you. But I worry, just the same. Marriage isn't easy, son. You should know that. What happens to these feelings of love when the honeymoon is over? Will you stop loving her? Will you ever walk out on her? These are the things that bother me."

My chest feels heavy. Is he right? If he knew what I did . . .

I've been quiet too long. "Are you having doubts? Because if you are, I want you to tell me right now. I'd rather break my daughter's heart today, while she's still young and innocent, than have it broken later on down the road. Are you sure you're ready to marry her and commit to her?"

Should I tell him? *No, I'm not sure. Four days ago, I was sitting in my car, making out with my ex-wife. I'm not sure I can do it. But I do love her. I hope that's enough.*

No, I can't tell him. I look down. "Honestly, that's what I worry about, too. I've spent most of my life being weak. It's just been the last couple of years that I've tried to do the right thing. And, sometimes, I'm still weak. I don't know if I'll be the best husband for her. There might be someone who would be better. And I can't say that I'll never be weak again. What I do know is that your daughter has changed my life, and I will always be grateful to her for that. I want to make her my wife, the one I'll be married to for the rest of my life, so I can prove to her how much she means to me."

He's still frowning. "What do you think, Tony?"

"I've known Joshua for several months now. At first, I didn't like him at all, and he knows it. But I've seen him change during these months. And I know he wants to change. I've also watched him, closely, to see how he treats Angela. He's never been rude to her, or disrespectful, or uncaring. Once, when Angela was rude to him, he walked away rather than fight with her. He walked away, but then he forgave her and asked her to marry him. I think that's a sign of a good relationship."

The Doc smiles. "You didn't tell me about that. So you know she has a sharp tongue sometimes. I'm glad. You have passed a test, then." He sighs deeply, as if he's been holding his breath. "I'm glad we had this talk. It makes my heart feel easy."

Yes, I have passed a test. I don't have to walk away. I can marry her. I can forget about what happened. Thank you, Umar. Thank you, Allah.

The Doc looks at his watch. "We've still got an hour or so before you have to get ready. Why don't we just take some time to get to know each other better? So, Joshua, who do you like, the Sox or the Cubs?"

"I've always liked the Cubs. They keep losing, year after year, but they never give up." *And I don't have to give up. I don't have to always be a loser.*

We talk, for the next hour, about less important things in life. We find that we're both Cubs fans, just hoping for the day when they finally get to the World Series. The Doc tells me a little about his childhood in East St. Louis and his struggles to get where he is. It turns out he knows a lot about weakness, but he's never given in to it.

Marcus doesn't talk much. He's on a soccer team, like Michael. And he hates doing homework, but loves playing basketball. He's never been up in the Sears Tower. I promise to take him someday soon.

Umar just listens, smiling. In the beginning, he wanted to keep me away from Aisha. Now he's the one bringing me into the family.

"Well, I guess we'd better get going soon. You need to get ready, Joshua. I know you're not going to wear those jeans. Did you get a tux?"

"No, Abdul-Qadir sent me something from Pakistan." I show him my wedding suit.

"Very nice. Well, go put it on. We don't want to keep the bride waiting."

❧

The hall is already crowded by the time we get there. A woman is standing on a step stool near the door, putting up a white streamer. "There, that should do it."

"It looks good, Arlene. Here he is. Joshua, do you remember my little sister, Arlene?"

"Oh, Joshua, you look so nice."

"Thank you. The hall looks beautiful. Angela said you were talented."

"Oh, I love to do it. We're all so excited for our little Angela. And I just know you'll take good care of her." She hugs me.

I look at Umar. He shakes his head and smiles. When Aunt Arlene is gone, he whispers, "You'd better get used to it."

Umar and I walk around the room, meeting and greeting more relatives. I look back toward the door just in time to see Brad and Beth walk in. "Come on, Umar, I'll introduce you to my big brother.

"Hey, Brad. I'm glad you could make it. Hi, Beth. This is Umar, Aisha's brother."

"It's nice to meet you. Joshua, could I talk to you for a minute?" Brad turns to Umar. "Would you excuse us? I'll be back in a minute, Beth."

He takes me outside the room and leads me to the far end of corridor, away from the main entrance. He whispers, "Heather came to see Mom. Is what she said true?"

"What did she say?"

"That you forced your way into the apartment and started coming on to her. The way she tells it, you nearly raped her. She had to threaten to call the police before you would leave. She has taken out a restraining order against you."

I didn't think she'd go that far. My face is turning red. It's hard to stay calm. "No, that's not it." I tell him what happened. "Believe me, I've been beating myself up for it, for being so weak. But what she's saying is a lie."

"And, even admitting what you did do, you're ready to marry this girl?"

"What happened—what really happened, not what Heather is saying—was just a moment of stupidity on my part. I was weak for just a moment, and I held her and kissed her. After I remembered Aisha, I pushed her away. Of course she's angry."

"You'd better watch out. She's out to get you now. You won't be seeing Mom or Chris here. They believe Heather."

"That's too bad. I thought I was making progress."

"Have you told Aisha?"

"No. I've just been trying to make my peace with Allah. Hopefully she'll never have to know."

"You'd better keep her far away from Heather, then. Look, Umar is signaling you. We'd better go back in. I just wanted to get that cleared up."

As we walk back in, I pat his shoulder. "Thanks for giving me a chance to explain."

Umar grabs my arm. "Brother Mustapha is here. He wants to meet you."

He leads me towards the front, where Aisha and I will be

seated. Brother Mustapha is waiting there. His beard is black with streaks of gray. He's wearing a simple white robe, with a green shawl draped around his shoulders.

"Assalaamu alaikum, Brother Isa. Umar has asked me to perform your wedding ceremony."

"Walaikum assalaamu. Thank you very much for coming."

"First, I'm sure Umar has told you that I'm also qualified to sign your marriage license for the state of Illinois. You do have your license with you?"

I panic for a moment, then I remember. "Yes, here it is." I put in my suit pocket before leaving Chicago.

"The ceremony will be very simple. Brother Umar tells me the father wants to walk his daughter in?"

"Yes, that's right."

"That's not always done in an Islamic ceremony but I don't think that there will be a problem.

"Aisha and you will be seated up here in front. You will sit here. Do you have witnesses from your side?"

"My brother is here. Some of my friends should be coming soon."

"They will sit next to you. On your other side will be Aisha's brother, Umar, and then Aisha herself. Her parents will be sitting with her. I will give a short sermon about the importance of marriage. Then I will turn to the bride and ask her if she accepts you and the dowry you have agreed upon. She can either answer on her own behalf, or ask her brother to do so for her."

"I will be answering for her," says Umar.

"That's fine. Then I will ask you, the groom, if you accept her as your wife. You will sign the marriage contract, which specifies the dowry, and you will be married. Do you have any questions?"

"Is that all? It sounds so simple."

"The important part is the marriage. It's not hard to get married, but you must have the right intention to stay married."

"Yes, I know. I do."

"Brother Umar, has your sister arrived yet?"

"She should be here any minute. I can wait by the door until she comes."

"That would be good. And I'll stay here with Brother Isa."

Umar leaves and I just stand here, waiting for it all to begin.

Brother Mustapha turns to me, once, with some final advice. "Remember, Isa, faith is the foundation for a good marriage. You must help each other become stronger in faith and righteousness. Are you very clear in your intention?"

I think briefly of my first marriage. There was never anything righteous about that relationship. It is so different this time. "Yes, I am."

I keep looking at the door, waiting for the signal that she has arrived. But I see some other friendly faces first. Ismail, Tariq, Mahmoud and Halima are here, followed by Fawad and his wife. They all come to greet me.

"Assalaamu alaikum. I am so glad you could come. I was wondering, with all the snow."

"Man," says Ismail, "how could I not be here? If it wasn't for me, you wouldn't be here."

"That's for sure." *No one else knows how true that is.* "And Fawad. What about the restaurant?"

"Friendship is more important than money. Tonight I couldn't rest if I wasn't here with you."

Everyone is introduced to Brother Mustapha.

"I think we're ready. If you could take your seat, Isa. Which of your friends will be sitting with you?"

"Ismail and Fawad."

"And you can call your brother to come up."

"That's okay. Brad's a good guy, but these are my truest brothers, the ones who have always stood by me."

"All right. If you'd please be seated, I think we're nearly ready."

Umar signals from the door. Aisha is here.

Brother Mustapha addresses the gathering. "I would like everyone to take a seat now. We are ready to begin. Oh, and please do not rise when the bride comes in. That is not done in Islam."

I'm waiting, sitting in front of everyone, with Umar and Ismail on either side. First I see Dr. Evans in the doorway. Then,

I see Aisha. Her gown and her scarf are white, with blue ribbons and embroidery for decoration. She takes her father's arm and starts to come my way. She smiles at me and continues walking. She reaches her seat. She's so close now. Just a little longer.

Brother Mustapha gives a short sermon about the importance of marriage and the duties of husband and wife. I pay close attention. First, he says, the husband, who is the head of the household, must be kind and not abuse his authority. The husband must also take care of all of his wife's material needs, such as clothing and housing, to the best of his ability. And, most importantly, he must always act lovingly toward her. The wife must also be kind and loving toward her husband.

He ends the sermon with a verse from the Qur'an. "And among His Signs is this, that He created for you mates from among yourselves, that you may dwell in tranquility with them, and He has put love and mercy between your hearts. Surely in that are Signs for those who reflect."

Then Brother Mustapha turns to Aisha. "Do you, Sister Aisha, Angela Evans, allow your brother Umar, Tony Evans, to act on your behalf in this ceremony of marriage?"

"Yes, I do."

"And do you, Tony Evans, accept Joshua Adams as a husband for your sister, with the dowry that he has offered?"

"Yes, I do."

I am so glad Umar likes me now.

"Do you, Isa, Joshua Adams, accept Aisha, Angela Evans, as your wife?"

"Yes, I do."

"Then, in the sight of Allah, and in front of those gathered here, Isa and Aisha, Joshua and Angela, you are now husband and wife."

Fawad shouts, "Takbir," and the guys answer with "Allahu akbar."

I wonder if her relatives will start looking around for the terrorists.

Aisha and I each sign the marriage contract, with Umar and Ismail as our witnesses. We wrote it last Monday, on the same day we went to get our marriage license. In the contract, I promise to provide for her, which is my duty. She also asked to include the provision that I would not marry another wife, even though I would be allowed to according to the teachings of Islam. At the time, I joked lightly about spending the rest of my life with just one woman. That was before I kissed Heather. Now I worry. Even as I sign the marriage contract, the weight of my betrayal stays with me. I will have to work hard to show Aisha that she is the only woman I love. For the rest of my life.

"We will close with a short prayer, and then you may come to congratulate the new couple.

"O Allah. Please bless Isa and Aisha, Joshua and Angela, on this, the first day of their lives together. Please grant them peace and happiness throughout their lives. Bestow your mercy upon their household. You, Allah, are the One who has brought their hearts together. Please help them in every trial, and keep their hearts together always. Amin."

We're married. I want to see my wife. But that will have to wait. The first person I see is Umar. He hugs me tightly.

"Welcome to the family, Isa. I'm glad to have you as my brother."

Then it's Dr. and Mrs. Evans, or Sharon and The Doc. Sharon hugs me. "I know you'll be good for Angela. I'm proud to have you as a son."

The Doc looks at me and offers his hand. "Welcome to the family, son." I accept his handshake, and he grabs me in a bear hug.

After I get free, I find Aisha. I'm about to hug her, but Brother Mustapha stops me. "No, brother, not now. Not in public."

"May I at least give her the ring?"

"Go ahead."

I touch her hand. She looks into my eyes, and smiles. I slip the ring on her finger. We stand and look at one another, smiling, until her aunts swallow us up in their hugs.

We're surrounded by family. I'm hugged so many times, I lose count. Many times, I completely lose sight of Aisha as she's taken away by the crowd.

Brad comes up and shakes my hand. "Congratulations, little brother. I think you'll get it right this time."

"Thanks. I think so, too."

"So are you going to introduce me to my new sister-in-law?"

"If I can find her."

❧

The party goes on for hours. We sit at the head table with Aisha's family. Aunt Vivien and Aunt Debra bring us plates heaping with food. I don't know about Aisha, but I'm starving. I haven't eaten all day. She and I sit together and have our first meal as husband and wife.

Brad and Beth come over to sit with us. They left Kyle with Mom.

"We told her we were just going away for the weekend. She wouldn't have kept him if she knew we were coming to the wedding."

"Why not?" says Aisha. "Why wouldn't your own mother want you to come? And I was wondering, why isn't she here, too?"

I look at Brad. He's said too much.

"It's nothing. Our mom still isn't too crazy about Joshua being a Muslim and she thinks we need to stay away from him until he comes to his senses." Not quite true, but it will do. That was close.

"That's a shame. Doesn't she know he's not going to change? So, how old is your little boy?"

We talk a while longer, until Brad looks at his watch. "I guess we'd better get back on the road. Congratulations, both of you. And Aisha, welcome to the family."

What family? Do you mean those people who always believe the worst about me?

The guests are leaving. Those who came in from Chicago leave first. Before Ismail goes, I take him aside.

"Thanks for coming, man. Thanks for everything."

"Remember, fifty years."

"Yeah. Hey, are you and Tariq still looking for a roommate?"

"We sure are. Our old ones keep getting married."

"There's a brother who just made Shahadah at the masjid last week. Bilal. Maybe you should hook up with him."

"Good idea. Thanks, man. And congratulations. It'll be good. I know you're going to do it right this time."

"Yeah, me too." He gets in the car with Tariq, Mahmoud, and Halima, and heads back to Chicago.

Soon it's just the Evans family—with all their aunts and uncles—and us.

"You two can go on now. We'll finish up. We'll take the wedding presents to our house and you can come over tomorrow to open them."

"Thanks, Mrs., Sharon. Thank you for everything."

Aisha hugs them all before we leave. Her longest hug is for The Doc.

Before we leave, The Doc puts his arm around my shoulder. "Remember, son. Marriage is supposed to last for a lifetime."

"Yes, sir, I'll remember that."

And Aisha and I drive away together, back to the hotel.

❧

The first thing we do is say our prayers. When the prayers are finished, I take her hand. Then I kiss her and hold her tight. I want to hold her forever.

❧

We go over to their house for brunch in the morning. It's a little awkward at first, with the change in our roles. Aisha is with me now. But she gets The Doc his coffee, and we eat Sharon's pancakes, and we open the presents, and everyone starts to relax. This is my family now. Finally, I have a real family.

We've received many nice presents. They include two blenders, three sets of dishes, and four sets of bath towels.

"That's okay. You can keep them on hand, just in case. When we got married we received five toasters, and what are you going to do with five toasters?"

"We ate a lot of toast that first year," says The Doc. Sharon pokes him in the arm.

So this is a family.

~

We head back to Chicago in the afternoon. There are more hugs and handshakes. "We'll come see you soon in your new home," says Sharon.

"Great. Then I'll take Marcus up to the top of the Sears Tower. Okay, buddy?"

"Yeah, sure. I'd like that."

The Doc looks a little sad. I can see it in his eyes. I wonder if I can ever be as close to my daughter as he is to Aisha.

"Drive carefully, now. Call me when you get there."

"Okay, Daddy." She kisses him one more time and climbs into the car. We pull out of their driveway, out of their street, heading home together.

Umar leads the way, with Aisha and me close behind. Most of the presents are in his car. Aisha sits close to me while I drive. No more loneliness.

When we pass the place where I was stuck, I tell her my story. Most of the snow is cleared away now, and what's left has started to melt. It doesn't look dangerous. Why did I panic back there? Was it guilt?

We talk about our plans for the future. After she graduates, in a few more months, she'll get a job in the suburbs. We'll find a little house. She'll teach for a couple of years. Then we'll have children. At least three, maybe four. By the time the children come, I'll have my degree and she can stay home with them. We might even home school.

We're almost to Chicago when Aisha touches the scratch on my face.

"What happened? Did you get that when you were digging

out of the snow?"

I touch my cheek. It still hasn't healed completely. "Oh, this? Yeah, I guess so."

I don't know if I can keep this up for fifty years.

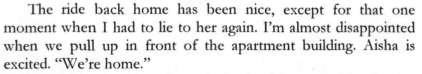

The ride back home has been nice, except for that one moment when I had to lie to her again. I'm almost disappointed when we pull up in front of the apartment building. Aisha is excited. "We're home."

We grab a few things from the back of the car and head up to the apartment. I don't carry her over the threshold, but I do kiss her as soon as we're inside.

Umar is standing in the open doorway, holding some wedding presents. "Um, where do you want these?"

Aisha takes over again, directing the two of us as we bring everything in and put it all away. When we're done, Umar puts on his coat and heads for the door.

"I guess it's time for me to go. I'll be seeing you soon, insha Allah. Have a nice evening."

"Thanks for everything. I mean that."

"Yes, no problem. Well, I'll be seeing you."

Aisha laughs. "Don't worry. You haven't lost a sister, you've gained a brother."

"That's right. Well, goodnight. Assalaamu alaikum."

I feel sorry for Umar, going back to his apartment alone. But only for a little while. I have Aisha, and now we're home, alone.

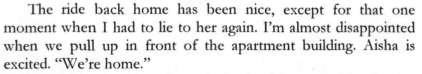

Neither of us has to worry about school for another week. The restaurant is closed, and I don't have to go to work until Tuesday. We spend our Monday morning relaxing together, still getting to know one another. There is so much to learn.

In the early afternoon, the phone rings. I don't feel like getting it. I don't want to let the outside world in today. The answering machine gets it.

"Assalaamu alaikum, Isa. This is Zakariya. Your custody hearing is on the calendar for the end of February. Call me when you have a chance."

We're going to court soon to get my kids. And we can be a family.

The Hearing

"Four things come not back.
The spoken word,
the sped arrow,
the past life and
the neglected opportunity"
- Arab proverb

The last six weeks have been a blur of paperwork and meetings. Joshua never imagined it would be so complicated. He has met several times with his lawyer to discuss finances, witnesses, and evidence. He knows Heather is doing the same.

Between preparations for the hearing, college classes, Aisha's student teaching, and Joshua's work at the restaurant, the newlyweds haven't had much time for each other. The pressure has made Joshua tense and restless. He paces, and twice he has snapped at his wife. Each time, she rubbed his back and reminded him it will soon be over. Soon he'll be with his children again. Each time, he apologized for being difficult. She said she understands.

Three weeks before the hearing, Joshua received a call from Heather. Aisha wasn't home. Heather informed Joshua that if he or his lawyer made any derogatory statements against her in court, she had decided to go to the police and formally charge him with attempted rape. Old Mrs. Johnson, who stays in the apartment next door, has agreed to support her story. After he hung up, Joshua was in a rage for almost an hour. He shouted and cursed and broke a few dishes. Then he cleaned up the mess. He hoped Aisha wouldn't notice.

The next day Zakariya called, telling Joshua to come by his office. He had evidence they could use against Heather. Her waitress job is at the Lion's Den, where she dresses in skimpy outfits and flirts with the customers. Zakariya also learned that a man sometimes spent the night at Heather's apartment. Joshua asked Zakariya not to use this information. Zakariya said he didn't understand.

The night before the hearing, Joshua and Aisha made plans for when Michael, Jeremy and Jennifer come to live with them. For now, the three will have to share a room. Later, as Jennifer gets older, they can all move to a house with three, or even four, bedrooms.

Privately, Joshua worried about seeing Heather again. Will she say anything to Aisha? And how will his mother act toward him? Of course, he couldn't share any of this with his wife. While she slept, he worried.

135

The night before the hearing, Evie thought about her decision to testify for Heather. Over these past two years, she has been impressed by Heather's ability to manage her life. She is a good mother. The children are clean, well-mannered, and properly fed. Jeremy is still a little too quiet, but he should outgrow that soon. Heather is not perfect, but she is a good mother.

Besides, how could she possibly support Joshua after what he did? She knew he was selfish and irresponsible, but she never knew he could be so violent. But Heather sat in Evie's office and told her how Joshua had actually attacked her. Not only that, but it was less than a week before his wedding. And he still married the poor girl.

The night before the hearing, Heather waited with anticipation. He has abandoned her twice. Now he will suffer. She will make very sure of that. She wondered if that new wife of his would be there. Heather would like to check out the competition. Not that she would ever take Joshua back, not after that time in front of the apartment building. He had his chance. Now he will have to pay.

She hadn't thought he would really leave, that first time. He had threatened to leave a few times before, and sometimes after they fought he would stay out all night. But he always came back to her. She waited for three days before she could admit he was gone for good. That second time, in the car, she was sure he had come back to her. The story of the attack, the lie which would help her humiliate Joshua in court, was true in Heather's mind. Joshua had come back and pretended to love her again. His attack on her emotions was worse than any physical attack Heather could imagine.

The night before the hearing, Chris sat and contemplated his testimony against his younger brother. He was always a bad kid, but who knew he could be this bad? That's what comes from leaving the church. They like to say how good they are, how peaceful they are, but their actions always prove otherwise.

The night before the hearing, Brad talked to Beth about his family. He thanked God he had found a wife as wonderful as

Beth, who provides a loving contrast to the dysfunctional home he grew up in. It's too bad Aisha had to get mixed up in all of this. She seems like such a nice girl.

Brad knows the names of the players, and their agendas. He has decided to sit on the sidelines. But he knows that Joshua is walking into a trap.

❧

They each arrive at the courthouse in the morning, ready to do battle.

Heather comes first. She searched through her closet for twenty minutes before finally settling on the dress she wore to Chris and Melinda's wedding. It's a simple cut, navy blue, with long sleeves and a high neckline. Joshua always liked that dress. She's never worn it since he left. Her less modest outfits remain hanging in the closet.

Joshua and Aisha arrive a few minutes after Heather. Joshua went out yesterday to buy a black suit, striped tie, and crisp white dress shirt for the occasion. It cut into their monthly budget, but it seemed like a necessary expense. Aisha is dressed as she usually is, in a long dress and matching scarf. Today she decided to wear blue.

Their witnesses are all lined up, ready to assist in the fight.

Ismail and Fawad come in shortly before the judge arrives in the courtroom. They will testify to Joshua's stability and overall strength of character. Fawad will go first so he can get back to the restaurant in time for the lunch crowd.

Chris will be coming in the afternoon. The lawyer said they wouldn't need him until then. He has morning classes and, although he could have asked for time off, he doesn't want to publicize his family's failings.

Evie won't be coming until tomorrow. This is a bad time to have to take off from work. Figures have to be collected and analyzed for the monthly report, and she has meetings scheduled all week. Hopefully, she will be able to testify right away tomorrow morning so she can get back to the office.

The stage is set for the confrontation.

Zakariya shakes hands with Joshua and urges him to relax. They have a good case. It should go smoothly. Joshua listens quietly to Zakariya's counsel, and braces himself for the explosion.

The judge enters, and they rise. The witnesses are asked to leave the courtroom and wait in the hall. Aisha remains to give support to her husband.

Zakariya takes the floor, presenting the case of the petitioner. He paints the portrait of a caring father who has been denied access to his children by a vengeful ex-wife. Zakariya enumerates the steps Joshua has taken in the past two years to build a stable home in the hopes his children will join him. He is financially stable, in pursuit of an undergraduate degree, and newly married to an educated and well-mannered young woman. Joshua and his new wife are both anxious to provide a loving home to the three precious children in question.

Joshua is the first to take the stand. Zakariya guides him through the last two years of his life. He urges Joshua to tell the judge about his success in working at the restaurant and enrolling in college. Joshua is reluctant at first, too nervous to open up. With Zakariya's encouragement, he tells of his struggle to improve himself. He is getting good grades in his classes and he intends to complete his undergraduate studies. Because of his ability and diligence, he has been promoted to assistant manager. Through determination and hard work, he has been able to get his life on track.

Then, before turning him over to Heather's lawyer, Zakariya asks Joshua to discuss the days before he began to change, before he became a Muslim. Joshua admits to youthful acts of indiscretion, which he regrets. He expresses his deepest regret for having turned his back on his children, and his strong desire to reestablish a relationship with them.

Zakariya asks him, also, about his time in Pakistan. Joshua credits that trip with motivating him to change. He states that in Pakistan he finally learned how to be a father and realized how much he loves his children.

Heather's lawyer challenges Joshua to prove he has truly changed, arguing no one could change that dramatically in so short a time. He also questions Joshua about the true nature of his trip to Pakistan, alleging he was actually training at a terrorist camp. Finally, he attacks Joshua for his failure to pay child support, except for the past two months, calling the timing suspicious. Joshua remains calm, occasionally looking to Aisha for support. He repeats what he said to Zakariya about being a changed man and wanting a true relationship with his children. His palms are damp, but he maintains his composure.

Joshua steps down and returns to sit with Aisha. She squeezes his hand and smiles. He did well.

The next witness is Fawad. He speaks of Joshua's good work ethic and dependability. He also talks of Joshua as a friend on whom he can depend. He tells the judge about their relationship, which is based on faith and trust. Fawad further states that Joshua has often talked about his children and his sincere desire to be with them again.

Heather's lawyer has few questions for Fawad. He simply verifies the date when Joshua began working, and his salary.

The judge orders a break for lunch. Fawad returns to the restaurant. Zakariya, Joshua, Aisha, and Ismail go for sandwiches. Joshua can barely eat.

Ismail testifies when they return. He tells the judge about the first time he met Joshua. At that time, Joshua worked with Mahmoud, one of Ismail's roommates, and he often came to the house to play video games and eat pizza. Later, Joshua came to the house to say he had just left his family and had nowhere to go. Ismail and his friends offered Joshua a place to stay until he could get back on his feet.

Zakariya asks Ismail to describe Joshua as he was when he first arrived at the house. Ismail admits Joshua sometimes went out drinking, and did little work of any kind. He then recounts Joshua's journey to Islam, as he began going to the mosque and stopped drinking beer. Ismail was there when Joshua made the Shahadah, pledging his commitment to Islam.

Ismail talks in greater detail about the Joshua who returned from Pakistan. He got a job on his second day back, and was diligent in both his work and his practice of Islam.

Ismail concludes by describing the Joshua he now knows. He replays some of their conversations in which Joshua has expressed his strong desire to be with his children. He portrays Joshua as a responsible and caring man who is now ready to fulfill his duties as a father.

In his cross examination, Heather's lawyer concentrates on Joshua's conversion to Islam. He again challenges the notion that a person can change so easily, and contests Ismail's assertion of Joshua's transformation. He also questions Ismail about Joshua's intention to raise his children as Muslims, even though they have never been exposed to the religion, which is foreign to most Americans, and contends this may threaten the long-term emotional stability of the children. Ismail, as always, remains in charge of the exchange, asserting that Islam would be a positive force in the children's lives.

Ismail steps down, and Joshua's case is finished. Heather's lawyer comes to the front.

He starts by outlining the case from Heather's perspective. Heather is a devoted mother who has always put her children first. He produces pictures of birthday parties and Christmases, three smiling children against a backdrop of decorations and presents.

When her husband left, Heather rose to the challenge of caring for them as a single mother. Receiving no financial support, Heather has worked two jobs to continue to provide for her children and meet all their needs. She is the only stable presence in the lives of these children whose world was tragically destabilized when their father walked out on them.

He then turns to portray Joshua as a man with no morals and no sense of fatherly responsibilities. Not only did Joshua refuse to provide child support for almost two years after he left, during much of that time he made almost no effort to see his children. The lawyer challenges the notion that Joshua was magically transformed by his conversion. Instead, he states, Joshua is an experienced manipulator who has brought this case to court not so much to see his children as to punish his long-suffering ex-wife.

The lawyer calls Heather to the stand. She recounts their five years of marriage, emphasizing Joshua's frequent acts of irresponsibility. He quit numerous jobs and often went out drinking with friends. She knows he was also seeing other women. She tells of her attempts to gently support and encourage him. She talks about the birth of their third child, and how Joshua refused to come to the hospital to see his new daughter or take his wife and daughter home. She becomes teary-eyed, remembering how he was out drinking while she was in the throes of labor. She starts to replay the events of the day Joshua walked out, while their two boys were begging him to stop screaming, but she is unable to finish. She breaks down and cries. The lawyer gives her a few minutes to compose herself.

Aisha sits next to Joshua, her arms crossed. Her eyes are riveted on Heather. She doesn't dare look at her husband. She knew the basic facts of the divorce, but never considered the emotional pain Joshua had caused. She knows he's changed. She has to believe he has changed.

The lawyer asks Heather about Joshua's behavior toward her since the divorce. She states she never heard from him until about a year ago, when he called and demanded to see the children. He still had not given her any child support, and when she reminded him of this, he became angry and hung up on her. She knows he has driven past the apartment on occasion and fears he may be stalking her. She received the first support check from him only two months ago, a few days after another argument. The lawyer doesn't ask for more details, and she doesn't supply any. Joshua's face turns red. Aisha doesn't notice. She's staring at Heather and wondering if what she's saying is true.

Zakariya knows there are some factual errors in Heather's testimony. Nevertheless, he fears his cross examination could provoke more tears, to which the judge would be sympathetic. After lunch, Joshua reaffirmed his decision not to use the evidence against Heather. Zakariya decides not to ask Heather any questions.

The lawyer calls Chris Adams to the stand. He asks Chris for a brief history of his relationship with Joshua. Chris recalls their teenage years when the two brothers fought often. Joshua, he says, had a violent temper and reacted with force at the slightest provocation.

What about Joshua when he became older, the lawyer asks. Chris responds that Joshua was selfish and uncontrolled during his marriage to Heather. He quit many jobs and was never able to provide adequately for his family.

The lawyer then asks Chris if Joshua has changed since his conversion, as has been previously claimed. Chris responds that, at first, he thought he saw some signs of maturity in his younger brother. He has come to the conclusion, however, that this was just a facade, and Joshua continues to be as selfish and uncontrolled as ever.

Aisha listens intently. The man they are describing cannot be the same man she married only two months ago. They must be mistaken.

Zakariya questions Chris about his personal bias. As a teacher at a Bible college, Zakariya states, isn't it possible that Chris is simply offended by Joshua's decision to embrace Islam. This bias could cause Chris to develop an attitude against Joshua no matter what the circumstances. Chris admits he is deeply bothered by Joshua's conversion, but he maintains that his religious convictions also require him to be truthful. He can truthfully stand behind his earlier assertions.

Zakariya does not want to further challenge the religious convictions of the witness, for fear he may alienate the judge. Chris is dismissed.

The judge asks if there are more witnesses. Heather's lawyer responds that he still has one witness scheduled to appear in the morning. The judge remarks that it is getting late, and he adjourns for the day.

On the way home, Aisha does not speak to her husband. She sits close to the car door and thinks hard, trying to reconcile the testimony she heard with the man she knows. They eat a quiet dinner at home and go to sleep with few words between them.

The next morning, Aisha tries to be positive. They don't know him. They never gave him a chance. She speaks encouraging words to her husband. He still says very little.

When the court is reconvened, the lawyer calls Joshua's mother to the witness stand.

Aisha has never seen Joshua's mother before. She can see some slight resemblance, though she thinks he must look more like his father.

The lawyer asks Joshua's mother to relate relevant incidents from Joshua's youth. She recalls him as being impetuous and irresponsible. He began to drink at an early age and later smoked marijuana as well. They had frequent arguments, and occasionally he became violent toward her. He had a long string of girlfriends, both before and during his marriage, and, in all his relationships, he exhibited a blatant attitude of disrespect toward women. Although she tried to be a kind and loving mother, she was unable to control him at all after the age of twelve.

That was in the past, Aisha thinks. He is so different now. Even his own mother doesn't know him. No wonder he has such a strained relationship with her.

The lawyer then asks the mother to describe Joshua's marriage to Heather. The mother states that the marriage was a mistake from the very beginning. Joshua was not mature enough to care for a wife or provide for a family. Throughout his marriage, he continued to act like an irresponsible teenager. He ignored Heather and her needs, preferring to spend time with his friends. Heather was raising the children by herself long before Joshua actually abandoned her.

What about his relationship with his children, the lawyer asks. The mother admits Joshua was thrilled when Michael was born, and he doted on his firstborn son for the first year or so. He was less excited about the arrival of a second child, and completely ignored the third, his only daughter.

Aisha can't help but think of the special relationship between her father and her, his only daughter. She wonders why Joshua wouldn't cherish his daughter the way her father cherishes her.

The lawyer asks the mother to describe Joshua's attitude towards the children at the time of the divorce. She recounts the conversation in which he expressed happiness and relief at being free of them. He stated he did not intend to pursue custody and seemed unwilling to pay child support. He wanted a clean break from his family, with no strings attached. The lawyer confirms those were his exact words.

The lawyer then asks the mother if Joshua has shown any changes in his behavior in recent months. The mother states he has been calmer, and less prone to violent outbursts. For a short period of time, he seemed to be acting responsibly. However, she is now convinced it was all an act. He is still the same irresponsible man who abandoned his wife and children.

Finally the lawyer asks the mother, in light of her statements, to summarize her opinion of Joshua's ability to be a father to his children. The mother states that placing the children in Joshua's custody would be foolish at best and dangerous at worst. Joshua, she states, is still an immature and irresponsible boy who is incapable of caring for anyone other than himself. His recklessness could cause irreparable harm to his children.

Aisha is stunned. She wonders how any mother could be so cruel, saying such hateful things about her son. She also wonders if she has been fooled. Maybe they are right.

Joshua works hard to control his emotions. He knows his mother is speaking out of ignorance, believing Heather's lie. Still, he feels crushed by her condemnation. He remembers that time in the office, when she hugged him. He wonders if she really did love him then, or if it was just an illusion.

Zakariya is also shocked at the brutality of the mother's comments. He takes a moment to gather his thoughts before standing to cross-examine her. Zakariya reminds the mother that Joshua has held a steady job for over a year, with a recent promotion, and he is now attending college. The mother remarks that anyone can attend college and hold a job. These small accomplishments, she states, do not compensate for Joshua's true nature. Zakariya has no more questions.

The judge advises both parties that he will consider the

testimony, as well as pretrial evidence submitted by both lawyers, and inform them of his decision within the next ninety days. The court is adjourned.

Before leaving the courtroom, Heather briefly studies the woman Joshua married, the one he said he loves. She's not unattractive, but nowhere near as beautiful as Heather. Heather wonders why Joshua prefers Aisha over her.

Before leaving the courtroom, Evie glances at Joshua's new wife. She is pretty. How long will it be, Evie wonders, before she is sitting in a similar courtroom, fighting with Joshua over their children. Poor girl.

Evie leaves without a word to either of them. Aisha wonders what kind of family she has married into.

The contest is over. Joshua knows he has been defeated.

Joshua: Learning to love

"I hold it true, whate'er befall
I feel it, when I sorrow most
'Tis better to have loved and lost
than never to have loved at all"
- Alfred Tennyson

Part One

I have been sitting in this courtroom, listening to my mother portray me as a monster. Does she really believe what she's saying?

Aisha's face is tense. Even after the judge leaves, she continues to stare into space. I hold her hand. She doesn't look at me. I shouldn't have let her come.

Since the day Heather called, I knew it would be bad. But I didn't know it would be like this. I've lost, I know that. I will probably never see my children again. Not only that, I have lost whatever love my mother once had for me. And Aisha still won't look at me.

I can't cry. Not here. Later tonight, maybe, after Aisha is asleep. But not here, not now. I almost wish that I was the monster my mother made me out to be. Then it wouldn't hurt so much.

"Isa." Zakariya puts his arm around my shoulder. "Listen to me, Isa. It's not as bad as it looks. We presented a good case."

I look at him and shake my head. "Don't lie to me. I know what just happened."

"It's okay, Isa. You still have a chance. Listen, why don't we go get some lunch. Maybe you'll feel better after you eat something."

"That's okay. I'm not hungry."

"Let's go. Try to relax a little. Things will look better after a good meal."

Zakariya keeps insisting. Aisha and I walk to our car and follow him to a nearby restaurant. All the way there, she continues to stare ahead. She still won't look at me.

We eat a quiet meal. I can barely swallow. Aisha contributes little to the conversation. Zakariya keeps talking. He tries to lay out a new strategy. All is not lost, he says. He won't give up.

When the bill comes, Zakariya takes care of it. We walk with him out to the parking lot. Before we get into our cars, he emarks, "I wish you had let me present the evidence I had against your ex-wife. It would have made a significant difference in your case."

"I know. I had my reasons."

"We did our best. Just keep praying. Maybe the judge will see the merits of our case when he reviews the pretrial report."

"Yeah, whatever."

We get in the car and I start to drive. I don't want to go home yet. First I want to get rid of this shroud over us. I drive along Lake Shore Drive. I try to get Aisha to look out at the lake. It's a beautiful, sunny afternoon. She continues to stare straight ahead. She hasn't said a word to me since we came into the court this morning.

She's quiet all the way home. But as soon as we walk into the apartment, she turns on me. "What evidence did Zakariya have against Heather? Why didn't you let him use it? You're talking about the custody of your children. Why in the world wouldn't you do everything possible to get them?"

"I don't want to talk about it. It's complicated." I try to kiss her. Maybe a little romance will make her forget what she heard. She pulls away.

"What's so complicated?" She looks at me, finally. "There's something you're not telling me, isn't there?"

"Aisha, I just don't want to talk about this right now." I take off my tie and suit coat. They're so uncomfortable. "I'm tired, and I'm behind in all my classes. I've got to get some rest so I can try to catch up tomorrow. Let's just relax for now and forget about it, honey."

"You're behind? I had to take two days off from my student teaching. I have lesson plans to make and my professor will be coming in to observe me on Thursday. But it was worth it, wasn't it, to get custody of your kids? That is what you wanted, isn't it?"

"Sure, honey. I'm just tired. Why don't we both go rest a little?" I stroke her cheek. She usually likes that.

"Or was Heather right? Did you do this just to punish her?"

"You should know me better than that." I try to hold her close. She pulls away from me again.

"Not now, Isa. We need to talk." She stands there, staring at me. "I thought I knew you, but I'm not so sure anymore. After listening to how Heather has struggled to raise those kids on her own, I'm not sure what I know."

"Honey, you know she's the one who wouldn't let me see the kids. It's not my fault. It's Heather. She's the manipulator. But I don't want to talk about her right now. Let's just concentrate on us." I rub her back.

"Then if Heather is so bad, why wouldn't you let Zakariya use the evidence to help your case?"

"I can't tell you, honey. Forget about it."

"Isa, I didn't think we had any secrets from one another." She comes closer and gently squeezes my arm. "This is too important. And if you start hiding things from me, how I can trust you?"

"You can trust me. You know that. But let me deal with Heather. You don't want to know about the evidence. You shouldn't have to worry about it."

"Don't try to patronize me. Let me decide what I want to know. Tell me." Her voice becomes harsher, and her gentle squeeze becomes a vise. "What happened to all that honesty? Was that just a facade, like your brother said?"

She touches a nerve. I push her arm away and yell, "Don't start with me. I have taken it from Chris all my life. Don't you dare turn against me, too."

She screams into my face. "Then tell me what is going on."

"You're not going to like it. It could change things."

"Don't you want to change things? Don't you want your children?"

"Yes, of course. And that's not what I mean."

"Tell me."

I have to tell her. Our relationship was built on honesty, and it's too much work to keep hiding it from her. Forget the fifty years. I can't do it. But it's going to be bad.

I hold her hand and look into her eyes. "Okay. I'll tell you. Zakariya found out that Heather works at the Lion's Den."

"You mean that place where the men go and—"

"Yeah, that's the place. Not only that, she's had a guy staying over at the apartment some nights."

"What? And you didn't bring this up in court? Your children could be in danger. Haven't you heard about those cases where kids are molested or abused by the mother's boyfriend? Why didn't you want Zakariya to use this? I know you're not stupid." She stops, and stares at me. "What's going on, Isa?" Her voice is lower now, and threatening.

"Look, I told you you're not going to like it. It was just something stupid, and I've been kicking myself ever since."

"What is going on? What did you do?"

"A few weeks before the hearing, Heather called over here and threatened me. She said that if I used any evidence against her, she would accuse me of attempted rape."

"What?" Her scream echoes through the apartment. "How could she say such a thing? Why would she even think of accusing you of something so terrible?" She's silent for a moment. "Unless you . . . you. You didn't, did you?"

"No, I didn't attack her." I stop, but she's still waiting for an explanation. "I didn't attack her. But I did touch her."

Aisha jerks away as if I had slapped her. Her eyes are wide. When she speaks again, it's almost a snarl. "What did you do?"

"It was a couple of months ago. I just wanted to see the kids. So I drove over there and parked outside the old apartment."

"She's right. You were stalking her."

"No, I just wanted to see the kids."

"A couple of months ago? After we were married?"

"No, a few days before our wedding. The day you and Umar left for Moline. I just wanted to see the kids. Anyway, Heather came out to the car and started screaming at me. We got into a big fight."

How can I tell her? I look away. "Um, anyway, we were fighting, and, somehow, she started crying. And, and I don't know what happened, but I felt sorry for her and, somehow, I don't know what happened, but, well, I, um, I held her and started kissing her."

"You what?"

"Until I remembered you. Then I stopped and pushed her away."

"And how long did it take you to remember me?" she shrieks. "You held her and kissed her four days before our wedding? I don't believe it. Four days! I was in Moline dreaming of our marriage, and you were fooling around with your ex-wife."

"I didn't mean to do it. It just happened. I felt so bad. Ask Ismail. I almost didn't marry you. But I fasted and asked Allah for forgiveness. And I did marry you, because you're the one I love."

"Do you always forget about the people you love?" She's still shouting. "You forgot your children, and you forgot me long enough to make out with your ex-wife. Is there anything else you're not telling me? Maybe you're sleeping with her, too."

"No, no, Aisha, it's not like that. It was just one moment of weakness."

"You cheated on Heather. You're cheating on me, too, aren't you?"

I shouldn't have let her go to the hearing. "No. It was just that one time."

"How do I know that? Mr. Honesty!" She slams her open palm against the wall.

"I don't believe you. You act like a pious Muslim and a loving husband. But you're sneaking around behind my back. How many times did it happen, Joshua?" She uses the name my family uses, the name which has come to mean failure. "How many times have you cheated on me?"

"It was just that once, before we were married. And I didn't mean for anything to happen."

"You never mean for anything to happen. You just stumble through life and expect everyone around you to pick up the pieces. Daddy knew it. He tried to warn me once. He said he was worried about you because of your past. But I just laughed and told him how good you were. Now you've made a liar out of me, too."

She sits on the couch and sobs. I walk over and stroke her cheek.

"Don't you touch me. Get out. Get out right now."

"Don't do this, Aisha. We have to talk."

"So you can tell me more lies? Get out of here. Now."

"But, Aisha."

"Maybe Heather will take you back."

"Aisha."

She stands up and pushes me against the wall. "I told you to leave. Now."

I've had enough. "Okay, I'm out of here." I grab my coat and slip on my shoes. I walk across the threshold, then turn to look back. She slams the door in my face.

As I trudge down the stairs, I can hear her sobbing.

It's a good thing I left the car keys in my coat pocket. I go to my car, the scene of the crime, and sit.

I have screwed up my life so badly. As long as I had Aisha, I had a chance. Without her, I don't know what I'll do. For a while, I just put my forehead on the steering wheel and do some sobbing of my own.

She's right. She can't trust me. No one can trust me. And what's left?

Maybe I could go back to Heather. Her standards aren't as high, and if I sweet talk her she might take me back. I could see the kids every day, and we'd look back on the divorce as just an unpleasant episode. Of course, if I go over there now, she'll probably call the police.

Do I want to go back to Heather? And do I want to go back to being the person I was when I was with Heather? They are all wrong, all of them. I have changed. But if I go back to Heather, I'll probably just slip into my old familiar ways. And I'm a Muslim now. Would I still want to practice Islam if I was with Heather, or would I give that up, too?

The thing is, I don't even want Heather. I want Aisha. Replacing one wife with another won't help anything. And Aisha is irreplaceable.

But I don't think Aisha will take me back. I never imagined

I'd hear her sweet voice screaming at me like that. And her face. I'll never forget the expression on her face. How can she ever trust me again? She doesn't know if it was just that one time, or one hundred times. And even one time was too many.

I can't imagine my life without Aisha. Much of who I am right now, the good in me, is because of her. She makes me feel like I'm worth something. She's the first woman who ever respected me and expected good things of me. I blew that, though. She'll never respect me again. I don't deserve it.

Without Aisha, my life is worthless. The old familiar thoughts taunt me again. Wouldn't I just be better off dead?

I've had these thoughts since I was thirteen. The first time was after my first really big fight with my mother. She was yelling at me about my grades, and I pushed her. She slapped me, hard, in the face. I ran to the garage and stayed there all night. The garage had many possibilities. But I fell asleep, and in the morning I decided to go hang out with my friends instead.

After that, sometimes even when things were good, I would lie in my bed and imagine the ways I might do it. I'd challenge myself to find the fastest, easiest way. I'd even plan how to do it for the greatest shock value when my mother found my body.

The game continued after I married Heather. When the collection agency called for the fiftieth time, or when they came to take the car away, I'd sit on the steps outside the apartment building and think about the relief it would bring. It was harder to plan, though, because of the kids. I wanted Heather to find me, but not the kids.

After I became a Muslim, the thoughts stopped for a long time. I thought they were gone for good. They came back, just a little, when I was stuck in the snow. But that time wasn't serious. That time wasn't anywhere near as intense as when I was younger. Or now.

I shouldn't be doing this. Suicide is wrong. I know that. But kissing and holding Heather was wrong, too. Hurting Aisha was wrong. Almost everything I have ever done was wrong. I was born to be wrong, and there will never be anything right about me. Sam knew it. That's why he left me.

I have been trying, these last couple of years. I thought I could change. I really believed it. I worked so hard for it. But it's no use. Heather, my mother, and my brother were all right. I haven't changed. I've just been fooling myself. Sooner or later, everyone around me finds out who I really am. Now Aisha knows, too. I'm a fake. I'm a failure. I'm a failure as a husband, a failure as a Muslim, and a failure as a human being. The best thing to do is to just stop pretending and put an end to it.

The first thing to consider, I guess, is who would find my body. Not Aisha. I would never do that to her. Not Heather, either, because of the kids. Wouldn't it be a hoot if my mother found me in her garage? How many times during the hearing did she call me irresponsible? Would she be surprised if I managed to be responsible for my own death?

I'm trying to remember. How did I plan it before, when I was a teenager? I would follow through with it this time, if I could just remember. But I can't quite get my mind around it. It's too hard. Will I be a failure at this, too?

Or maybe a drink will help me remember. I'll go drive by my old hangout first. After a few beers, I should be able to do it. Maybe some of my old friends are still there. We can have a farewell round together. I hope Lizzie is there too. She was there to comfort me when I left Heather. Now she can help me get over another wife. That's it. A couple of drinks, a final fling with Lizzie, and then I'll head over to my mother's garage.

I start up the car and get on the highway. I know where I'm going. It'll be hot there, but it's the perfect place for a loser like me.

On my way there, I drive past the lake. There were some good things in my life, like the lake. Like eating pizza. Like hanging out with the guys. But it's not enough. I've lost the best things in my life. I've lost my mother's love. I've lost my children. I've lost Aisha. And I've lost my faith. I wasn't cut out to be a believer. I am too messed up. Allah doesn't want me either. I'm only a loser.

I could stop somewhere for a final slice of pizza. One last meal. But I can't eat right now. My stomach is queasy.

I can't go see the guys. I want them to remember some good in me. They can't see me like this. Maybe they won't be surprised when they hear that I'm dead. Maybe I only thought I was fooling them. If they don't know by now how bad I am, they'll find out soon enough.

This is my last night. I have been trying to hold on for the last twenty-five years. But I can't do it. Sam knew I would fail. He didn't want to love me, because he knew who I was.

I'm ready. I've been anticipating this night for the last twelve years. And not very much has changed, for all the time I've been hanging on. I'm ready.

There's the hangout, just up ahead. It looks the same. It's just starting to bounce this time of night. There's a parking space right in front. Maybe this is my lucky day after all. I pull in and stop the car. The brakes screech.

Something falls off the dashboard. It's my Qur'an, now lying open, face down, on the floor of the car. That figures. My Qur'an is on the floor and my life is in the gutter. I put the car into park, turn off the ignition, and open the door. But I can't leave it there, open and mangled. I have to pick it up.

I glance at the open page, and some words catch my eye. "Say, 'Oh my servants who have sinned against their own souls! Do not despair of the mercy of Allah: for Allah forgives all sins for He is Oft-forgiving, Most Merciful."

I read it three times. Then a couple times more. And I get it. It means me.

The mercy of Allah. I remember. I sit in the neon light of my old hangout, with the smell of beer and the sound of laughter, and I remember.

I don't have to kill myself tonight. Do I really want to? I sit in my car, the door halfway open, and try to figure it out.

I've lost Aisha. I've lost my children. I've lost my mother's love.

But I guess I haven't lost my faith. Is that enough? I don't know. I can't think.

A guy in another car pulls up beside me and starts cursing at me to make up my mind. He wants this spot. I wish he would just shut up. He's too loud. I can't think.

I glance over at him. There's something about him. I take another look.

He looks familiar. That used to be me.

What am I doing? I don't belong here anymore. I shut my door, turn on the engine, and pull away from the curb. The guy pulls into the spot. He curses at me as I drive away.

I get back on the highway. I don't know where I'm going, but I have to get away from there. I have to get far away.

When I stop again, I'm in front of Umar's apartment building.

I shouldn't be here. Umar is the last person I want to see. I've betrayed him, too, and I don't know how I can face him. But I know, somehow, that he's the one who can save me from myself tonight.

As I climb up the stairs to his third floor apartment, I waver. I've lost Aisha. I've lost my children. I've totally messed up my life. I could still go up to the roof and throw myself off. I guess it wouldn't hurt too much. Umar might be the one who finds me. Then he would know that he was right about me from the beginning. He should have kept me away from his sister. But I have to remember the mercy of Allah. I have to remember. With each step I take, I have to remember.

I knock lightly on the door. Maybe he's not home. I'm relieved. And I'm terrified. I don't want to see him, but I have to see him. I don't know where else to go. Except back to the hangout, and my mother's garage.

He answers after a couple of minutes, when I'm just about ready to walk away.

"Isa? What are you doing here?"

"I don't know. Can I come in?"

He stands there for a long moment, glaring at me. He knows. I want to run away. But I know where I'd be running to. It's too hot. I stand instead in the heat of his glare.

Finally he nods. "Come in." That's all he says. Then he turns his back on me.

I sit on the couch. Home free. Umar won't hurt me because

he has faith. And as long as I stay here, I won't hurt myself.

He walks around the apartment, ignoring me. Finally he comes over and stands in front of the couch, looking down at me. "I'm too angry to talk. Go pray. I'll talk to you in the morning." He heads for his bedroom, then stops and looks at me. "You told me that was in the past." He goes into the room and slams the door.

I go to the bathroom to wash up. The cold water shocks me. I wash my face three times. What was I thinking? I wash my arms, up to the elbows, three times. Why did I drive over to the hangout? I wash my feet, up to the ankles, three times. How could I walk away from everything I've worked so hard for these last two years?

I say my prayers, and my mind becomes clearer. I'm beginning to understand the mercy of Allah. And my despair falls away.

I stay up all night, praying and reading the Qur'an. I keep going back to that verse in Surah Zumar, the one I found there in the car. I have messed up my life in so many ways. Do I still have the right to hope for mercy? I hope so. Otherwise, I should have just killed myself that night in the garage.

I thought I had left my demons behind me. But tonight they took control of me again. Tonight they almost won.

I try not to think too much about it, or about all the things I've done wrong. Thinking might open the door to despair. I don't think. I just read, and pray, and hope.

At dawn, I make the call to prayer. Umar comes out of his room and, without a word, steps to the side, silently inviting me to lead the morning prayer. I recite the Qur'an with my heart. I bow in submission. I touch my forehead to the carpet, concentrating on getting nearer to Allah. I end with greetings of peace. And I feel the peace.

When the prayer is over, Umar goes into the kitchen and sets up the coffee maker. As the coffee starts to brew, he sits down at the kitchen table. "Come sit here, Isa. Now we'll talk."

His voice is firm, but not angry. He looks down at the table while he talks. "My sister called me last night. She was crying.

You can imagine how I felt when she told me that the man I had given her to in marriage had betrayed her. If you had been with me in this room at that moment, I swear by Allah, you would have been a dead man." He gestures at the wall on the other side of the room. That hole didn't used to be there.

At the same time he wanted to kill me, death is what I craved. It's almost funny.

"It's by the mercy of Allah that you came here over an hour later. That gave me time to think, and pray. By the time you came, I was very angry, but not murderous.

By the time I came, I was desperate, but not suicidal.

"I am still angry. I'm sure you realize the extent to which you betrayed my trust in you. But you've suffered, too, I think, from your weakness. That's good. I pray that your suffering will purify your soul."

I pray that my weakness hasn't destroyed my soul

"It will take me a long time to forgive you for what you have done. I will never forget it. But I won't abandon you. For better or worse, you are my brother."

I have been waiting all my life to hear those words. And now I do, from one of the people I've hurt the most.

"My father told you we don't have divorces in our family. And I will not allow my sister to be the first. So we'll drink some coffee, because neither one of us slept last night. Then we'll go to my sister together. And you two will have to figure out how to stay married."

He strokes his beard, and frowns. "I remember now. You almost backed out of the wedding, there in the hotel room. Didn't you?"

I can't look at him. "Yes, I almost did."

"Because of what happened with your ex-wife?"

"Yes."

"And I was the one who stood up for you."

I just nod.

"I trusted you, Isa. You lied to me." He shakes his head. "Why didn't you say anything then?"

"Because I love her. I was too weak to walk away."

We drink our coffee in silence.

On the way to our cars, he turns to me, "You had better find out what her favorite flower is. It might come in handy. This time, I think roses will do."

As I get into my car, I notice the sun rising in the east. The darkness is gone. I've made it.

He waits in the parking lot while I run into a store for a dozen roses.

Umar knocks. "Assalaamu alaikum, Aisha."

She opens the door quickly. "Oh, Umar, I'm so glad you're here." Then she sees me. "Oh," is all she says.

I offer her the roses. "I got these for you."

She reluctantly accepts the peace offering, looking down at the floor. "Thanks, I guess."

"Can we come in?"

"Yes, Umar, please come in."

"And Isa, too."

"If you say so."

The apartment looks the same. I don't think she has broken anything of mine. There is a pile of tissues on the floor next to the couch.

Umar takes over. "I want you both to sit down. There, on the couch." We sit at opposite ends. "A little closer, please." I move. She stays where she is.

"On my way, I called in to the office and told them I had a family emergency. I'm going to sit here with the two of you for as long as it takes. Nobody leaves until you start to work this out."

"What about my classes? I've already missed two days this week."

"Your education is important, Aisha, but your marriage is more important. If you want to go to your student teaching assignment today, I suggest you try hard to resolve things with your husband."

"Some husband he turned out to be." She starts crying again.

161

"I don't want to do this, Umar. It's no use."

He ignores her. "I want each of you to tell the other how you feel right now. Isa, you go first."

"Aisha, I am so sorry for everything." I look at her, huddled at the end of the couch with her head down. I have to convince her that I'm sincere. "I hate to see you sad like this. I didn't want to hurt you. I messed up. I made a mistake. But I love you. I need you to forgive me." I try to look into her eyes, but she turns away. "Please."

"Your turn, Aisha."

She shakes her head.

"Go ahead, Aisha. Say what you feel."

"What I feel? You don't want to know what I feel. I feel like throwing you out that door and down the stairs. I feel like hitting you until I stop hurting. I feel used, betrayed, and disgusted. I feel like this marriage is based on a lie."

"Okay." I don't know how Umar stays so calm. I guess it's his job. "So, Isa, you want forgiveness, but Aisha is too hurt. She feels you've made a sham of your marriage. Now it's my turn, and I want you both to listen.

"Isa, you have made a real mess out of your life. When you became a Muslim, you had a second chance, but you haven't been able to escape from the echoes of your past. Until you can do that, your life will always be a mess." I put my head in my hands. Not even Umar knows how much of a mess I am. "But you can use the intelligence Allah gave you to get over your past. So far, you've sold yourself short. It's time for you to use your strengths rather than giving in to your weaknesses.

"What you did was reprehensible. If I had known, I never would have allowed this marriage to take place. I know you regret your actions, and I expect you to make sure you never come close to making that kind of mistake again.

"Aisha, you have every right to feel hurt, and angry. When Isa came to my apartment last night, I was so angry I couldn't bear to look at him. For a short moment, I was so angry I could have killed him. He betrayed you, and he betrayed the commitment he made to you. I can tell you, though, that he was up all night praying. I believe he sincerely regrets what he has done.

"I just said I would not have allowed you to marry him, if I had known, but the fact is that you are married. Now the two of you will have to find a way to get past this. You can begin by forgiving him."

"How can I forgive him? How can I ever trust him again?"

"Answer that, Isa."

"I don't know. Maybe if you just give me a chance to show you how much I love you."

"Don't do that to me. I thought I loved you, too. But now I feel like I don't even know you." She pauses. "Tell me, honestly, how many times did you go to see Heather?"

"I had been driving past the apartment off and on for months. Once, I saw her and the kids walking along the sidewalk. But I never talked to her, or touched her, except for that one time. That's the truth."

"But why did you go there at all?"

"I had to see my kids. I'm the one who walked out on them, and I'm the one who didn't want custody when we first got the divorce. The last time Michael saw me, I was cursing his mother. The same way Sam used to curse at my mother every time he bothered to come see me. And I don't want Michael to be as screwed up as I am. I have to see them again, and make things right."

"But what you did was wrong. When you didn't see the kids outside why didn't you just drive away? And why did you let yourself get close to her?"

"I don't know. I was married to her for five years. And when she was sitting there, close to me, in the car, and crying, some of the old feelings came back."

"Then why did you marry me?"

"My feelings for Heather were always just for the moment. When she was with me, I would lose myself in her. When she was gone, she was gone. But you, Aisha, you are in my heart. You've been in my heart ever since I met you that first time at the restaurant, and I saw you smile. For just one short moment, I lost myself again. It was four days before our wedding, and I was aching to be with you, not her. But she was sitting there, close to me, and it was just one stupid moment."

For a few minutes, we all just sit here. Aisha is still crying. I slouch over, my head down, waiting for it to get better. It has to get better.

Umar takes a deep breath. "When I was in high school, I had a bad temper. I wouldn't start a fight, but if somebody pushed me too far, I would make sure he didn't forget it. It was only after I became a Muslim that I learned how to keep myself under control. Now I'm almost never angry. Though I'm not kidding when I say I could have killed you last night because, for just a moment, my old habit overcame my faith. It's a good thing I took it out on the wall instead.

"Aisha, how would you feel if you saw Craig again?"

"Craig? How did you know about him? And what does that have to do with anything?"

"Never mind how I know. I know you were sneaking out of the house to see him during your senior year. You were pretty serious about him, weren't you?"

"Yes, but how did you know?"

"That's why I encouraged you to apply to Northeastern. I wanted you here with me in Chicago, where I could keep an eye on you. Mom and Dad didn't have a clue, did they?"

"No, I don't think so."

"And if Craig had come back one day and started coming on to you, would you have given in to him?"

"Of course not. I'm not weak." She looks at me. "And this isn't about me. It's about Isa."

"I know. Just think about it."

I never imagined Umar or Aisha could have a hidden past. I have been so wrapped up in myself.

I never thought about Aisha with another man. I feel a twinge of something. Jealousy, I guess. But she's right. This isn't about her.

"That was different, Umar. I wasn't married, or engaged to be married. I wasn't even a Muslim yet. Don't start putting anything on me."

"You're right, it is different. It's just something to think about. Because sooner or later, you're going to have to make up your mind to forgive Isa. And while you're sitting there, feeling hurt and angry, I want you to remember that no one is perfect."

"But what he did. You can't compare it."

"No. But you have to forgive it." He holds her hand. "You have to get past this and move on. For the sake of your marriage."

"This marriage was a mistake. It was based on a lie."

"Aisha, do you still love Isa?"

She looks down. "Yes, I do. That's what makes it so hard."

Umar looks at his watch. "You two still have time to get to your classes. I think we're finished, for now, but you must be very clear about one thing. You will both work very hard to make this marriage last."

"But how?"

"Give it time. Let your husband come back home, and give it time."

"I don't know, Umar. I don't think I can do it."

"Aisha. You will do what I say. And Isa, you will go straight to class, straight to work, and straight home. If you even come close to doing anything like this again, think about the wall. Only much, much worse.

"By the way, you both probably forgot that Mom and Dad are coming to visit this weekend. They don't know about Craig, and they're not going to know about this, either. If you are not ready to be happily married yet, then you will have to pretend." He picks up his coat and walks out.

I try to hold her hand but she pulls it away. I look at her. "What can I do to make it better?"

"Just leave me alone. I have to get to school. You can come home tonight, but don't ask for anything else."

She goes to change her clothes. I wait until she's finished before I go into the bedroom to change. We leave separately, in silence.

When I come home from the restaurant, she's working at the computer. She answers my salaam, but nothing more. On my way home, I bought a pint of mint chocolate chip ice cream. I put it next to her as she types. She keeps on typing. I heat my own dinner and go to sleep on the couch.

We keep this up for two days. On Friday evening, Sharon and The Doc come to town.

They're at the apartment when I get home from work. As soon as I walk in, Aisha comes over and kisses me on the cheek. Then she helps me with my coat. "I'll hang this up for you."

"Hi there, Joshua. How's the restaurant business, son?"

"It's okay." What's up with Aisha? "Friday nights are busy, of course."

"Oh yes. Joshua is so tired on Fridays. Come over here, Hon, and sit next to Daddy. I'll get you some tea." She pats my shoulder on her way to the kitchen.

"How are your classes this semester?"

"It's a little tougher, with four of them. But I'm hanging in there."

"I think that was so sweet, that you promised to get your degree as part of the dowry. I always thought a dowry was something the girl's parents paid to get rid of her. Angela explained it to me. That's a lovely custom."

"And he's working so hard, Mom," Aisha calls from the kitchen. "I'm really proud of him."

"You should be. You have such a nice little apartment, too. It reminds me of when Jim and I first got married."

Aisha brings me the tea. "Here, just the way you like it." She sits next to me, on the arm of the couch, and rubs my back.

Later, when we sit down for dinner, she brings out spaghetti. She knows that's my favorite.

We talk a little after dinner, but it's getting late, so her family heads back to the hotel.

"You don't have to stay in a hotel, Mom. You could stay here with us."

"That's okay. Your father has a bad back. He looks forward to sleeping in that nice hotel bed. But thanks for the offer."

"Okay, Mom. I guess we'll see you in the morning, then. Goodnight, Daddy."

Umar walks out behind them. On his way out, he looks at me and nods.

As soon as the door is closed, I get the spare blanket from the closet and spread it out on the couch. It's been a long day and a tough week. I'm exhausted.

"You don't have to do that, Isa."

"That's okay. They're gone now. I appreciate the tea and the spaghetti and everything, but you can stop pretending."

"I'm not pretending. I forgive you."

I put the blanket back in the closet.

~

I wake up in the middle of the night, feeling uneasy. Everything is so much better now. I beat the demons, and I think they are gone for good. Aisha has forgiven me, and she's sleeping peacefully beside me in the bed. But something is wrong.

I sit in the dark for a long time before I realize what it is. It's the lies. Not Heather's lies about me. My lies to Aisha. Our relationship is built on honesty, and she trusts me again. I can't lose that. I can't lose her.

I won't wake her now. I'll wait until morning. But I can't sleep.

I'm restless. There's a hunger inside of me. And I know what it is. I remember what Ismail said, after I told him I had betrayed Aisha four days before our wedding, and after I told him I couldn't pray. He told me that Allah already knows. That's what I keep forgetting.

I have to remember that I'm not alone.

I wash up, and go to the living room to pray and read Qur'an. At dawn, I wake Aisha, and we make the morning prayer together. After the prayer I hold her hand.

"I love you, Aisha. I love you so much. I want to thank you for forgiving me, and for loving me. But there's something I have to tell you."

"No, Isa, not again." She tries to pull away from me but I pull her closer.

"Just listen. I lied to you. Twice. Because I didn't want you to know what happened with Heather. My mother didn't come to the wedding because she believes I attacked Heather. It had nothing to do with my being a Muslim. And that mark on my cheek came from Heather. She scratched me after I told her that I love you and planned to marry you. I'm sorry I lied. I won't lie to you again."

She looks down and doesn't say anything for a long time. Finally she reaches up and touches my cheek, the one Heather scratched.

"Thank you for telling me. And thank you for loving me." She leans against me and I put my arms around her. I hold her for a long time.

❧

The Doc, Sharon, Umar, and Marcus come over a couple of hours later, bringing doughnuts for breakfast. After eating, we head out on the town. It's a family day. First we take Marcus to the top of the Sears Tower and impress him with a view of the city. The day is windy, as usual, but a little warm for this time of year, so after the Sears Tower, we take a walk along the North Avenue Beach. Then we stop in at Giordano's for some authentic stuffed crust pizza. I've lived in Chicago all of my life but I have never had a day like this with my family.

During lunch, Sharon asks about my mother. "Why don't we all go over there later for a visit? Here you've been married for two months now and I haven't even met her."

That's not possible. My mother still believes Heather.

I look down. I am so tired of lying.

Aisha squeezes my hand. "I'd rather just concentrate on being with you and Daddy today, Mom."

"Is everything okay? You're not having trouble getting along with her, are you, Angela?"

"No, Mom, that's not it. It's just that, well . . ."

"Sharon, my mother has never really met Angela yet. She saw her at the custody hearing, but she walked right past us."

Sharon shakes her head. She can't comprehend the mess that is my family.

Sitting in the restaurant with them, listening to their friendly, lively conversation, it occurs to me that if I had lost Aisha, I would have lost them, too. That would have made it all the more painful.

They come over for breakfast the next morning before heading back to Moline. I make the eggs and pancakes while Aisha handles the coffee and serving. She hasn't said anything more about my betrayal. While I cook, she bustles around the kitchen, often touching me when she passes. I say a prayer of thanks for the mercy of Allah, and inwardly shudder at how close I came to throwing it all away.

Before they leave, The Doc takes me aside while the rest of the family chats. "You know I had my doubts about this marriage, Joshua. I was very worried that my daughter would show up one day, crying on my doorstep. But I can see how happy she is. And I like the way you treat her. I'm glad you're a part of our family, son." He pats me on the back.

I came so close.

Part Two

Aisha and I settle back into a pattern of school and work. We're more comfortable now than we were before the fight. I think we both take our marriage more seriously.

We've been talking more about the things that are important to us. I'm starting to realize how important it is to talk in a marriage. Heather and I never did very much talking. Yelling, but not talking.

Sometimes we talk about the house we want to live in someday. She wants to plant a garden. I want a garage where I can go to fix things. I've never been very good at fixing things, but now that I'm settled down maybe it's time for me to learn.

Sometimes we talk about having kids. We both want them, of course. The only question is when, and how many. She's looking forward to being a teacher, but last week when she visited a friend from college who has just had a baby she told me, "I can't wait to be a mother." I want to have kids with her. Someday. But first I want to have some time for just the two of us. I'm not ready to share her yet. She says she won't take any pills that could mess up her hormones, so I guess we'll just leave it all in the hands of Allah.

We never talk about Heather. We don't even talk about my kids. But I'm silently counting the days, waiting for the judge's decision. Maybe Zakariya was right. Maybe I do have a chance of seeing them again.

On a Sunday evening, almost two months after the fight, we decide to go visit Umar for a while. We go over there sometimes, just to talk. I know he misses Aisha, and I think he still feels a little awkward at our place. I want them to always be close. Especially now, after he saved me and saved our marriage.

It's raining. We dash from the car into the apartment building. At the same time, a woman holding an umbrella is hurrying from her car. We almost run into her at the door.

When we get inside she lowers her umbrella. It's Heather.

"Hello, Joshua. Oh, and this is Aisha, isn't it?"

"What are you doing here?"

"It's none of your business, but I came to see a friend."

"Where are the kids?"

"They're at home. Michael is seven. He can take care of things for a while."

"You left them at home alone?"

"Like you care. You left them long ago."

"Don't start with me."

"Excuse me, Heather. I'd like to talk with you, woman to woman."

"What's your problem? Don't blame me for how he treats you."

"No. I blame you for how you treat him. I know all about the lie you told his mother."

"Do you? And you stayed with him?"

Aisha squeezes my hand. "I want you to tell everyone you've been lying. His mother and Chris have pretty much disowned him over your lie. You're breaking up a family. How do you sleep at night?"

"He's the one who broke up our family. Don't put anything on me. I'm just trying to survive."

"Don't give me that. I know you've had some difficulties, but Joshua wants to see his children, and you're keeping them from him. You're getting child support now. He wants to be a father to them."

"He should have thought about that before he walked out on us."

"It's always the same old song, isn't it? 'Joshua left me, and I have to raise my children all on my own.' You'd better try a different tune with me."

"If you don't want to hear it, you shouldn't have married the bum."

Aisha's voice gets louder. "If he was a bum when you were married to him, it's because you didn't know how to take care of your man."

"Oh, I took care of him all right. He was plenty happy with

me when the lights were out."

"You slut! Is that what everything is to you?"

"That's all he ever gave me. That, and three kids. I had to take what I could get."

"You are so shallow. No wonder he left you."

"You don't even know him, do you? Talk to me again in a couple of years, when he walks out on you and your kids."

"Don't worry about me. I know my man loves me."

"Yeah, he really loved you when he was making out with me in his car."

"If that's all love is to you, it's no wonder you can't keep a man."

"That's the only love he wants, and I know how to give it to him."

"You are so desperate, it's pathetic. Give it up, Heather. He married me, remember? You're history."

"You are so blind. Did you ever ask yourself why his own mother believes he attacked me? She wants him in jail."

"I'm warning you, Heather. The lies have to stop."

"And what are you going to do? You have my man. What else do you want?"

"I want you to stop the lies. And I want you to let him see his kids."

"Then you want too much." She shakes her wet umbrella at me. "Next time, Joshua, don't make your woman do your talking for you. You're still a bum." She flashes me a finger and walks quickly up the steps.

Aisha is shaking. "She makes me so angry. How can she be so cold? And those kids are at home all alone. What if there's a fire? Let's go get them now, while she's here."

"We can't. She has a restraining order against me, remember? I have a test tomorrow. I can't afford to spend the night in jail."

Aisha is still breathing deeply, and her hands are clenched. "Someone is going to have to teach that woman a lesson."

I squeeze her waist. "You're woman enough to do it, honey, but it's not worth the trouble. I don't think anybody's going to make her change." I kiss her cheek, and whisper, "Thanks for taking care of your man."

We stop at the first floor landing for a long kiss, and I hold her tight. I don't deserve Aisha. Sometimes I have to pinch myself, because I'm still amazed that she loves me.

As we walk up the stairs to Umar's apartment, she keeps saying, "Something has to be done to help those kids." I went to court. I don't know what else I can do.

❧

When I get home from school the next day, Aisha's not there. She almost always comes home before I do. And Mondays are special because I don't have to work. We can spend the entire evening together, going out or just being together. Maybe she had to do some work at the library.

She's still not home by six, and I'm starting to worry. I've made chicken and rice, Pakistani style, her favorite Monday night dinner. I wait a few minutes longer and call Umar.

"Assalaamu alaikum, Umar. Is Aisha over there?"

"No. She's not home?"

"No, and she's never this late. Especially not on Mondays."

"Call me if she hasn't come by six-thirty."

Could she have had an accident? Maybe she's lying somewhere, calling for me. There has been a string of assaults against women in the city in the last few months. I hope she's not hurt. Or worse. I pace the floor, trying to come up with a rational explanation.

I wish I could call the police, but they wouldn't take it seriously. Unless they're trying to notify me. No, not that. I make sure the phone is firmly on the hook, just in case. There's nothing I can do, except pray.

She's still not home at six-thirty. Umar is coming over. I try to think of places we can look. All I can think of is the library. And if she were in the library she would have called me by now. To make sure I didn't worry.

When Umar comes, we pace the room together. After a few minutes he decides to go look for her on campus. I'll stay home and wait for her here. I keep on pacing.

It's almost seven-thirty when I hear her key in the door. I rush to open it and hug her tightly in the doorway.

"I was so worried about you. I didn't know what had happened. Thank God you're safe." All I want to do is hold her.

"I'm fine, Isa. Nothing happened."

I take her things and we walk into the apartment. "We were so worried."

"We?"

"When you weren't home by six, I called Umar. He's over at the campus looking for you."

"Go ahead and call him first. Then I'll tell you why I'm late."

She gets settled in, I call Umar, and we sit down to dinner. "So what happened? Where were you?"

"I went to see Heather."

I almost choke. "You went where? To the apartment? Why?" I pause. "Did you see the kids?"

She smiles. "Yes, I did. Oh, they're adorable. Michael looks just like you, but Jeremy reminds me more of you. He's so quiet and hesitant, but you can see how smart he is. And Jennifer is a little princess. She was dressed all in pink, from her headband to her sneakers. She was the talkative one."

My kids. I can barely picture them anymore. And I've never heard Jennifer talk.

"Why did you go there? You were bored, and felt like getting into a fight?"

"No. I wanted to see if Heather and I could work things out, woman to woman. You said yesterday that I was woman enough to do it."

"Sure, but I didn't mean it like that. I didn't want you to take her on."

"No, but I'm glad I did."

"Wasn't she angry when you showed up?"

"To put it mildly. For the first ten minutes or so, all she did was scream at me. She thought you were with me, and she was ready to call the police. Then she thought maybe you had sent me to take the kids away from her. We almost took up from where we left off yesterday, astagfirullah, but I held my tongue this time. I stood there in the hall for at least twenty minutes, listening to her rant, before I could convince her to calm down and let me in. I told her I just wanted to talk."

"And she bought that?"

"Finally, yes. It was the truth."

"So then what?"

"After she let me in, I continued to let her do most of the talking. She went through her whole laundry list of complaints against you, starting with things that happened before you two got married."

"Way back then? She sure didn't act unhappy. She's the one who called me all the time."

"You don't understand. Maybe it's a woman thing. I'll let her tell you herself."

"Sure. That's going to happen."

"She's coming here this Saturday."

Now I do choke. Aisha has to pat me on the back a few times.

"Here? To our apartment? I don't want her here."

"But she has to come and see where we live. Otherwise, she won't feel comfortable letting the kids come over."

"The kids? She's going to let me see the kids?"

"We worked out a deal."

"You did? What kind of deal?"

"You'll have to wait until Saturday, when she comes. She'll tell you then."

"You're not going to be friends with her now, are you?"

"No, I don't think so. We're very different. But I do understand her now."

"Then you're ahead of me."

There's a knock at the door. It's Umar. He hugs Aisha, and then scolds her for making us worry. When we tell him where she was, he just looks at her and shakes his head. "That sounds like my sister."

While he eats, Aisha tells him a little about her conversation with Heather and their agreement to meet again on Saturday.

"You told her to come here? I don't think that was a good idea."

"But she insisted on seeing the apartment before she'd agree to let us bring the kids here."

"I don't like it, Aisha. There's already been trouble between her and Isa. What if she comes over someday when you're not home?"

"I hadn't thought of that."

"You'd better think things through, little sister. Isa, don't you ever let Heather in here if Aisha's not home."

"No. I think I've learned my lesson."

"And in case you're tempted again, think about the wall."

"I will."

"And, I am going to be here on Saturday. Just in case."

I'm restless all week. This time I don't need beer or hot curry, and I sure don't need Heather. I'm just waiting to see what will happen on Saturday. Will she really agree to let me see the kids? That's what Aisha thinks. We'll see.

On Saturday morning, Aisha makes sure everything in the apartment looks just right. She even bakes brownies to go with the tea she'll be serving.

"This isn't a tea party, Aisha. We're going to meet with my ex-wife. After what happened, I thought you hated her as much as I do."

"I did, until I actually sat down and talked with her." I ask her what she means by that, but she won't say anything more.

By the time we hear the knock at the door, the apartment is perfect, and the brownies and tea are ready. Aisha is wearing her favorite blue dress. She's told me to go change into one of my newer Pakistani suits, out of the old brown one I usually wear on Saturday mornings.

Aisha opens the door. "Hello, Heather. Welcome to our home."

Heather looks around. Aisha has done a lot of decorating these last few months. "Thank you. It's nice."

"Come in and sit down. I'll bring the tea."

Heather walks over to the couch. I'm coming out of the bedroom, buttoning my shirt. She scowls. "Hello, Joshua."

"Hello, Heather." Before I can say anything more, there's another knock at the door, and I rush to get it. I'm glad Umar is here.

As soon as he walks in, he glances at Heather, and frowns. She didn't bother to wear that modest blue dress she had on in court. Even though it's early May, and still cool, she's wearing a sleeveless top with tight-fitting slacks. In court, she put her hair up in a bun. Now it's full and wild. At least she didn't wear shorts. If I tried, I could still remember those legs. But I won't.

That time in the car, even the sight of Heather was enough to tempt me. Not now. I'm uncomfortable. But now I have Aisha, and I don't want to even come close to losing her again.

I introduce Heather and Umar, and they both nod. We're quiet, and uneasy, until Aisha walks in with the tea.

"Good, we're all here. Here's your tea, Heather. How do you like it?"

"A little sugar would be nice."

While Aisha fixes the tea, Umar and I look at each other. They're acting like it's perfectly normal for the current wife and the ex-wife to get together for tea. I don't understand.

"Okay," says Aisha as she sits on the couch next to Heather, "let's get started. Before we talk about the kids, I think Heather needs to tell Joshua some things he doesn't know about her. Things she told me the other day. Go ahead, Heather."

"Okay." I can tell she's nervous. She bites her lip. "I can't believe I'm doing this, but maybe it will help." She looks at Aisha, not me. "The thing is, you never really knew me, Joshua. I didn't plan on getting pregnant and dropping out of school. I wanted to be an art therapist."

"You don't know how to draw."

"How do you know? You were too busy looking at my, um," she stops, and glances at Umar. "Anyway, you never bothered to find out what I could do."

"Okay, I wasn't perfect. But this isn't supposed to be about me. I know Aisha didn't bring you here just so you could rag on me."

"No, she didn't. But you didn't know that I wanted to be an art therapist, and that's important. When I was a freshman, I knew exactly what I was going to do with my life. I'd get good grades and try to get a scholarship to a good college, or maybe an art institute. Either way, I wanted to be like my older sister and go away to study.

"I was a sophomore when I met you. I thought you were cute, and I was excited when you asked me out. But you started coming on to me right away. And I didn't want you to lose interest, because you were my first serious boyfriend."

"Oh, come on. What about Dylan and Jeff and those guys? They were always talking about how hot you were. Dylan told me all about how you came on to him, out on the football field. Jeff, too."

"It was all talk. Dylan tried to put the move on me and I brushed him off. That's why they said those things about me. I know how it is to have people believe lies about you."

What do I say? When I was sixteen all I wanted in life was a good-looking girl with a bad reputation. That's why I asked her out. "I'm sorry, Heather. I didn't know. I really was a jerk, wasn't I?"

"It was my fault, too. I wanted you to like me. And then, when I was a junior, I decided to get pregnant. My parents were driving me crazy and I would have done anything to get out of that house. We were fighting almost all the time. A lot of our fights, though, were about you."

"Wait a minute. You meant to get pregnant?"

"By then, I had forgotten about my dreams of college. I just wanted you to love me. I thought if we had a baby together, maybe you would."

I didn't know. I thought it was just another accident in my screwed-up life.

"I love Michael, and in the beginning I tried to love you. But it wouldn't work. I don't know what to say."

"I know. I guess I was expecting too much."

My life isn't the only one I screwed up. I look at Aisha. I hope she's not angry. She smiles at me.

"I already knew, Isa. Heather told me the other day. And I knew you were wild when you were young. That's all in the past, as far as I'm concerned, but I thought you needed to hear Heather's side."

Until now, I never thought about what I had done to Heather. It was always about me. "I was a real jerk."

"And what are you now?"

"I don't know, Heather. I'm trying to be better. I've been trying hard for the last two years. That's a lot of why I had to leave. I hated myself, the way I was then. I wasn't any good for you and the kids, anyway."

"No, you weren't. In some ways, things were easier after you left. But I still felt abandoned."

I feel trapped. I look at Umar, hoping he'll rescue me. He comes through.

"I believe everything you're saying about the old Joshua, but in Islam, we believe in second chances. In these last few months alone, I've seen him become more responsible, and more caring. If you're not letting him see the children because of whom he used to be, I think you need to reconsider."

"It's not just that. The main reason I'm bringing up all this ancient history is because, in many ways, I blame Joshua for how my life is now. I should have my degree by now, and be working to help people through art. I should have had the time to choose when and whom to marry, and when to have children. I know I had a part in it, but I blame him for believing bad things about me and taking away my self-worth. The way he degraded me, it was like he abused me."

"I never hit you."

"No, but you never loved me, either. I know that now, especially after talking with Aisha and seeing how you are with her. You used me."

I hang my head and take a deep breath. "You're right, I did. I'm sorry."

"I need something more than an apology. If you want to see

the kids, I need you to help me get my life back on track. I think you owe me that much."

"What do you want me to do?"

"First of all, I need to work on my education. Remember, I quit school at the end of my junior year. I can take G.E.D. classes for free at Daley College, but then I need to work on my degree. Daley has a program in art I could sign up for. The problem is, they want over a hundred dollars for registration and other fees. I can probably get financial aid to help with the tuition, but I need the money for the fees to get me started. Can you cover that?"

"Sure. Let me know when it's due and I'll send in a check for you. Is that all?"

"I need a good job. You know I work at the Lion's Den, and I hate it. But it's all I can get that pays fairly well, at least with my education. And by the time I finish flipping burgers at the other place, I'm too tired to enjoy the kids. I want you and Aisha to help me get a job that pays well so I can quit the two I have now. You know, look around for openings and provide references for me, that kind of thing."

"We can do that. Anything else?"

"That will be enough. Just help me get my life, and my dreams, back on track. If you do that, I'll let you have the kids two weekends a month. Aisha can pick them up on Friday afternoons and bring them back on Sunday evenings."

"What about the lies?"

"I'll ask them to lift the restraining order, and I'll tell your mother what really happened. But I need some kind of insurance, something to make sure you're going to follow through on your end of the deal."

"In Islam," says Umar, "we often write contracts. These are usually related to borrowing money, but I'm sure this situation would fit. Heather, if you dictate the terms, I'll type everything up. Then we'll print it off, and each of you will sign it. Aisha and I will be witnesses."

"But a contract is just a piece of paper. How do I know Joshua will follow through? You all keep saying he's changed, but all I can think of is how good he was at breaking his promises."

"That's why you need witnesses. Between Aisha and I, we'll make sure he keeps his promises this time. Besides, as a Muslim, Joshua knows the importance of keeping his word."

"I don't know much about Islam. I just want to make sure he does what he says he'll do."

"Don't worry. I'll make sure of that. There is one more thing you need to consider, Heather. As a Muslim, Joshua must teach his children about Islam. How do you feel about that?"

"I don't know. I'm not very religious, but Islam is so strange to me. Besides, there aren't many Muslims in this country. I don't want my kids to feel left out. They're fine the way they are now."

"Heather, I need to teach them about Islam. That's my duty as a father. And no more wisecracks. I am trying."

"I know. I'll have to think about it. I sure wouldn't let you force anything on them. If they were to come back from your place and tell me that you made them pray or something, I'd think hard before I let them come back. But maybe if you just tell them about it, now and then, it would be okay. I guess it would, anyway."

"That will be good enough, for now. When they get to be teenagers, I'll probably have to be stricter. I don't want Michael or Jeremy to be like I was growing up."

"If Islam could keep them from being wild like you were, I think I might support it. We'll see."

"There is one more thing. I don't want you bringing any strange men around my kids. And I don't want you leaving the kids alone again while you go to see your boyfriend."

"Wait a minute. I didn't come here for this. You can't tell me how to live my life. You left, remember?"

Heather picks up her purse and heads for the door. Aisha stops her.

"Heather. Wait. He's not telling you how to run your life. We're just concerned about the kids, that's all. I'm studying to be a teacher, and I know all about the potential for child endangerment and abuse. When we have the kids, you can do what you want. But bringing a strange man into the house, or leaving them alone, just isn't safe. How would you feel if your friend molested Jennifer?"

"He would never do that!"

"It happens. It happens way too often. Please, for the sake of the kids."

"But I deserve to have a life, too."

"Yes, you do. Just not around the kids."

She puts her purse down. "All right. I'll figure out a way to see him when the kids aren't around. I promise." She pauses. "But I need something else from you, too, then, Joshua. When you left us, you also left a ton of debt. Your mom has helped some, but I'm still struggling to pay it all off. I want you to pay at least half of whatever we still owe to the credit card companies. I think that's only right."

I had forgotten about that. I ran up most of those charges supporting my old habits. The beer, and the women. Heather shouldn't have to pay for that. She already paid enough just by putting up with me. "Okay, send me the statements, and I'll get to work on it." I don't know how long I'll be paying for my mistakes.

Umar types up the contract, listing what each of us is promising. Then he prints two copies, which we all sign.

Heather studies her copy for a moment, then folds it and puts it in her purse. "I'm glad I came. I almost didn't, but I decided to give it a try. The kids need to see you too, Joshua. Especially the boys. Michael is getting so big. And Jeremy is so quiet. He just withdraws into himself sometimes. Yeah, I guess this is good."

"I think so. On Monday I'll call my lawyer and tell him we reached an agreement. I hope you'll call your lawyer, too."

"I will. Well, thank you, Aisha. When you came to my door, I was ready to run you off. But I'm glad you came, and I'm glad you made me come today."

"I am too. Oh, do you want to see the room we have for the children? It isn't furnished or anything yet. We've been waiting. I guess we'll have to start, won't we?"

Heather looks inside the empty bedroom. "This is a good size. Yes, that'll be okay for them. I want to talk to them first and get them used to the idea. How about if we start in two weeks?"

"I've waited this long. Two weeks will be just fine. And, for what it's worth, I'm sorry about the way I was, before."

"You know what? I'm glad I finally got that off my chest. I feel better now. Well, I have to go get the kids from your mom's house. I didn't tell her where I was going."

"Could you hug them for me?"

"You can do that. In two weeks."

Aisha walks Heather to the door. I collapse onto the couch. It's been a long morning. But I'm finally going to see my kids.

I turn to Umar. "I was pretty bad, wasn't I? Are you going to let me keep your sister?"

"I'm not kidding when I tell you I did a background check. I talked to all the people I needed to talk to and I knew everything I needed to know. Almost everything. I didn't know about that time in the car. Heather has already told me quite a bit about you, by the way."

"But she didn't recognize you."

"No, I wouldn't expect her to." He smiles. "I have my ways."

"I wonder if I will ever be able to get away from my past."

"When you became a Muslim, all your past sins were wiped out. Now they're just echoes, real but distant."

When Umar leaves, I hug Aisha. "If not for you, I wouldn't be able to be with my kids."

"I'm looking forward to it. They are such sweet kids. I can't wait to spend more time with them. Besides, it can help us get ready for our own."

"Are you ready?"

"Not yet. Soon, maybe."

"Really? What about your teaching?"

"My mother managed to build her nursing career around us three. I think I could do it, too. What about you? Are you ready?"

"My life has had so many surprises that I've learned to leave everything up to Allah. But," I say, holding her close, "I'm really enjoying my time alone with you."

We're running around all the next week. I call Zakariya and fax a copy of the contract to his office. And we have to get ready for the kids.

We find bunk beds at a garage sale, and a pretty little pink bed at a thrift store. I don't know what kids play with, but Aisha goes shopping one day while I'm at work and comes home with bags full of books and toys. Next week, we'll paint the walls and put up new curtains.

And Aisha is graduating on Sunday. Her family, her whole family, will be coming. I don't know if I'm ready for that.

When I come home on Saturday night, I hear the noise as soon as I get out of the car. Are they all there in our little apartment? I can barely squeeze through the door. They're all here. And, just like on Thanksgiving, Aisha is talking and laughing her way through the crowd. It takes us five minutes to reach one another.

"I thought you were going to wait until we had a house."

"What am I supposed to do, tell them to go back home? Besides, it's only for a few more hours. They'll go back to their hotel, and it'll be quiet again. Okay?"

"It's your weekend, Hon. Whatever makes you happy."

We have to get to the campus early on Sunday. Her relatives will be coming straight from the hotel. Then we'll go to Karachi Kitchen to celebrate. Fawad and I already have it planned.

I feel so proud as I watch her walk across campus in her cap and gown. She made it. This semester was tough, for both of us, but she hung in there. Of course, I always knew she could do it.

She's been applying for teaching jobs in the Chicago area. She's sent her resume to a few different school districts. We'll find out in the next couple of weeks, I think.

She has to go join the other graduates. I wait for the relatives. They arrive in a convoy, all together, about forty minutes before the commencement. She must have one of the biggest families here.

"I am so proud of our little Angela," says Aunt Arlene. "And when will it be your turn, Joshua?"

"I still have a few years to go. I started late. But Angela is the one who helped me get started."

"That's my Angela," says The Doc.

The ceremony itself isn't very interesting. There are speeches, and some music. The best moment is when they read Aisha's name. "Angela Evans, Bachelor of Science in Education, Elementary Education." The whole family cheers for her.

Seeing her there, getting her diploma, I start to get chills. I can do that. If I work hard for the next three years, then one day they'll be calling my name. For the first time, I really want it. And if my family doesn't come to cheer for me, I know Aisha's family will be there.

She finds us after the ceremony. There is a round of hugs, and then it's time to take pictures. Sharon's youngest brother, Uncle Paul, is the designated photographer again.

He takes pictures of Aisha with me, with her parents, with her grandparents, with Umar and Marcus, and with various assortments of aunts, uncles, and cousins. Then, of course, he has to get one big group picture. It takes a few minutes for everyone to get into position. Uncle Paul finds a willing bystander to help out so he can be in that picture, too.

As soon as we get into the car, she rips off her cap, which was bobby-pinned to her scarf, and gown. "I'm glad that's over. It was getting hot in there."

I lean over to kiss her. "Congratulations. I am so proud of you." I hold her for a minute, until we hear a knock at the window. It's Marcus.

"Mom and Dad said I could ride with you guys." He climbs into the back seat.

I don't know if we're ready to have children of our own yet.

On the way to the restaurant, we talk with Marcus about his life and plans. "I want to be a biologist. Mom and Dad said if I get good grades I can come to Chicago for college, and live with you guys."

At least when we do have children we'll have Uncle Marcus around to help change diapers.

Fawad has prepared a banquet of curries, samosas, and baked chicken, served with rice and salad. He's ready for us, in a room set aside for private parties. All of the relatives file in, remarking on the wonderful aroma.

The dinner reminds me of Thanksgiving, and our wedding. Everyone is talking, with Aisha's laughter floating above the crowd. They ask us about our future plans – where Aisha is going to teach, how my education is going, how my job is going, and if we're excited about my kids coming.

The Doc is the one who asks the question everyone really wants to ask. "So, when am I going to be a granddad?"

"Oh, Jim, that's kind of personal. They haven't been married that long yet, and Angela is looking forward to being a teacher first."

"That's all right, Sharon. I just want to know."

"You'll be the first to know, Daddy. After Joshua, that is."

I pick a time when everyone is busy talking to see Fawad about the bill. I'm opening my checkbook when he stops me. "No, I'll take care of it."

"But this is a lot of food for a lot of people. It's going to hurt your business."

"Isa, Muslims know that when we give more, we receive more. And you're my brother. I want to do this for Aisha and you."

I hug him. "Thank you, brother."

"And don't worry. The business is doing fine. You're doing a great job, and I have been looking for some way to thank you for giving me more time with my family. So, thank you too."

Before everyone leaves, they compliment Fawad on the food. Aisha's father and uncles get together and leave Fawad a large tip.

"Thanks for bringing us here, son. That was some of the best food I've ever tasted."

"And he knows about food." Sharon pats The Doc's stomach. "So, Jim, when is your baby due again?"

He laughs and grabs her in a bear hug.

After more hugs, the aunts, uncles, and cousins get in their cars and head back to Moline. The Doc, Sharon, Umar, and Marcus are coming back with us to the apartment.

Marcus climbs into our back seat and whistles. "Wow, look at this."

There is a mound of presents back there, left by some of the aunts, uncles, and cousins.

"And look at this." Aisha shows me a small stack of envelopes. "Uncle Paul and Aunt Helen and everybody gave me these on their way out."

At the apartment, Aisha opens her presents and cards.

"Why don't you use the money to buy some new clothes? New clothes for a new teacher."

"That's a good idea, Mom."

"I'll come back to Chicago sometime this summer and we can go shopping together."

We show Sharon and The Doc the kids' room. "What do you think?"

"It's looking nice, Joshua. I'm sure they'll like it."

"Remember, son, they haven't seen you for a long time. Give them some time to get to know you."

"I know, Doc. I've been thinking about that. I just hope that they, well, that they like me. I haven't been a very good father so far."

"But you are their father. And they're still young enough to be able to forgive you. I'm sure they still love you. Just give them time."

They head back to Moline in the late afternoon. Fawad has given me the day off, and Aisha and I spend a quiet evening together.

Late at night, while Aisha is sleeping, I try to remember when I got to be too old to forgive Sam. I think it was when I was ten. He wrote me a letter and promised to visit soon. Of course, he never came.

The next week passes quickly. School is out for both of us.

I've decided not to take summer classes. We want to spend more time together.

We paint the kids' room a nice shade of blue, and Aisha finds some curtains full of balloons.

On Wednesday while I'm at work, she paints white clouds on the walls. She gives them one of her bookcases and fills it with books and toys. I think we're ready.

On Thursday while I'm at work, two different school districts call and schedule her for interviews. She hugs me as soon as I walk in the door. "Oh, Isa, I can't wait to be a teacher. It's what I've wanted ever since I was a little girl."

Everything is coming together. For the first time in my life. I close my eyes and remember the mercy of Allah.

❧

I've been working extra hours this week, and will work more next week, so I can have the weekend off. I want to spend every minute with my kids.

Aisha goes to get them at around four. I start to get nervous when an hour has passed and she still isn't back. I hope nothing happened. Maybe Heather changed her mind. I have the contract, but I don't want to have to go back to court to enforce it.

It's about five-thirty when I hear some noises in the hallway outside. They sound like women's voices, not children's. I open the door to find Aisha and Heather coming up the stairs. Heather is holding Michael and Jeremy's hands. Aisha is carrying Jennifer.

I am so happy to see them, but I have to stay calm. I don't want to scare them away.

"You're here. I'm so glad you made it."

"Heather had to come, Isa. The kids were too scared to come on their own. I am still a stranger, after all."

And so am I. "That's fine. Come on in. I'm so happy that you're here."

Heather tows the boys into the apartment. They follow reluctantly. Jennifer is talking to Aisha about her favorite cartoon or something like that.

I crouch down and look at my boys. "Hi, Michael. Hi, Jeremy. How are you guys doing?" I reach out with both hands to tousle their hair, but Michael pulls away from me and Jeremy buries his head in Heather's side.

"That's okay. We haven't seen each other in a long time. Why don't you guys take Mom over to the couch and have a seat. I think I have some chocolate chip cookies for you in the kitchen."

Heather drags them over to the couch. They stay close to her and practically sit on her lap.

I turn to Jennifer. "Hi there, Princess. Do you want to come to Daddy?" I reach for her, but she clings to Aisha.

"Okay, that's fine. I'm going to get the cookies now. We'll sit down and have a snack first. And while we eat, we can get to know each other all over again."

While I'm in the kitchen, getting the milk and cookies, I hear them whispering.

"Maybe this wasn't such a good idea. They're not ready yet."

"Give it some time, Heather. It will be okay."

"Mom," says Michael, "I want to go home."

This is what I deserve. I'm the one who left. It's those echoes again. No matter how hard I try to change, they keep coming back at me from the canyons of my past.

"Here we go, guys. Milk and cookies."

"I'm not hungry," says Michael.

"Me either," says Jeremy.

Jennifer was starting to reach for a cookie, but pulled back when she heard her brothers. "No milk or cookie."

I try to keep it up. I take a cookie and bite into it. "Oh, this is good. You guys don't know what you're missing." They just look at me.

"Isa, can I talk to you in the kitchen?" We take a timeout, leaving Heather with the kids.

"I don't think it's going to work. Not today, I mean. Can't you see they're scared? Heather is all they've had. They're not ready to leave her, not yet."

"They're not ready to come to me, that's what you mean. I don't understand it. I would have loved it if my father had wanted me in his life."

"Would you? Or would you have taken some time to size up the situation first and try to figure out his angle?"

She's right, but it hurts. I had pictured a full weekend of getting to know my kids. Not yet, I guess. We go back into the living room.

I sit down and look at my kids. "You know, guys, Daddy really wants you to stay here with me. But it looks like you might not be ready just yet. So I'll give you a choice. Do you want to stay here with Aisha and me or go back home with Mom?"

"I want Mom," Michael says quickly.

"Me too," says Jeremy.

"Mommy," says Jennifer.

I turn to Heather. "I guess you can take them back if you want. But can we try again, next week?"

"Okay. Next week."

Aisha picks Jennifer up. The two boys stay close to Heather. I stand in the doorway and watch them walk away. "Bye, kids. See you next week." They don't look back.

I punch the couch cushions. I should have known better. It was stupid to get my hopes up. I know how it feels to get left by your father. I should have remembered.

When Aisha comes back in, I meet her at the door, car keys in hand. "I'm going to work. No use staying here."

"But Isa, you don't have to leave."

"No, I do have to leave. I'll see you tonight." I close the door a little harder than necessary.

At work, I throw myself into greeting customers and supervising operations in the kitchen. I've been here for two hours before I realize how I treated Aisha. She didn't deserve that.

On my way home, I buy a dozen roses. It turns out they are her favorite.

Part Three

Aisha has the first of her two interviews on Monday afternoon. "I think they're going to offer me a job," she says when she gets home. "I can't wait to have my own classroom."

"What about the other school district?"

"I'm meeting with them tomorrow, insha Allah. We'll see how that goes."

I'm excited about her successes, but I can't help brooding over my failure as a father. I keep trying to think of what I can do, what I can say to make things better with my kids.

While they were here, I noticed that Michael is the leader of the pack. If I can get to him, maybe I'll be able to get to the others, too. But I don't know how to do it.

Aisha's second interview goes well, too. She'll wait for an offer before she decides. She's been good at winning over her potential employers. I need to figure out how I can win over my kids.

On Wednesday morning, we get a call from Heather. Aisha talks to her briefly, and then hands the phone to me. She shakes her head.

"Joshua? I just remembered, the kids won't be able to spend the whole weekend with you. Michael is starting soccer season. They have games every Saturday morning."

"Why can't I take him to the game?"

"Not yet. You saw how he was with you. It's better if I do it for now."

"So what should I do? Just forget about the kids?"

"No, I don't think so. You're right. They do need a father."

"You're not talking against me to them, are you?"

"No, not lately. Michael and I talked in the car on the way home from your place. I told him that he should try to get to know you. But he's angry. He remembers the yelling. And he's angry at you for leaving."

What can I expect? I know how it feels.

"I wish there was some way for me to connect with him again." The whole thing seems impossible. But . . . "Tell me where his soccer game is. I'll show up there to cheer for him. We can all go out for burgers afterwards, and maybe then they'll be ready to come with me. What do you think?"

"I don't know. Yeah, I guess that would work. I have to tell you, part of me doesn't want to let them go. But they do need a father."

"Yes, they do. And I need them."

She gives me the directions to the soccer field.

I'm about to hang up when I think of something. "Oh, by the way, what are his team's colors?"

"Blue and white. Why?"

"You'll see."

After I hang up, I talk with Aisha, and together we come up with a plan to campaign for my children's affection.

❧

On Saturday morning, Aisha wears a blue dress with a white scarf. I wear my jeans with the blue and white striped polo shirt I bought yesterday. On the way to the game, we stop to buy a bunch of blue and white helium-filled balloons.

We get there a few minutes before the game starts. I spot Michael on the sidelines with his team, listening to last minute instructions from their coach. I wave, but he doesn't see me.

Heather does. "What in the world are you doing?"

"We're showing our team spirit."

"Okay." She shakes her head. "You don't have to try so hard, Joshua. The kids will come around."

"What's wrong? I'm just here to cheer for my son's team. What are they called, by the way?"

"If I tell you, you won't go out and get costumes, will you?"

"Give me a break, Heather."

"Okay, already. They're called the Roadrunners."

As the teams take the field, I hold up the balloons and yell, "Go Roadrunners!"

From his position as forward, Michael looks my way. For a moment he looks right at me. Then the game begins.

Jeremy and Jennifer are sitting near us on the sidelines. Every time I look at Jeremy, he turns away. Jennifer is shy at first, until her fascination with the balloons overcomes her. Near the end of the first half, she walks up to me. "I want a balloon." I choose a white one and tie it to her wrist. She smiles at me and bounces away, the balloon bouncing with her toward the sky.

I cheer at every good play the Roadrunners make. Aisha, who doesn't usually yell (except when she's really mad at me) sticks to clapping.

The game is almost over. The Roadrunners have a one-point lead but the other team has the ball. They're making their way down the field. I'm shouting, "Defense, Defense."

Then I hear a small voice.

"Can I have a balloon too, Daddy?"

I look down, even as the other team gets into position for the goal. "Sure you can, Jeremy." I crouch down to tie a blue balloon to his wrist, then reach up to brush the bangs from his forehead. I smile, and he smiles back. Behind us, the crowd is cheering as time runs out and the Roadrunners win the game. But my victory is in front of me.

Michael is busy whooping it up with his team. I'm still crouching next to Jeremy. Jennifer is running around chasing her balloon. And the sun is shining.

As the crowd leaves, some of the other children ask me for balloons. I give most of them away, but keep one blue balloon for Michael. From the corner of my eye, I see him leaving his teammates and running toward us.

"Did you see me, Mom? I helped score two goals. And we won. It was awesome."

"Great job, Michael. That was a good game."

"Michael, are you too old for a balloon?"

"Hi, Dad. Did you see me score?"

"I sure did. You were great."

"I was just running down the field, kicking the ball. They tried to stop me, but I went right through them. The goalie didn't even know what hit him."

"You did a good job. I'm proud of you." I reach out and pat him on the shoulder. He doesn't move away. "So, do you want a balloon?"

"Nah, give it to Jennifer."

"Balloon!" says Jennifer as she runs around the field bearing the colors of the winning team.

"Okay, guys, let's get in the car. Your daddy's going to take us out for hamburgers."

"All right! Can I have a cheeseburger?"

"Sure, Michael."

"And I want a toy!"

"Okay, Jennifer. Let's go."

I climb into my car with Aisha. Heather puts the kids, and balloons, into her car and follows us to the hamburger joint. I look in the rearview mirror every few seconds, just to see them.

I take them to a fast food place and, after a few minutes of confusion, manage to get everyone's order in. Michael reminds me several times to "make sure they don't put pickles on my cheeseburger." I emphatically relay his message to the skinny teenager behind the counter.

Aisha helps me carry the two trays to the table where Heather is waiting with the kids, who have clean hands and hungry stomachs. The three of us distribute the sandwiches, fries, and drinks around the table. The boys start eating while Jennifer plays with her toy.

"Thank you, Heather, for letting us come today. I think it helped."

"I think so too, Aisha. We've been fighting for so long, but it's not good for the kids. I just couldn't believe it when you two showed up with those balloons!"

"You've got to have team spirit, especially when you're the father of the best forward in Chicago."

"I'm not the best yet, Dad. I'm working on it, though."

As we eat, I wonder if the kids will come with us today. It's better now, much better. But I don't know if they're ready.

Heather waits until they're finished eating. The boys are

finished eating, that is. Jennifer has been so busy with her toy that she's barely touched her food. "What do you think, guys? Do you want to go to your daddy's house now?"

Their chatter stops. Even Jennifer becomes quiet.

"Do we have to?"

"No, you don't have to. I want to spend more time with you. But it's up to you, Michael, and your brother and sister."

Jeremy and Jennifer look at Michael. It is up to him.

"I'm really glad you came today, Dad. It was great. But I want to go home with Mom."

It's going to take some time. "Okay, then how about next week? Do you have another soccer game?"

"Yeah. Can you come?"

"We'll be there."

"More balloons?"

"Sure, Jennifer. More balloons."

Aisha laughs at me on the way home. "You should have seen yourself out there. Some of the other parents were staring at you. You were a real soccer Dad."

"You know, I liked it. I tried baseball once, when I was about Michael's age. But I wasn't that good, and there was nobody there to cheer for me. My mom dropped me off, and then went to the office to get some work done. I tried it for about a year before I gave it up. Michael's good though, isn't he?"

"He is. Your mom worked a lot when you were growing up, didn't she?"

"All the time, it seemed like. She said she was working hard to put food on the table and help us afford nice things. I used to think she worked to avoid spending time with me. But I've been thinking about it. She probably worked so much to avoid facing her own life. After Sam left she filled the emptiness with her work."

"I can see that. What do you remember about Sam?"

"The last time I saw him, I must have been about seven or eight, something like that. He gave me a football. We threw the ball around together for about ten minutes, then he got tired. He promised we'd do it again, but we never did. Before he left, he got into another fight with my mom. Then he got into his car and went back to Cynthia and their brats. I've got a half-sister and half-brother somewhere but I don't even know their names. And I've hated Sam for so many years that I can't even remember what he looks like. In my mind he has horns and a pointed tail."

"I'm proud of you, Isa."

"Why? Because I know how to yell at a soccer game?"

"Because you're trying to be a dad to your kids. My dad is great, and I am so thankful to have him. But there were lots of kids in my school who didn't have dads in their lives. I'm proud of you for trying so hard."

"It's all I can do. I know how it feels to be abandoned, and I'm not going to do that to my kids again."

❧

Aisha gets two job offers during the week. She thinks and prays about it, and decides to work for the Lincolnwood school district. They're going to give her a class of third graders.

"I love that age. They're still innocent, but they are so aware of the world around them."

She calls her parents and tells them the news. Sharon will be coming in a few weeks to help her buy her "teacher wardrobe."

I'm counting the days until the next soccer game. On Saturday morning, we buy twice as many balloons. By the time the game starts, we're there on the sidelines, cheering and handing out balloons. The Roadrunners lose this time, so we go out for burgers afterward to cheer up the star forward.

On the third Saturday, Jeremy sits next to me all during the game. On the fourth Saturday, he holds my hand as we head back to the cars.

I wait until the fifth Saturday before I ask again. Michael smiles.

"We'd like that, Dad. We're already packed."

I can't hug Heather to show her my appreciation. Aisha does that for me. The three kids climb into my back seat. It takes me several minutes to figure out how to put in Jennifer's car seat. I used to do that, before, when Michael was little, but that was a long time ago and, besides, it seems like every car seat is different.

When they're safely in, I look back at Heather, standing alone next to her car.

"Can you give me a just a minute? I promise I'll be good," I say to Aisha, winking.

"You'd better be. I'll be watching."

I walk up to her driver's side as she gets into her empty car. "I really do appreciate this. Thanks for working things out with me."

She smiles. "It's going to be quiet tonight. But we do have to think about the kids, don't we?"

I nod. "Thanks."

❧

The kids ask to stop by a video store on the way home. I let them each pick out a DVD. Michael gets a movie about a dog that plays soccer. Jennifer wants something with pink on the cover. Jeremy takes a long time to decide before he finally settles on something about dinosaurs.

Before going home, we make one more stop, at the restaurant. I told Fawad I was going to ask them today. If they said yes, I wouldn't be coming in to work. I'll make it up to him by working all day next Tuesday.

"Let's get out of the car, kids. This is where Daddy works."

"I have to go to the bathroom," says Jennifer.

"Then we've come to the right place." I hesitate. "Um, Aisha, could you take care of that?"

"Sure. Let's go, honey."

They go running in ahead of us. I take my boys' hands and we walk in together.

"Assalaamu alaikum, Fawad. I want you to meet my boys."

"Oh, look at you two. Your daddy is always talking about you. Michael, how was your soccer game today?"

"We won, and I scored the winning goal!"

"That's great. And Jeremy, your daddy tells me you like to

read. Is that right?"

Jeremy just nods.

"I am so glad to finally meet you. And I have something here for you." He reaches over by the cash register. "Here it is. You like candy bars, don't you?" He hands one to each of the boys. Michael rips his open and starts eating it. Jeremy just holds his.

Aisha and Jennifer come out from the restroom. "Oh, and here's the princess. I've heard all about you, too. Here's your candy bar, Jennifer."

She squeals with delight.

"Oh, I forgot, thank you," says Michael, his mouth full of chocolate. Jeremy mumbles his thank you.

"I know you've already had lunch today, Isa. But why don't you bring the children back here for lunch tomorrow? I'll have Khalid make something special, just for them."

"That's okay. You don't have to bother. And Sunday is too busy."

"It's no bother. It's a celebration. I'll see you tomorrow, then."

I shake hands with Fawad before we leave. "Do you boys want to shake hands with Uncle Fawad?" Michael reaches out with his chocolate stained hand, which Fawad readily accepts. Jeremy just looks down at the floor.

Fawad pats him on the head. "That's okay. After we get to know each other, right, buddy?"

Jeremy nods.

❧

I'm glad that the kids have been to our apartment before. At least it won't be quite as strange to them.

"Okay, which movie should we watch first?"

"Mine," says Jennifer.

"Go ahead," says Michael. "She always gets her way. Anyway, it's almost her nap time. Then we can watch our stuff."

Jennifer's movie seems to be about ponies and rainbows and princesses, things like that. I sit down and try to watch it with her, but I'm soon bored.

"Boys, if you don't want to watch this you can go play in your room."

"Our room?"

"That's right, Jeremy. Let's go see it." I open the door and the boys walk in and look around.

"Wow. I've been wanting this action figure. Cool."

"Look at all these books. I like these. They're a little scary, but not too much." That's the most I've ever heard Jeremy say at one time.

The boys quickly become involved with the things in their room. Jennifer is still sitting quietly, watching her movie. She looks sleepy.

"Here you go, Jennifer. You can lie down here." She puts her head on the pillow, her eyes never leaving the screen.

"Let's go pray," I whisper, "while we have a chance." Aisha and I take the prayer rugs into our bedroom and say our early afternoon prayers.

When we finish, I see Jeremy standing in the doorway. "What are you doing?"

"We were praying."

"That's not how Uncle Chris prays. He makes us put our heads down and fold our hands like this." He shows me.

"Come over here, Jeremy. I want to tell you something."

He sits next to me.

"You go ahead," says Aisha. "I'll check on the other two."

"A couple of years ago, I became a Muslim. Do you know what that means?"

He shakes his head.

"A Muslim is someone who follows a religion called Islam. Just like Uncle Chris is a Christian who follows Christianity."

"Oh, okay."

"Just now, Aisha and I were praying the way Muslims pray. That's also why Aisha wears a scarf when we go out."

"Is that why you have a beard now?"

"That's right." I pull him close to me and kiss his soft cheek.

"Oh, Daddy, your beard tickles."

The rest of the day is mostly movies and toys, punctuated by pizza for dinner. When Jennifer wakes up from her nap, Aisha takes her to see her new bed and toys. Jennifer stays in there and plays, while Michael watches his soccer movie. Jeremy is reading some of his not-too-scary stories.

When the prayer times come, Aisha and I make sure the children are safe, and then go into our bedroom to pray. Each time, when we finish, I find Jeremy watching us. I don't say anything except to answer his questions.

After the evening prayer, he asks me, "Why do you pray so much? Uncle Chris just prays before we eat."

"Well, I'm sure Uncle Chris prays more than that, but he doesn't do it out loud. And that's just something Muslims do. We pray five times every day, to help us remember God."

"Uncle Chris prays to God, too."

"That's right. We both pray to God."

"Oh, okay."

Things have been going smoothly, but now it's bedtime. Jennifer was delighted when she first saw her new bed, but she doesn't want to sleep in it. Two minutes after we put her down, she's up again. "I want to sleep with Aisha."

Aisha looks at me. I shrug my shoulders. Aisha takes her hand. "Okay, honey, let's go."

"And I think I'll go sleep in the other room with those brothers of yours."

Michael stakes out the top bunk and Jeremy seems happy with the lower one. But as soon as I turn out the light, they're full of requests. They need to go to the bathroom, get a drink of water, eat another cookie. Then Jeremy needs a story.

By the time they've fallen asleep, I've read three stories. I'm too tired to go anywhere, even to brush my teeth and change my clothes. I lie down on the floor next to the bunk beds. That's the last thing I remember until morning.

"Isa, Isa, it's time to pray." Aisha is gently shaking my

shoulder. The early morning light is already coming through the balloon curtains. Sometime during the night, I pulled Jennifer's pink blanket over my shoulders and chest.

"What? Where am I?" It takes me a moment. I look around the room, and then raise myself up on my elbow to see Jeremy sleeping peacefully in his bed. They're here. It's a beautiful sight.

After praying, we start on breakfast. I make chocolate chip pancakes.

Jennifer is the first one up. We hear her crying, and Aisha runs to her. She must be confused, too.

I wake the boys up when the pancakes are done. "Let's go, guys. Breakfast time."

Jeremy opens his eyes right away. "Good morning, Daddy."

It takes a little more prodding to get Michael up. He groans, and rolls over. Finally he opens his eyes. "Oh, hi, Dad."

I lead them to the kitchen, where Jennifer is already up, dressed and digging into the pancakes. She has a chocolate ring around her mouth.

After breakfast, we decide to take the kids for a walk. After half a block, Jennifer gets tired and I end up carrying her on my shoulders. Aisha holds Jeremy's hand and Michael walks on his own, like a young man already.

We don't walk far. There's nothing much to see on a Sunday morning, and Aisha is getting tired. We do find an area of grass where we can sit and watch while they can run and play for a few minutes. Then it's back to the apartment. Jeremy hasn't finished watching his movie yet.

We hang around for a few hours, until it's time to go eat lunch with Fawad. I don't think the kids are very hungry but Fawad is expecting us. Besides, I'm getting tired of junk food.

As soon as we walk in, Fawad greets the kids. "There you are. I've been waiting for you. This way, please." He leads us to a table near the back.

The food is already on the table. He has hamburgers, hot dogs, and French fries. "Just for my niece and nephews."

I was looking forward to some rice and curry, but he knows my kids aren't used to that. I could go back to the kitchen and fix myself a plate, but I decide to go ahead and eat with the kids. These hamburgers are good. Maybe we should add them to the menu.

By the time we're finished eating, it's almost two. Heather is expecting them back by six. We take them to the lake and walk along the beach. Michael wades in a little. Jennifer approaches the water, then runs back giggling every time it touches her toes. Jeremy is content to stay on the shore.

Next time, I want to take them to the zoo.

It's about five-thirty when we pull up in front of her building. I don't want to push my limits, especially not the first time. I look up at the second floor window. I think I see the curtain move. She must be waiting.

"Okay, guys, you're home now."

"Already?" says Michael.

"Yeah. Your mom's waiting for you. You can come back to my house in two weeks, okay?"

"Can we get movies again?"

"Sure, anything you want."

We get kids and bags unloaded from the car. We're about to cross the street when Aisha reminds me, "Don't forget the car seat." Michael carries that.

We walk up the stairs together and down the hallway to the apartment. A man is walking toward us. He has just come out of Heather's apartment.

"Hi Bryan."

He stops for just a moment. "Oh, hi, Michael." He glances at me, and then quickly walks away.

Aisha and I exchange glances, too. She didn't spend her quiet night alone, I guess.

Heather opens the door after the first knock. "Hi guys. I've missed you. Did you have a good time?"

"Yeah, we sure did." They start to tell her about their adventures.

"Okay, okay, hold on. Let me talk to your dad for just a minute, and then you can tell me everything. Now go on in and get ready for supper."

She turns to me. "How was it?"

"It was good. It was great, really."

"They look happy."

"Yeah, I think they had a good time."

"So we'll see you at the game next week?"

"Sure. Oh, no, not next week. I just remembered. Fawad's taking his family on vacation and I have to cover for him. In two weeks. Can I have them again?"

"That's what we agreed to."

"Let me tell Michael that I won't be there next week."

"That's okay. I'll tell him."

"Well, I'll see you in two weeks then."

"We'll be there." She closes the door.

As we walk back to the car, I ask Aisha, "Does she seem a little cool to you?"

"A little. But I'm not surprised. The kids enjoyed being with you. Maybe she wasn't ready for that."

"Besides, she knows we got a glimpse of that boyfriend. She wasn't too lonely."

"At least she's seeing him when the kids aren't around."

At least. But . . . When we get into the car, I pound the steering wheel.

"What's wrong, Hon?"

"That jerk knows my kids. He's probably spent more time with them than I have."

She rubs my back. "Don't worry. That's going to change now. And they know who their daddy is."

She's right. I don't know what I would do without Aisha.

Part Four

They were here for only a few hours, but the apartment seems so much quieter with the kids gone. I miss their energy, and their laughter. Two more weeks.

On Wednesday afternoon, when I go in to work, Fawad is grinning. "I can't tell you how much I appreciate you taking care of the restaurant for me. I haven't taken my family for a vacation in over five years. My wife is so happy. She and the kids are all packed up and ready to go. We will be leaving in a couple of hours, insha Allah."

"Where are you going?"

"Niagara Falls. My wife has always wanted to go there. And, if we have time, we might drive up to Toronto to see my cousin."

"That sounds nice. Don't worry about a thing. I can handle it."

"I know you can. And if there's an emergency, call my cell phone."

"Nothing will happen. Just relax and enjoy yourself. You deserve it. Have a great trip. I'll see you next Thursday, insha Allah."

After everything Fawad has done for me, I'm glad to be able to do something for him this time. And I'm looking forward to the challenge. I want to prove to myself that I can do it.

I'm getting ready to go open the restaurant on Thursday morning when the phone rings. Aisha has gone back to bed. I get it.

"Joshua, this is Sharon. I need Angela. It's urgent."

I call into the bedroom. "Aisha, it's your mom. She says it's important."

"I'll be there in a minute," she says sleepily. "Ask her what time she's coming on Friday."

"She wants to know when you'll be getting into town."

"Jim has collapsed. I'm afraid it's his heart. We're at the hospital right now."

I sit down. "When? How is he?"

"Just over an hour ago. I had to call an ambulance. I don't know anything yet."

"Hold on, I'll get her." I run to the bedroom. "Aisha, you have to talk to her. It's your dad."

"What?" She hurries to the phone. "Mom? What is it? Oh my God. Yes, yes, I'll be there. Don't worry. It'll be okay. Yes Mom, I'm on my way."

She hangs up. "I have to go. I have to be there."

"I'll help you pack."

She stops, and buries her face in my shoulder. "Oh, Isa, what am I going to do. If anything happens to him . . ."

"Just go and be with him. But, Hon, I can't go with you. I promised Fawad."

"That's right. The restaurant. I'll call Umar."

Umar comes ten minutes later. "I was on my way when you called. I can get a week off from work. Hopefully, by then, he'll be out of the woods."

"Hopefully. And tell them I'll come as soon as Fawad gets back." I hug Aisha. "Give them my love. And don't worry. It will be okay."

She nods, with tears on her cheek. "I know. Just keep praying."

❧

All day, all I can think about is The Doc. I keep saying the same silent prayer, "Please, Allah, please make him strong." But I'm worried.

I have to smile for the customers. That's part of my job. But Khalid notices. I ask him to pray for The Doc, too.

As soon as I get off from work, I call their house. There's no answer. They must still be at the hospital. I could call Umar on his cell, but I don't want to disturb them there. They'll call when there's news.

I can barely sleep, waiting for the phone to ring and thinking about The Doc. Aisha doesn't call until after sunrise.

"How is he?"

"He's still bad. They had to resuscitate him in the ambulance. He's in ICU. I think he knows we're here. But, it's bad."

She's crying, and I can't do anything to comfort her.

Over the next few days the news doesn't get any better. They're keeping him alive, but he's extremely weak. They've found the blockage, but they have to wait until he gets stronger before they can operate. He needs a quadruple bypass.

The restaurant is closed on Monday, as usual. I sleep a few hours on Sunday night and head out early Monday morning. I get to the hospital by nine.

I ask about him at the information desk.

"Jim Evans. Oh, yes, Sharon's husband. He's still in ICU. Only family members can see him."

"I am family."

"Oh really?"

"I'm his son-in-law. Angela Evans is my wife."

"You can go on up then." They still look skeptical.

I start to get the same routine when I get to ICU, but Umar sees me. "Isa, I'm glad you're here. Don't worry," he says to the nurses, "he's family."

We walk down the corridor together. "How is he?"

"The doctor says he's a little stronger. They should be able to operate by Wednesday, maybe Thursday. But," he pauses, "you won't recognize him."

Umar takes me to his room. There are wires and machines everywhere. He looks so small. And so old.

Sharon, Aisha, and Marcus are by his bed. Aisha sees me first. "You came." She hugs me.

"Hi, Joshua. I guess Tony told you. Now we're just waiting."

"It will be okay. We have to believe that."

"Joshua?" The whisper is coming from the bed, but it can't be The Doc. It's so small, so weak. "Come here, son."

He tries to reach out. I go over and hold his hand.

"Glad you could come."

"I had to be here. Just rest now. It's okay. We're all here for you."

I spend much of Monday next to his bed, holding his hand. Sitting here, next to him, I feel a closeness I've never experienced before. It's a new emotion. Maybe this is how it feels to love a father.

But I have to get back to the restaurant. By midnight, I'm on the road to Chicago.

When Aisha calls on Tuesday night, she tells me the surgery is scheduled for Thursday morning. The doctor thinks he'll be strong enough and, anyway, there's not much choice. It has to be done.

I try to call Fawad as soon as I get home from the restaurant on Wednesday night. I finally get an answer on the third try. It's his oldest son.

"Assalaamu alaikum, Abdullah. I need to talk to your dad."

"He's gone to bed. We just got back, and he's very tired."

"Tell him it's Isa, and it's important."

It takes a few minutes for Fawad to come to the phone.

"Assalaamu alaikum, Isa. How are you? The vacation was wonderful. I'll tell you all about it tomorrow."

"I can't come to work tomorrow, Fawad. I have to be in Moline." I tell him about The Doc, and tomorrow's surgery. "I have to be there."

"Yes, you must go. You took care of the restaurant, as you promised. Go to your family now. They need you more."

I sleep a few hours before getting back on the road. By the time I walk into ICU, they've just wheeled The Doc into the operating room. All we can do now is wait, and pray.

Sharon is curled up on one of the hard plastic seats in the waiting room. There are dark circles under her eyes.

I rub her shoulders. "It will be okay. We have to believe that."

"I keep thinking about him, there on the kitchen floor. One minute he was laughing with Marcus and talking about going for a walk, and the next minute he was so helpless. His heart stopped once in the ambulance. They wouldn't let us see him for hours. This isn't my Jim. I want my Jim back." She stares into space, tears running down her face.

Umar brings her coffee. "Here, Mom, you might need this. It's going to be a long day."

"Thanks, not now."

Aisha sits next to her mother and holds her hand. "He'll be okay, Mom. I know he will."

"I hope so, Angela, but I just don't know. I feel so helpless. I've worked at this hospital for almost twenty years, but it's not some stranger this time. It's my Jim. And I don't know what to do." She buries her face in Aisha's shoulder.

Aisha strokes and comforts her mother. After a while she says, "Why don't we go down to the cafeteria and get something to eat?"

"No, Angela, I can't eat right now."

"You have to, Mom, to keep up your strength."

"Okay, maybe just to take a walk. He will be in there for a long time, won't he?"

Aisha and her mother walk away, hand in hand, down the corridor.

Umar sits next to me. "I'm worried about Marcus. He was with Dad when it happened. He hasn't said ten words all week. I've tried, but I haven't been able to get through to him. I think maybe, in some strange way, he blames himself."

"He is still just a kid, isn't he?"

Is it better to have had a dad, and love him with all your heart, only to face losing him, or to have never had a dad at all? Between Marcus and me, right now I think I'm the lucky one.

"Hey Marcus, do you want to talk?"

He shakes his head.

"You have the coolest dad I've ever met. But you know that, don't you? He loves you guys so much. He is really a great dad."

"Yeah."

"You know, my dad left me when I was a baby. I never had the chance to know him."

"Yeah, I know."

"But your dad is really great. He's always there for Tony and Angela and you. He even has a sense of humor sometimes, doesn't he?"

"Yeah."

"I was so afraid of him that first day, though, when I first met him. Could you tell? I think my hands were shaking."

"Yeah, I noticed. It was kind of funny."

"Thanks for not laughing at me. You know, it means a lot to me, that I can be part of your family. I never had much of a family when I was growing up."

"Really?"

"My dad was gone and my mom had to work all the time. And my big brothers thought I was a loser. But you guys have a real family. Your mom, and your dad, and Tony and Angela and you. You all really care about one another."

He turns away.

"What is it, buddy?"

"It's hurts to care about people."

"Yeah, I know. It does. But we have to keep praying that he'll get through this."

"You didn't see him."

"That must have been scary."

"I'm the one who wanted to go for a walk. And we were horsing around. I should have known better."

"Listen to me, Marcus. His arteries were blocked. It would have happened anyway. You didn't have anything to do with it."

"Why? Why did it have to happen?"

"I don't know. But sometimes things happen. And we just have to do what we can."

He squints his eyes. A tear rolls down his cheek. "I'm scared."

"I know, buddy. Me too."

Many of the relatives are in the waiting room with us. And together we all pray and hold on to each other, trying to get through the long day. It's been over five hours by the time the doctor comes out. Everyone is quiet.

"Well, Mrs. Evans, he made it through the surgery. It's a good thing we went ahead and operated. Now we will just have to wait and see."

"How long?"

"The next forty-eight hours will be critical. If he can make it through that, then we've got a good chance for full recovery."

Aunt Arlene walks up to him. "I need to see my brother."

"They've just wheeled him back into ICU. You will be able to see him soon. But I suggest his wife and children go first. Only immediate family will be allowed in for at least the next forty-eight hours. You can come see him now, Mrs. Evans."

Sharon follows the doctor. The rest of us sit here, waiting and hoping.

She comes back over an hour later. "He's so weak. I never thought I'd see him like this."

Umar takes her hand. "Come sit down, Mom. We've been talking – Angela, Joshua, and I. You have to go home and get some rest. We'll take turns. I don't have to leave until Sunday, and Joshua can be here until Tuesday. Angela and you need to take a break. Joshua and I will stay here with Dad and take care of Marcus. In the morning, when you come, we can go back and rest. This way, when you can come back tomorrow, you'll be stronger and you can help him more."

"I don't know, Tony. I can't leave him. What if he needs me? What if something happens?"

"We'll call you right away. You can be here in ten minutes or less."

"Let's go, Mom. I'll fix you some tea. And you need to try to get some sleep."

"Okay, I guess. Thanks, kids. Your father would be proud of you."

"I love you, Mom." Umar kisses her on the forehead. Then Aisha leads her down the corridor to the parking garage.

We're only allowed to go in one at a time for now. Umar goes first. Aunt Helen and Aunt Arlene are still here, waiting to see him. The other relatives have gone home. Marcus and I sit, silently waiting.

Umar is gone for almost two hours. When he comes back, he says, "Marcus, you can go in. But remember, he looks different. He's been through a lot. Don't be scared. It's still Dad in there."

"Can he talk?"

"Not yet. But I'm sure he'd like to hear your voice."

While Marcus is gone, Umar and I say our prayers together. I brought my copy of the Qur'an in with me this morning, and we take turns reading from it.

After a few minutes, Umar looks up from the Qur'an. I've never seen him cry before.

"It's bad, Isa. I don't know if he's going to make it. And if, if he doesn't, we need to figure out how to take care of Mom and Marcus. I don't know if Mom could take it. And Marcus is so young yet. Don't tell anyone, but I'm scared, too." He looks down and goes back to reading. Tears fall on the pages.

When Marcus comes back, his face is tear-stained but he looks calmer. "I talked to him, and I think he heard me. Once, I thought he smiled. I told him what a great Dad he is, and how much he means to me. I talked to him about basketball, and how I'm excited to be going to high school next year. I just kept talking so he would know I was there. I didn't want him to feel like he's all alone."

"Come here, buddy." I hug him. "You're not alone either, you know."

"I know. I have you guys, and Mom and Angela. But Dad looks so lonely in there."

"I'll go sit with him awhile," says Aunt Arlene. She's gone for a long time. Umar tells me that The Doc is very close to both his sisters. When Aunt Arlene comes back, her eyes are red. She goes to a corner of the waiting room and reads from the Bible. Aunt Helen goes in after her. When Aunt Helen comes out, they sit huddled together. Now it's my turn.

There are even more machines than before, and he looks even smaller. His eyes are closed and his body is still. The constant beep of the monitor keeps the rhythm of his heartbeat.

It hurts to see him like this. But I have to stay positive. "Hi, Doc. How are you doing? I mean, besides being stuck in that bed with all those wires attached to you. We're here for you, you know. A lot of people love you. A whole lot of people are praying for you."

I don't know what else to say. So I just open my mouth, and tell him what's in my heart. "I wonder if I could ask you a favor. Doc is nice, but what I'd really like is to call you Dad. I know, we haven't even known each other that long. Just since Thanksgiving, the day you accepted me into your family. But I've spent more time with you than I ever spent with my real father. And you've taught me a lot. Isn't that what a dad is supposed to do? So I'm going to start calling you Dad now." I don't want to cry. I have to keep it light. "If you don't like it, then you're just going to have to get well enough to tell me so.

"You've got to get well. We still haven't gone to that Cubs game yet. They're doing a little better this year, but I don't think they'll ever get to the Series. It's just one of those things.

"And I'm looking forward to that big barbecue in a couple of weeks. I bet it's good. Maybe not ribs, though. Hamburgers will be fine.

"And we want you to stick around and play with your grandkids. Angela and I have been thinking about having some kids soon. Any kid would be pretty lucky to have you as his grandfather. You have to be here for them. When they act up, we'll bring them to you so you can scare them, the way you scared me the first time I met you.

"I love you, Dad. I need you to stay around and teach me how to be a good father, like you are. I need your strength. I want to hear you laugh again."

I hold his hand. He doesn't move. It feels like I've lost him already. Except for the beeping.

I recite some verses of the Qur'an. He doesn't understand what I'm saying, but I hope he hears me. I think he does.

I stay with him for a long time. Just sitting here, looking at him, and praying he'll get well. And the machine keeps beeping.

❧

Aisha and Sharon come early in the morning, soon after sunrise. They both look better. They must have rested a little. Neither one of them says much. They go straight to see Dad.

We all go back to the house in Umar's car. Sharon promises she'll call if anything changes.

Nobody feels like eating, but we cook a little breakfast anyway. I remember the way Dad glared at me and almost made me drop the pancakes. I remember having brunch with him the morning after the wedding. There are too many memories here, and I've only known him for a few months. I wonder how the others handle it.

After some breakfast, I stretch out on the couch, the same place I sat on the day he decided to accept me. My own Thanksgiving Day. I drift off to sleep, but I don't sleep well.

I have many dreams, but only one that I can remember. Dad and I were sitting out on the patio, next to the barbecue grill. It was a nice day. We were listening to a Cubs game on the radio, and they were winning. Suddenly, a strange man came around the corner of the house. I looked at him two, three times before I realized it was Sam. He grabbed The Doc, my Dad now, and tried to force him into a car. I screamed and tried to rescue Dad. But I couldn't get to him. I wake up, breathing hard. I'm relieved when I realize that it was only a dream, but the sense of loss stays with me.

Frisky is curled up next to me. I stroke her for a long time, trying to erase the image.

When I finally get up, I peek in at Marcus. He's still asleep. I find Umar sitting at the kitchen table, staring into space. His breakfast is sitting in front of him, untouched.

"I remember one time, when I was twelve, I got into a fight with this kid at school. He sat here at this table and gave it to me twice as hard as I gave it to that kid. The funny thing is, he never touched me. But by the time he was finished, I felt all beaten up. I got into a couple more fights after that, but I sure never started one again.

"And the time when I came home and told them I'd become a Muslim. At first he acted worried, like he was going to lose me. So we sat here and talked about it, and he kept listening until he felt he could understand.

"I keep thinking about Marcus. Who's going to teach him how to be a man? You and I can't, because we're still learning. He's too young. I know Allah has a plan. Right now, I just can't accept any plan that takes him away from us.

"But he looks so bad. I don't think he's going to make it. And I don't know how any of us can make it without him."

We go back to the hospital in the late afternoon. Aisha is waiting for us.

"Good news. He woke up, about an hour ago. Mom is with him now."

"How does he seem?"

"He's weak, but he can talk. It's not much, Umar, but it's progress."

"It is, alhamdulillah. Do you think I could go in?"

"Yes, he'll be glad to see you."

She turns to me, and smiles. "So, how are you?"

"I'm okay. Just worried. So he's really talking?"

"Yes. His voice is so soft, we could barely hear him. But it was so nice just to hear him at all. It was so scary when he didn't move."

"I know." I glance at Marcus. I don't want him to pick up on our fears. "So now you can talk to him, buddy."

"I want to ask him if he heard me last night. I think he did."

"Could be."

When Sharon comes out, she looks a little better, too. "Did Angela tell you? I think he's coming around. I sure hope so. He's not out of danger yet, but I hope this will be the beginning of his recovery." She crosses her arms and quietly shivers. "I've seen death happen to other families, but I'm not ready to let him go yet."

Umar is still gone when the doctor comes over. "Hello, Mrs. Evans. Our patient is looking better today, isn't he?"

"I hope so. How is he, really?"

"His heartbeat is regular. He's in a lot of pain, but, as you know, that's normal. We need to watch him closely for several days yet. But I'm a lot more optimistic than I was yesterday. We're doing everything we can. We'll just have to wait and see."

"How many times have I heard doctors say that to other people's families? It's all I can ask for, I guess."

When Umar comes out, Marcus jumps up. "Can I see him now?"

"In a minute. First he wants to see Angela and Joshua, together."

"Don't worry, buddy. We'll be back soon and you'll get your chance."

The machines are still there. He still looks much too small. But his face is brighter. He smiles weakly when we walk in.

"Hi, Doc. How are you doing?"

"It hurts like hell, but at least I'm alive. Weren't you going to start calling me Dad?"

"You heard me?"

"I heard all of you. But don't tell Marcus. I want to surprise him."

"Okay, Dad."

"And Angela said something, too. Something about me becoming a granddad next March."

She smiles. "I thought you heard me. That's right, Daddy. So you have to get well."

"I guess I do, then. Imagine that. My own little grandbaby." He slowly raises his right hand and reaches out to us. "Give me your hands, both of you. I want the two of you to promise me that you'll always take care of one another, no matter what happens. Can you do that?"

"Yes, Dad, I can." I look at Aisha.

"Yes, Daddy, I promise."

"Good. Because after I'm gone, I want to make sure that my grandchild always has a loving home."

"But, Daddy, you're going to be with us for a long time yet."

He grunts. "We'll see. Can you send Marcus in? I want to talk to him about high school."

After we leave the room, I look at her. "It was nice of you to say that, to make him feel better. But later you're going to have some explaining to do."

"No, I won't." She smiles. "It's true."

"You are?"

She nods. "I've been feeling so tired lately, but I thought it was just because of the stress of Daddy's illness. Then yesterday I threw up after Mom and I had breakfast. She told me I should check, to be sure. I picked up a test on the way home last night."

"So she knows, too."

"I wouldn't tell her the results until I told Daddy and you. I promised, and I think she understood. But I'm sure she knew."

I was kind of hoping it wouldn't happen this soon, but I can't stop grinning.

It must be pretty obvious. When we walk into the waiting room, Sharon takes one look at me and says, "It's true, isn't it?"

"Yes, Mom, it is."

She hugs us both. "I'm going to be a grandma."

Umar looks up. "What's that?"

"You heard her, uncle."

He nods. "That is good news. Congratulations, both of you."

He smiles, but he looks troubled. I know he's very worried about Dad. And maybe he's still not used to the idea of me touching his sister. Or maybe he's just being Umar.

Dad is awake and we're having a baby. I hope the news stays good from now on.

Aisha and Sharon leave for the house as we take over the night shift. "Be sure to get a lot of rest. And eat something. You need to keep up your strength."

Sharon smiles. "Don't worry, Joshua. I'll take good care of her."

"I love you." I hold Aisha tight. "See you tomorrow."

Marcus is excited after his talk with Dad. "He really did hear me last night. I knew he heard me."

216

"That's right, buddy. I think he's coming back to us." It's good to see Sharon and Marcus smile again.

We continue to take turns sitting with him, and reading Qur'an in the waiting room. When I go in, he seems anxious to talk to me.

His voice is a little stronger. "Come over here, Joshua. Hold my hand again, like you did last night. I want to tell you something. We never know if we're going to get another chance."

"But you're stronger now. I know you're going to make it."

"Just listen, son. Remember when I told you that we don't have divorces in our family?" I nod. I remember well.

"I've got to tell you, that's a new rule. I grew up in East St. Louis, I told you that. It's a tough area. A place where you have to be strong to survive. Especially back when I was coming up, during the sixties.

"My momma, she had a real tough time raising us. Because she had to do it alone. When I was ten, my daddy walked out on us, too.

"Another thing. I used to have a little brother. He couldn't have been more than two when our daddy left. I tried to be a daddy to him, but I was just a kid myself. He got himself killed when he was nineteen, fooling around with drugs. I wanted to help him, but he always seemed like he was lost. I couldn't save him." The Doc becomes quiet. For a moment he just stares into space. Then he blinks, and looks at me. There's a tear on his cheek. "Now it's just my two little sisters and me. Momma passed a couple of years ago. She was the toughest one of the bunch."

He closes his eyes and takes a deep breath. He's silent for a few minutes. Then he opens his eyes and looks straight at me. "Anyway, son, what I wanted to say is that life was always so rough, and my momma always told me not to do like my daddy did. No matter how hard things get, she said, you have to stand by your family. And I have. We all have. No divorces for any of us, or our children.

"That's why I was so hard on you at first. I didn't want to see Angela suffer the way my momma did. You've got a new child coming now with Angela, and you've already promised to take good care of my daughter and my grandchild.

"But you also have to be sure to take care of the children you already have. You left their mother, but don't you ever leave them. They didn't ask to be brought into this world. You and their mother did that. And they need you, son. You know they need you. We both know how they would feel if they lost their daddy again.

"I want you to promise me that. Don't you ever let your children get lost because they don't have a daddy."

"I won't, Dad. I'll take care of them. I promise." After spending the weekend with them, I don't see how I could ever turn my back on them again.

"Good. I believe you. Now, can you read some of what you were reading to me last night? I don't know what you were saying, but it brought me peace."

I recite to him for a long time, until he seems to be sleeping. I kiss him on the forehead and quietly leave.

I was already planning to call Heather to tell her that I'm not going to make it to the soccer game tomorrow. After talking with Dad, I start to feel that I should go. But I can't leave him yet. Not this Saturday. After Dad is well and I get back to Chicago, I'll spend all the time with them that I can.

I borrow Umar's cell phone. He doesn't tell me if I should stay or go. But I know I can't cheer at a soccer game while Dad is lying so weak in his hospital bed.

She answers on the second ring. "Hi, Heather, it's me."

"The kids are so excited about tomorrow. They're all packed."

"That's why I'm calling. I won't be there."

She's silent for just a moment, before she starts screaming. "I knew it. It was just too good to be true. Pretending to be Mr. Soccer Dad. It's the same old story. You get what you want, and then you run."

"Heather, wait, listen. Don't hang up. I'm in Moline. Aisha's father has had heart surgery. He's still in critical condition."

A longer silence. "Is that the truth? Because I don't want you messing with me again."

A doctor is paged over the intercom.

"Did you hear that? I'm at the hospital. I swear it. He had the surgery yesterday, and the doctor said that he's looking better, but we just have to wait and see. I have to be here. He's the closest thing I have to a father."

She's calmer. "Okay. Just make sure that your kids don't have to go looking for substitute father figures when they grow up."

"Can I talk to Michael?"

"That's okay. I'll tell him. What about next week?"

"I don't know yet. I hope so."

"You'd better call me before the kids start packing. That's not right."

"No, it's not. I'm sorry, but I can't be in two places at once. Besides, I wouldn't be any fun these days."

"Okay. Call me when you can. And tell Aisha I'm sorry about her father. I like her. I just don't know how she got stuck with you."

"Yeah, Heather. Whatever. Talk to you later."

Over the next couple of days, Dad seems to get stronger. He's still in a lot of pain, but he's talking more, and eating. On Sunday afternoon, the doctor tells us he plans to move Dad to a regular room on Monday. Sharon calls the relatives and tells them they can see him tomorrow. That's what they've been waiting for.

Umar leaves soon after talking to the doctor. "It looks like the crisis is over, insha Allah. Now we'll just have to make sure he gets some exercise and lays off the salt."

"When I get your father home, I'm going to watch him so closely he won't know what to do. Forget the salt and ribs. I'll do whatever I can to keep him from having to come back here again."

"Then you'll have your work cut out for you. I love you, Mom. I'll be back on Friday. Call me if you need anything." He kisses her, and heads back to Chicago.

I don't get to see too much of Dad on Monday. Visitors keep popping in – relatives, friends, and students. Aunt Arlene controls the flow of traffic.

When a group of teachers walks in on Monday afternoon,

Sharon shakes her head. "I hope he doesn't get worn out."

"I'm sure he enjoys the attention. He's looking so much better too. It's great to hear him laugh again. Anyway, I know Aunt Arlene will start keeping people away if she thinks he can't handle it."

"That's the truth."

I have to leave on Tuesday morning. Aisha will stay a while longer, maybe a week or so. She plans to go shopping with her mother one day soon, while Dad is still in the hospital with Aunt Arlene watching over him. "It isn't Chicago, but it will do. Besides, now we have to shop for maternity clothes."

I stop in to see Dad before I leave. He's sitting up, and he doesn't look so small now. He smiles when I walk in.

"Joshua, son. How are you this morning?"

"I'm good. I'm glad to see you looking better."

"I've still got a lot of pain, but I guess that's normal. I've been feeling a little dizzy, too, but the old man isn't what he used to be."

"I have to leave, Dad. I need to get back to work. I'll try to come back on the weekend to see you. Angela will be here for as long as you need her."

"You better not make me that kind of offer, or she'll never get back to Chicago. Thank you, Joshua, for staying by me when I needed you. It meant a lot. Can you promise me one more thing?"

"Sure. Anything."

"If something happens to me, I want you to help Tony take care of my family."

"But you're getting stronger. You don't have to think like that."

"I know, son. I just need you to give me your word. Do you promise you'll take care of Marcus and your mother-in-law? I know Tony will do what he can, but it will be easier if you're there to share the load. I just want to know that they'd be okay without me."

"Of course, I'll always be there for them. You, and Sharon, and Marcus, you are all my family now. But you can't talk like that. You'll be going home in a couple of weeks. And you'll be coming to Chicago next March to hold your first grandchild."

"I just need your promise, that's all. A couple of weeks ago I sure didn't expect to be in this hospital bed. We never know what the Lord has planned."

"Okay, I promise." I don't like it when he talks like that. It worries me. "Um, Dad, do you believe in God? Do you believe in the One God?"

"I do, son. I may pray a little differently than you do, but I believe our prayers go to the same place. I have to say, there must be something awfully good about Islam. I can see what it's done for you, and for Tony and Angela. And, like I said, those verses you read brought me peace. It's good to have faith."

"Yes, it is. It really is. Well, I guess I'd better be going. I love you, Dad." I hold his hand. His grip is getting firmer.

"I'll see you this weekend, son. Drive carefully now."

I lean down to kiss him on the forehead, and he hugs me. "I love you, son," he whispers. "Remember that."

I start to cry. And I can't stop. I wonder if he knows how long I have wanted to hear the words I never heard from my father. I sit on the edge of his bed, and he holds me while I cry. He strokes my head. "I know, son, I know."

I don't want to leave him, but I have to go. When the tears are gone, I wipe my eyes. One more hug, and I have to head back to Chicago.

"I'll see you this weekend, Dad."

"If the Lord wills."

Aisha walks with me to the parking garage. She doesn't ask why my eyes are red. "I'm going to miss you."

"I'm the one who has an empty apartment to go home to. I'll come this weekend. You can show me your new clothes."

"I wish I could come home with you, but I can't leave him yet."

"No, not yet. It's good that you're here. Call me tonight when you get back from the hospital."

"I will. Drive carefully."

"I will. Take care of yourself, and take care of little Ismail, too."

"Ismail?"

"Remember? He's the one who introduced us. He said I'd be so happy with you that I'd name all our kids after him. I think one should be enough."

"Okay, then. Ismail. Or Maryam."

"Maryam?"

"After my grandmother, Mary. Daddy's mother. I wish you could have met her. She was so loving, and so full of life."

"Okay. Ismail or Maryam. I love you."

"And I love you back."

It's a lonely highway from Moline to Chicago. But my loneliness is eased by knowing that I finally have a dad who loves me.

Part Five

She calls at night, right after I get home from work. He's still in a lot of pain. And he has developed a cough. But he's sitting up and talking, and he's eating well. He just needs more time.

They went shopping today. "We got some nice things. Wait till you see them."

I told Fawad earlier today that I need the weekend off again. I'll be going on Saturday. I have to remember to call Heather and let her know I won't be there. Not now, though. I'm tired. And I miss Aisha too much.

We're in the middle of the Wednesday night dinner crowd when Aisha calls the restaurant. She's crying. "Isa, you need to come. His cough is much worse, and I think he's coughing up blood. Mom told me to call. You have to come right away."

"Don't worry. I'll be there, Hon. Don't cry. It'll be okay." I wish I believed that.

The restaurant is full of customers. I call Fawad, who is in the middle of his own dinner at home.

"I have to go, Fawad. It sounds bad."

"Don't worry, Isa. I'll come as soon as I can. Tell Khalid you're leaving. He can handle things until I get there. Go to your family. Don't worry about the restaurant. Let me know if there is anything I can do."

"Just pray."

Umar is waiting for me at my apartment. "Grab your things and we'll go together. And, Isa, I think you need to pack a suit."

I stop and look at him. "Why?"

"I told you, I'm scared."

My suitcase is still packed. I throw in my toothbrush, and the suit I bought to wear in court. I hope I won't need it.

We make it to Moline in less than two hours. The highway patrol must be on break.

He's back in ICU. We find them there, in the waiting room. They're all here. Umar goes to Sharon and puts his arms around

223

her. Aisha buries her face in my shoulder. After a minute or two, the doctor comes out. "It's a blood clot, a rare complication from the surgery. He's been on anticoagulants, but they don't seem to be taking effect. We have him on oxygen. I can let family members see him, a few at a time. But please, try not to get too upset in front of him. This might be the last chance you get. I'm sorry."

All of us—Sharon, Marcus, Umar, Aisha, and I—file into the room. He looks so small again. I touch his hand. It's cold.

"Jim, we're here. We love you."

"Dad, it's Tony. I love you, Dad."

"I love you too, Dad."

"I love you, Daddy, and the baby does, too."

"I love you, Dad." I don't have the words to say what I feel for him.

We stay and talk quietly about good times, trying to give him the strength to get through this. He doesn't talk but he looks at us, his eyes damp.

He starts to cough. He can't stop. Umar holds a small bowl, and he spits blood into it. But the coughs keep coming. When it's finally over, he is gasping. He reaches out. "Sharon?"

"I'm here, Jim."

She holds his hand and strokes his head and whispers words of love and encouragement. His breathing slows, and he relaxes back into the bed.

His sisters need to see him. The rest of us leave, except for Sharon. She holds him and comforts him as he struggles to hold on, or let go.

We're sitting in the waiting room, holding on to each other, when Aunt Helen comes out. "You children need to come back in and say goodbye to your daddy." She's shaking. Umar puts his arm around her shoulders as we walk back into Dad's room.

His breath is labored, even with the oxygen. He starts coughing again. Umar holds the bowl, and holds Dad while he coughs. He's sweating. I wet a washcloth and gently wipe his forehead.

He lies back down and looks at us all, scanning us with his

eyes. Then he whispers, "I love you all so much. And there is only One God." He coughs again.

Then he's quiet.

There's nothing more to say. We silently gaze at him for a long time, wishing for one more word, one more breath. Then Umar gently closes Dad's eyes and kisses him on the forehead one last time. "We all belong to Allah, and to Allah we will all return," he says softly. His voice breaks. But he's the only one who isn't crying.

The funeral is on Saturday. Aunt Arlene and Uncle Paul made most of the arrangements. The church is packed. Umar and I are two of the pallbearers. I wear my suit.

Sharon is trying to be strong. She greets people at the funeral home. She doesn't cry during the funeral. She waits until everyone is gone, and then she breaks down.

I'm worried about Aisha. She keeps throwing up. I make her sit down as much as possible. I bring her white soda. I hold her while she cries.

Marcus hasn't talked since Dad died. It's hard to reach out to him, and it's impossible to hide our own grief. He needs time.

I called Fawad yesterday. I need another week. I promised Dad I would take care of them. It's too soon to leave.

I didn't call Heather. I can't talk to her now. I'll tell her later, and I hope she'll understand.

We all came back to the house after the funeral. People brought casseroles, talked quietly, and held Sharon's hand. They have just left. The house is quiet. But he's everywhere.

None of us has said much since Wednesday night. First there was shock. Then there was crying. We have to start talking.

At least Umar and I do. We sit at the kitchen table on Sunday afternoon. Sharon and Aisha are resting. Marcus is brooding in his room. Umar and I have to come up with a plan.

"I've called my work," says Umar, "and they'll give me another week. We need that time to figure out what to do."

"I promised him I would help you."

"I know. He told me. I called him on Tuesday, the day before . . ." He stops, trying to control himself. The tears come anyway. He puts his head on the table and sobs.

All this time, he's been so strong. He didn't cry at the hospital or the funeral. He took care of Sharon and Marcus, and spoke quietly with relatives and friends. He's tried so hard to be strong.

I put my hand on his shoulder and quietly remind him, "We all belong to Allah, and to Allah we will all return." He looks at me, and nods. He's quiet, but the tears keep coming.

It takes several minutes before he can talk again. "I'm sorry. I didn't want to do that."

"You don't always have to be strong."

"Yes, I do." He clears his throat, and goes to rinse his face at the kitchen sink. "They need me. Dad," his voice catches, and he stops for a moment. "Dad told me to take care of them. He's depending on me. I can't disappoint him."

"How could you ever be a disappointment to him?"

"You don't understand. Dad used to have a younger brother. His brother died, about a year before I was born, from a drug overdose. Dad talked about it sometimes. It broke his heart. That's why he became a high school principal. He wanted to help other teenage boys fight the despair that killed his brother, Tony."

"Tony?"

"He named me after his brother. I think he wanted me to erase his brother's failure. And he needed me to be strong. I can't fail him now."

"You won't."

"I have to take care of them."

"And I'll help you."

He nods. "I know you will. It's going to take the two of us, working together. And no matter what we do, even the two of us can't fill his shoes." The tears start again. He shakes his head. "To

hell with it. I guess a man can be allowed to cry for his father."
He puts his head on the table.

I leave to go check on Aisha. She's sleeping. There is a pile of
tissues next to her on the bed. She hasn't been able to stop
crying. And she hasn't been able to eat without throwing up. I'm
worried.

I sit and watch her sleep. And I keep thinking about it. I
finally found a dad who loved me. Someone who wouldn't
abandon me. But now he's gone. While Aisha sleeps, it's my turn
to cry.

It's dark outside when Umar knocks on the bedroom door.
"It's time for the prayer."

I open the door and step out into the hallway. His eyes are
still red. He looks at me. "You too?"

I nod. "I guess a man can cry for the dad he finally found."

He grabs me and hugs me, just like he did at the wedding. It
reminds me of Dad and his bear hugs. Thoughts of Dad
overwhelm me. I sit on the floor and put my face in my hands.

Umar sits next to me and waits until I get my emotions under
control. When I'm calm again, he pats my shoulder. "Let's go
pray. Why don't you go get Aisha, so she can pray with us?"

"She's having such a hard time. I want to let her rest. She was
so close to Dad. And now there's the baby too. She's been so sick
she can barely eat. I'm worried about her."

"Don't worry. My sister is strong. She'll get through this,
Insha Allah. But I'm glad you're in her life, to help her get
through it." He's quiet for a moment, and then he shakes his
head. "I didn't even like you, but she was so stubborn. If it had
been up to me, you wouldn't be with her now. She was the one
who saw who you were beneath the surface."

"I'm glad you listened to her."

"What could I do? You know how bossy she gets. And then
you walked away from her. I think that's when I started to respect
you, because it took strength for you to stand up for yourself.
And Ismail told me you were still going to college, without Aisha
pushing you. She wouldn't want me to tell you this, but she cried
a few times during those months. I told her to wait, and pray

about it. She spent all of Ramadan thinking and praying. When I saw the two of you standing there together on Eid day, I knew you would be my brother."

"What if Dad had said no?"

"I don't think he would have. He knew Aisha wanted to marry you. He wouldn't have said no to her."

"You mean I did all that sweating for nothing?"

"Remember, brother, suffering builds character."

"I was so afraid of him at first. He seemed so stern."

"That was his principal mask. He talked to a lot of his students that way, especially the difficult ones. He had to test you. Just like I did. We didn't want to see Aisha get hurt." He's quiet for a moment. "Why did you come to my place that night? You knew I would be angry."

I've never told anyone. Not Brad, not Ismail, not even Aisha. I know I can tell Umar. But how can I make him understand?

"You know that I had a troubled youth. When I was younger, before I became a Muslim, I often had dark thoughts. These thoughts turned into urges, which sometimes controlled me. They felt like demons inside my head. They were trying to control me again that night, and I almost gave in to them. I knew that you were the only one who could protect me from them. From myself."

"I almost didn't let you in. I wanted to slam that door in your face, but something stopped me."

"The mercy of Allah."

"I guess that's it."

"I know it is. Without the mercy of Allah, I would have destroyed myself that night. I thought I had lost Aisha, and she was the first woman who loved me for who I am. Without her, I didn't want to live. Suicide was my greatest demon, and I almost gave in to it."

"What about your faith? Even if you had lost Aisha, you still had your faith."

"I forgot my faith. Believing in God is still a new experience for me. I spent my first twenty-three years feeling empty, alone. That night, I felt alone again. As if I was falling into a bottomless pit. That's why suicide seemed to be such an attractive option."

Umar looks at me as if he's never seen me before. "I didn't know you were suffering that much. I wish I had done more to help you." He looks down. "I feel like I failed you."

"No, you didn't fail me, brother, you saved me. You let me come in, and you took me back to Aisha. I knew you hated me at first, but by then I had come to depend on you. You're strong and steady, and you have a deep faith." I pause, and try to smile. "I hope I can be like you when I finish growing up."

"You're a different kind of man, Isa. You say you've had demons, but that's not what I've seen. What I've seen is a man with a tremendous need to love and be loved. I think that's what Aisha first saw in you."

"I can't believe she saw any good in me. I still had a long way to go back then. In some ways, I was still the screwed-up guy who walked out on his kids."

"And who are you now?"

"That's a good question. I'm a Muslim. I'm a father and a son, a husband and a brother. I feel like I've walked through hell to get where I am. And I think that I'm almost where I should be."

"What about the demons?"

"Something changed in me that night. I came so close. But by the mercy of Allah, I stopped and came to you instead. You didn't turn me away. And I prayed. You know that I prayed all night. And sometime during that night, I lost my feeling of despair. After that night, for the first time, I began to feel a kind of peace inside my soul. And since then everything has been better. Aisha forgave me, and I've been given the chance to get to know my kids. And even though losing The Doc hurts more than I could ever have imagined, I know he loved me. You're right. I've had this deep need all my life. Up until these past few months, I've often felt empty inside. Now I do feel loved, and there's no more room for the demons."

"You are loved, brother." We stand up and hug again, briefly. "Well, let's go pray."

We pray in the living room. After the prayer, Umar turns to

me. "We still need to decide what to do. I have a plan. I want Mom and Marcus to move to Chicago, to be with us. But I don't think Mom will do it."

"Have you tried to talk to her yet?"

He shakes his head and sighs. "No, I can't. But I don't want to leave them here alone."

I can't imagine them staying here in this house without Dad. The memories are too strong.

"It would be hard for us to move here, because we all have work and you have school. And your kids are there. But Mom could take a leave of absence from the hospital, and Marcus could go to high school in Chicago. I don't think she'll leave, though. They moved here right after I was born, when Dad was still a teacher. This is her home."

"Where would they live? Neither of us has a big enough apartment."

"What if we find a house where we can all live together? We could pool our money and rent a place out in the suburbs. Mom could even keep this house to come back to. I'm sure she wouldn't sell it. I don't think I'd let her."

"That would work. Then Sharon could help Aisha through her pregnancy, and you and I could help Marcus adjust."

"It's the best solution I can come up with, but I don't think Mom will like it."

"No, I don't think so, either." She's standing in the doorway. "I just lost my husband. Now you want me to uproot my whole life?"

"No, Mom, we'll think of something else. It was just an idea."

"When Jim and I first moved to Moline, we lived in an apartment. You were a baby then, Tony. We bought this house a few months before Angela was born. Don't you remember? You were six. You fell in love with the backyard. The first weekend after we moved in, your father went out and bought a swing set kit. He spent the next two weeks putting that thing together. It's still out there.

"We had a life together here. If I leave this house, it will feel like I'm leaving my last piece of him behind."

230

"I know, Mom. Never mind. It was a bad idea." Umar holds her. Since Wednesday, he has been holding back his own pain so he can comfort her. Except for that one time, in the kitchen.

All of us are having a hard time moving on. All of us are hurting. But Sharon is hurting the most. Of course she can't think about making changes in her life right now. She's built a life around him for more than thirty years. And now he's gone.

I go to check on Aisha again. She hasn't made her evening prayers yet.

She's lying on the bed, staring into space. I kiss her cheek. It's wet.

"You need to go pray, Hon. Umar and I already did."

"I can't believe he's gone. It's too soon. I still need him. He was supposed to be a grandfather."

"He is a grandfather. I wasn't expecting us to have a baby this soon, but it made his last days happier. We'll have to tell the baby that. We'll tell him, or her, everything about who he was. So they'll have a connection."

"I'm worried, Isa. I feel so sick. I don't know what's normal, but I'm scared. I just lost my father. What if I lose my baby too?" I hold her while she sobs, and recite the verses that brought peace to Dad.

❧

On Tuesday, I finally call Heather. I still don't want to talk to her. She won't understand. If she starts with me, I don't know what I'll do.

"Hello, Heather. Don't say anything, please. Aisha's father died last week. We're all still trying to come to grips with it. I want to see the kids, but I have to deal with this first."

She actually listens. When she does talk, her voice is softer than I've heard it in a long time. "Oh, I'm sorry. I didn't know it was that serious."

"We thought he was getting better. It was sudden."

"I'm sorry. I don't know what to say."

"Let me talk to Michael. I need to tell him what's going on."

"Okay. I'll get him."

I tell Michael, as gently as possible, why I didn't come last Saturday. I don't know how much he understands about death. He's still so young. "Michael, Aisha's father has been very sick. I've been spending a lot of time with him here in Moline. He was a good man. But, well, he's not with us anymore. He died. And we're all very sad."

"I know, Dad. My best friend, Caleb, had a grandmother who died last year. He was real sad. Sometimes he didn't even want to play."

"That's right, Michael. That's how I feel right now. I miss you, I really do. And I'll come back to Chicago soon, and you can spend the night with us again. I love you, son. I want you to always remember that." In my mind I flash back to that moment with Dad. I wish I had stayed with him instead of going back to Chicago.

"I know, Dad. But my last soccer game is in two weeks. Do you think you can be there?"

"I think I can. The Doc would like that."

"Who's he?"

"That's what I called Aisha's father. He was very smart, like you."

"Okay. I have to go, Dad. I have to get ready for soccer practice."

"Okay. Can I talk to your mom again?"

"Hi, Joshua. I wish there was something I could do."

"Just keep on being understanding, like you are now. I told Michael I'll come to his last game. That's the best I can do."

"All right. We'll see you then."

∾

I'm very worried about Aisha. She can eat saltine crackers, but not much else. I need to take her to see a doctor as soon as we get back to Chicago. We have to go back soon.

∾

On Tuesday night, when everyone else is asleep, I talk with Umar again. "We have to figure this out. Aisha needs a doctor, and you and I have to get back to work. And I told Michael I'll come to his soccer game the week after next. It's the last game of the season. And I'm all mixed up.

"Until now, I never really knew about death. I thought about death all the time when I was younger, all those times when I wanted to destroy myself. I thought I knew death. But now I know that my suicidal urges were just a dark and selfish game I played. Though I did come close sometimes. But I never understood the reality of dying. Until now I never knew how it felt to lose someone this way."

"I've lost some people who were important to me, but I never thought I would lose Dad. When I was seventeen, one of my best friends wrapped his car around a tree. One day we were playing basketball and goofing around together, and the next day he was gone. My ideas about life were shattered. Dad was there to help me understand. He helped everybody get through it. And when our grandmother died, a couple years back, he was there to help us all get used to life without her. Now I know how much he must have been hurting, but he never showed it. He has always been there when I needed him. I never could have imagined my life without Dad. I don't know, either, how to get through this without him."

We sit at the kitchen table for a long time without another word. The tears are gone but there is a sadness hanging over us. I finally break the silence.

"Why is it so hard? Is it because we're weak?"

"No, it's because we're human. That's why we need Allah. And I keep on praying, but the hurt isn't going away."

"So what do we do? Our small world has crashed. But the larger world goes on. How does that work?"

"I don't know, but we have to think of something soon. We can't go back to Chicago without a plan."

"But the plan has to involve Sharon. And she's not ready."

"Let's talk to Mom tomorrow. We'll see what she has to say."

I nod, and leave Umar sitting alone at the table.

Part Six

I go into the bedroom and crawl into bed next to Aisha. She has been sleeping almost all the time since the funeral. That worries me too. I can't sleep at all.

While I've been lying here, unable to sleep, I have come to realize something. Umar is different now. I have always respected him for his strength and determination, but he's changed somehow. He's trying, just like he tried to hold back the tears. But part of his strength, I think, came from Dad. It's going to take him a while to recover and learn how to be strong on his own. Dad must have known that. That's why he asked me to help. In the morning, I am going to take charge. And by morning I know exactly what I'm going to do.

❧

I get up at dawn and make the call to prayer. Umar comes right away. I have to practically drag Aisha out of bed and make her pray with us. Then I ask them to come with me to the kitchen. While I make the eggs and pancakes, they sit and watch.

"I have to go back to bed, Isa. I'm so tired."

"I know you are, Hon, but I want you here with me. Just a little while."

"Are you up to something?"

"Of course I am, brother. You'll see. Right now, I want you to make tea for your mom."

When the food is ready, I set the table. "Umar, go get your mom. We're going to eat breakfast together."

"She's still sleeping. I think we should leave her alone. She's having such a hard time."

"She's having a very hard time, but I think you need to go get her. Breakfast is ready."

I go to Marcus's room, open the door, and turn on the light. "Let's go, buddy. Time to get up."

He moans.

"I mean it. Breakfast is ready. And we're going to eat it together."

I have to shake him by the shoulder a few times before he opens his eyes. "Aw, Joshua, leave me alone."

"No. You're going to get out of this bed. Come on. I'll help you up."

It takes some doing, but I finally get him to the table. The others are already here.

"What's going on, Joshua?" Sharon is staring at me.

"We're going to start by eating breakfast together. Then I'll tell you my plans for the rest of the day."

"I can't eat. I'll throw up again."

"I know you're sick, Hon. Try just a little. Eat half a pancake, without syrup. That should stay down."

It's a quiet breakfast, but they do eat. Aisha manages to finish an entire pancake.

They're almost finished. "Okay, this is what we're going to do today. First, Marcus will wash the dishes. Then we're getting into Umar's car and driving out to Sunset Park. After we get there, I'll tell you what's next."

"What are you talking about, Joshua? We don't want to go to any park."

"I know, Sharon, but that's where we're going."

"Honestly, that's about the last place I want to be right now."

"Aisha, you need to get dressed. Why don't you wear your favorite blue dress?"

"I can't go anywhere. I don't feel well."

"The pancake stayed down, alhamdulillah. A little fresh air will help."

Marcus moans about doing the dishes, but he does them. Soon we're all in Umar's car on the way to Sunset Park.

Sharon complains in the car. "I don't know what's going on with your husband, Angela. Is he crazy?"

"No, I'm just trying to help."

When we get to the park, I ask Umar to drive up to the overlook. He parks up there and we get out. It's a beautiful July morning.

"I'm not crazy. I just wanted to get you all out of the house. We're all going crazy in there. Aisha is sleeping all the time, and not eating anything. Marcus spends all of his time in his room, shutting himself inside. Sharon, you're going through the motions, but you don't know how to go on living without him. And Umar, you hurt, but you're afraid to show it.

"I love Dad. He was a great man. But if he saw all of you like this, he would be doing just what I'm doing. He asked me to promise him that I would help Tony take care of his family. That's what I'm going to do.

"I want you all to look over there at that river. The Mississippi has been here for thousands or millions of years. And it just keeps flowing. That's how rivers are, how God made them to be.

"But people don't last that long. We wear out. Each one of us is going to die. And, whenever it comes, the people who love us will think it's too soon.

"God gave Dad fifty-six years of life. And he lived it well. Someone else could have wasted all those years. But Dad lived well. He worked hard, and he loved, and took care of everyone around him. It was too short for us. But if he had lived another fifty-six years, it still would have been too short, because he was the kind of man you want to have with you forever.

"I love Dad. And I love each of you. And I can't stand to see you like this. We're allowed to mourn, but we have to live, too. Not just exist."

They're quiet. Umar is looking down at the ground. Aisha is absentmindedly playing with the grass. Marcus is looking up at the clear sky. And Sharon is looking out at the river.

"I'm going to take Angela back to Chicago with me in a few days. She needs to start seeing a doctor. She also needs to get ready to teach her third graders. When I get back to Chicago, I'm going to help Tony look for a house to rent. Sharon, I don't like leaving you and Marcus in Moline. Without Dad, I'm afraid you'll both be lost. The only way we can get through this is to do it together. I know your life is here, but I think you need to start making plans for a new life in Chicago. You can keep the house and come back here for visits. But if you stay, I'm afraid you'll just keep on going through the motions. The new school year starts next month, so you need to move soon enough for Marcus to start high school there. None of us likes it, but we all have to learn how to live without Dad. And we have to do it together.

"That's all I wanted to say. Now it's your turn."

They're quiet for a long time. Umar is the first to speak.

"I think you're right, about everything. Including what you said about me. This last week, I've tried, but I haven't been able to do it anymore. Mom, I think I know how you feel, but I want you to be in Chicago with us. I don't want to leave you and Marcus here alone. Like Joshua said, we have to do it together."

"I'd like that, Mom. I want you to come live with us, especially now with the baby coming."

Sharon shakes her head. "I'll think about it, I guess. But you kids don't know what you're asking. I've lived here for almost thirty years. I can't just pick up and leave." She stares out at the river. "I still can't believe he's gone. I keep waiting to hear him pull up in the driveway. Or I start thinking maybe he's out of town for a conference, and he'll call any minute. Then I remember him, how he looked there in the hospital. And I blame myself. I'm a nurse. I should have taken better care of him. I tried to make him watch his diet, but he just laughed, and I let him do what he wanted. I didn't make him exercise, and I didn't make sure he had all the tests. He hated going to the doctor, but I should have forced him to go more often. And the night before, he complained about some discomfort. I thought it was indigestion from the lasagna I made for dinner. I gave him an antacid and we went to bed. He seemed okay in the morning, at first. I should have known. I should have taken him to the ER that night. It's my fault he's gone. And I'll never see him again."

Umar holds her while she cries. "It's not your fault," he whispers. "You did everything you could. He loved his life with you. On that Sunday before he died, he told me to let you know how much he loved you. He also told me to tell you that he knew how much you loved him, and how grateful he was to you for all your years together. He told me to tell you, after he was gone. I didn't want to hear it, but I think he knew he wasn't going to make it. And you did everything you could for him."

She cries for a long time. I can't imagine if I ever lost Aisha. I reach for her hand. She puts her head on my shoulder.

Marcus is crying softly, too. I pat him on the back.

"How are you doing, buddy?"

He looks at me, and tries to smile. "I keep thinking about Dad, and how good he was, and how I miss him so much. And it's weird, because Dad is gone, but the sun is still shining."

We stay up at the overlook for a long time. There are a lot more tears, and then we're silent. But it's a calmer silence now, I think.

Eventually, we drift back to the car. I want to take them out for lunch.

In the car Sharon says, "Jim always liked coming here. Remember, kids? We would drive up here sometimes on Sundays after church. Some days, we would pick up some chicken or burgers on the way and have a picnic. Other times, we would just sit and enjoy the view. Sometimes, if he had a hard day at school, he would come here alone before coming home. You didn't know that, did you, Joshua?"

"No, I didn't."

"I think he's the one who brought us up here today. I don't know what the religions would say about this, but I think he hasn't left us completely. He wouldn't leave us all alone."

I don't know about that, but I do know we're not alone. I remember the mercy of Allah.

❧

Umar chooses the restaurant. When he pulls into the parking lot, Marcus jumps up. "This is Dad's place. He always liked coming here."

"I know."

The waitresses recognize the family. One by one, they come over and express their sympathy.

Before we're finished, the manager comes to our table. "We are all going to miss Dr. Evans. He made a difference in the lives of many people. I was one of his kids at the school, a few years back. He was the one who helped me stay out of trouble. Please, feel free to come here any time. No charge."

～

The first thing Umar does when we get back to the house is to open all the curtains. The sunlight comes streaming in.

When he's finished, he turns to Sharon. "Mom, I want to remember the good things about Dad. There is so much good to remember. Before we go back to Chicago on Sunday, I want to go ahead and have the barbecue, in Dad's honor. I want to invite everyone who was close to him, to come together and celebrate his life. Is that okay with you?"

"I don't know, Tony. I feel so sad that I can't imagine ever feeling anything else. I like the idea of celebrating his life, but I don't know when I'll be ready to do that." She pauses, and almost smiles. "I know what your father would say. He would want you to have the barbecue for him, since he can't be here to do it himself." She starts to cry again. "If you and Joshua want to do it," she whispers, "then go ahead." She goes back into her room.

"What do you think, Isa?"

"I don't know how to barbecue."

"Don't worry. Dad taught me everything."

"Okay. If you can handle that, I'll do whatever I can. I know he'd like it."

～

By evening, Umar has written up a list of people to invite. It's long.

"I'll call a few of our relatives and have them pass the word. I'd like you to call some of his friends—I've written the names down over here—and let them know. Tomorrow, we can go buy what we need."

"Are you sure you want to do this?"

"Remember? Dad told you he always has a big barbecue around the middle of July. He loved it. Everyone came. He'd stand over there next to the grill, in his apron, holding his tongs and laughing at somebody's joke. He started the tradition. It's up to us now."

I make the calls, then go to check on Aisha. She smiled a little today, out at the overlook, but when we came back to the house she went to bed. I don't think she threw up at all today.

I sit on the bed and stroke her cheek. She opens her eyes.

"Hi there. How are you doing?"

"Better, I guess. I haven't thrown up. Maybe I just have to figure out what I can eat."

"I think so. And it should get better in a month or two."

She turns and looks at me. "You've been through this before, haven't you?"

"Yes, with Michael." And Jeremy and Jennifer. Every time Heather threw up, my stomach tightened because I knew it meant another mouth to feed. That was so long ago. I lived in a different world then.

She looks away. "So it's not special to you, is it?"

I hold her hand. "It is very special, because you're very special. This is our first baby. And it's all going to be new, and different, and special, because I'm with you. And I love you so much."

I lie down with her, and hold her. We haven't been this close since The Doc got sick.

❧

Umar, Marcus, and I go shopping on Thursday. We have to go to a few places to get everything on Umar's list. In each store, someone comes up to Umar to talk about Dad. I never imagined that one man could touch the lives of so many people. But, he was The Doc.

While we're out, I buy a bottle of prenatal vitamins for Aisha. That should help, at least until she gets in to see a doctor.

When we get back, Umar marinates the meat. I watch. I know Pakistani cooking, and pancakes. I'd like to learn Dad's barbecue secrets, too.

On Friday, Umar and I go to the Islamic center for the weekly prayer. Mustapha greets us afterwards.

"Assalaamu alaikum. I was so sorry to hear about your father, Umar. I met him just that once, at the wedding. They say he was a good man."

"Yes, he was. Can we sit for a while? I have some questions."

We go to a corner of the mosque and sit with Mustapha for the next hour. We ask him about life, death, and mourning. At the end of an hour, Umar smiles. He hasn't smiled since the night Dad died. "Thank you, brother. You've helped me."

"I hope so. We need to remember that life is a struggle. For those who believe, death brings peace."

"Then I think he's at peace."

❧

Umar puts us all to work on Saturday morning—all except Sharon, of course. She's still very quiet. She needs more time. Aisha and I can find comfort in each other's arms. But her comfort is gone, and she's alone.

People start coming at one. Umar is out in the backyard, in Dad's apron, carrying Dad's tongs, and greeting the guests. Sharon stays inside.

There's laughter again, cautious at first, as the guests remember Dad. There are so many stories. As Marcus walks through the crowd, people come up to him and tell him things he never knew about the man who brought him through his first fourteen years. He smiles.

Aisha stays by my side. We greet everyone and share our good news. She sips a little white soda, and eats a little chicken. When she gets tired or nauseous, she sits down, and people come to sit with her.

Sharon's parents come late. Grandma looks around. Then she walks straight over to Aisha. "Where's my daughter?"

"She's inside, Grandma. She didn't want to come out."

"I'll go talk to her." Grandma heads for the back door.

Grandpa sits with us. "I heard our little Angela is going to be a mother."

"That's right, Grandpa. Sometime next March, I think."

"Did your daddy know?"

"Yes, I told him."

"Good. I know that made him happy. He knew he would live on, through you and your brothers, and through that baby."

Grandma stays inside with Sharon for a long time. Finally they come walking out together. Grandpa gets up to meet them. He puts his arms around his youngest daughter.

"Hi, Dad. I'm glad you're here." She smiles at him, but the tears start again. "Oh, Dad, what am I going to do?"

He holds her while she cries into his shoulder. "You're going to be okay, baby."

❧

We leave on Sunday afternoon.

"I'll be back next weekend, Mom," Umar says as we head out to the car. "Just think about coming to Chicago. I talked with Grandpa about it yesterday."

"I know, Tony. He told me I should go to be with my children. He said your father isn't in this house. He's in our children." She touches their faces, one by one. "He's right." They all hug. I watch. That's something I can't be a part of. But our child is a part of Sharon and The Doc.

"I love you all so much, and I want to live with you and share in your lives, but it's still not easy for me to just pick up and leave. I'll think about it. Give me another week or two to decide."

There are more hugs and kisses. We drive away, leaving Sharon and Marcus standing alone in the driveway. They look so small.

Umar drives while I sit in the backseat with Aisha. She leans against me, her head on my shoulder. As we head out of Moline, she whispers, "Jamal."

"What?"

"Oh, I was just thinking. If it's a boy, I'd like to name him Jamal Ismail."

"Jamal Ismail? Why?"

"After my father. It's not an exact match, but it almost sounds like Jim. What do you think?"

"Jamal Ismail Adams. I like it."

We're quiet most of the way back. Halfway there, Aisha puts her head on my lap and falls asleep. I stare at her, sleeping peacefully, and stroke her cheek. She is so much more precious to me now. Not just because of the baby. Now I know how precious life is.

As we near Chicago, Umar glances back at us.

"I've been thinking, Isa. Life is too short to spend it alone."

"Why don't you talk to Ismail? I bet he knows just the right woman for you."

He's quiet for a long time. The traffic is heavier as we get closer to the city. He takes the exit that leads to our apartment, and signals left. While we're sitting at the stoplight, he nods. "Yes, I think I might just do that."

He walks with us up to our apartment. "I'd better be going."

"Don't you want to come in?"

"No, I have to get ready for work tomorrow. And I might give Ismail a call."

"Good."

The minute we get inside, Aisha falls into the couch.

"It feels like ten years since I've been home."

"That's how it felt to me when I was here without you."

"It is so good to be back. All I want to do is curl up in our bed and take a nap. Do you want to join me?"

"Not now. We need to go somewhere first."

"Where?"

"We're going to go see my mother. I have to make things right with her, while I still have the chance."

On our way to her house, I stop to buy some daisies. They're her favorite.

Evelyn: Finding Peace

"We have enjoined on man kindness to his parents:
In pain did his mother bear him,
and in pain did she give him birth."
- Qur'an (Surah Al Ahqaf (46), Ayah 15)

When I leave the courthouse, I don't feel good about what I have just done. But it was necessary.

My testimony was strong enough to prevent Joshua from gaining custody of the children. Heather's lawyer built a strong case, with the intent of portraying Heather as the victim of Joshua's manipulations, but I believe my testimony "put the nail in the coffin." If a man's own mother cannot trust him, then who can?

After Joshua's visit to my office, I had some doubts about testifying. I still believed the children were better off with Heather, but I was touched by Joshua's change in demeanor. He no longer slouched, and when he spoke to me, it was with confidence rather than defiance. I was thinking about speaking with Heather's lawyer, telling him I wanted to soften the blow of my testimony. I would state, truthfully, that Heather was the better parent of the two, but if asked, I would have to confess that I was impressed with the changes I had seen in Joshua.

I changed my mind one afternoon, right before Christmas, when Heather showed up at my office, crying. She said she had to speak with me. It was urgent. I closed the door and postponed my next meeting.

"Joshua came to see me today," she said.

I was surprised. I knew Joshua was about to be married. I wondered why, after all this time, he would return to the apartment he had once shared with Heather.

"He came to the door, begging to talk to me. He said that our divorce was a mistake. He was thinking about calling off his engagement. He wanted to know if I would take him back."

That sounded like Joshua. A few days away from getting married, and feeling restless.

"I told him no. I told him to go away and leave me alone. But then he forced his way into the apartment and . . ." She stops, crying harder.

"What is it, Heather? What did he do?"

"He tried to force himself on me. I fought him and pushed him away. I had to threaten to call the police before he would leave. He tried to rape me."

My heart dropped. I held Heather, consoling her as she sobbed in my arms. I asked her if she wanted to press charges. After she stopped crying, she said, "No. I don't want to publicize it. It's too embarrassing. But I have to make sure that he never gets close to the kids."

I tried to convince her to press charges, but she refused. I did persuade her to take out a restraining order against him. At that moment, I became more determined than ever to help present the strongest case possible against my son in court.

And I did. He looked beaten. He just sat there, staring into space, as I chronicled his misdeeds. We had agreed not to bring up the attempted rape unless it was necessary. It wasn't.

His wife had a blank expression on her face. I felt so very sorry for her. I'm sure she didn't know what to expect when she married him.

As I left the courtroom, I knew I had done my job. I said what I had to say to make sure Joshua will never gain custody of his children.

The hearing is over. I made my choice. And I am satisfied that I did what I had to do. I'm settling in for a night of television when the doorbell rings. It's Brad.

"How did it go?"

"The children are safe. Joshua will not be granted custody. The official judgment may take another ninety days, but I could read the expression on the face of that judge."

"How did he take it?"

"How am I supposed to know? He didn't look happy, I can tell you that. That new wife of his didn't look happy, either. I think she'll have some questions for him when they get home. I hope she realizes what kind of person he is before they have any children together."

"Mom, there's something I need to tell you. Back in December, when Beth and I asked you to take care of Kyle, we didn't just go out of town. We went to Joshua's wedding."

"You did what? After I expressly told you not to? How could you think of associating with him after what he's done? As far as I'm concerned, he's no longer a member of this family."

"I needed to hear his side of the story. I talked with him before the ceremony and he told me he didn't do it. He did go there, he admits that, and he parked across the street. He did touch Heather, in what he called a moment of weakness, but he never went into the apartment. And he never attacked her."

"And you believed him? What about that 'moment of weakness'? Did he clarify that for you? He had a 'weakness,' that's for certain. If I had my way that 'moment' would have landed him in jail, but Heather refuses to press charges. She has been very brave throughout this entire ordeal."

"Are you sure she's telling the truth?"

"I don't have any reason to doubt her. She was visibly shaken. And you know Joshua. After everything else he's done, isn't this just the next step in his depravity?"

"I don't believe her, Mom. I believe Joshua."

"Then I don't want to talk to you right now. I did what I had to do for the sake of those poor children."

"If you say so. I'll leave. But I think one day you'll regret this."

He walks out, and I return to my program.

❧

Heather continues to bring the children over at least once a week. It is wonderful watching them grow. Michael is such a capable little man now. He is getting so tall, too. Jeremy is still very quiet. I worry about him sometimes. Some children are more vulnerable than others, and I am concerned that he has been more negatively affected by the divorce. He should grow out of it with time. There is no telling what would have happened to him if his tender nature had been exposed to Joshua's evil. He is better off this way.

Jennifer is, of course, a little princess. She loves to talk, and always wants to dress in pink. Most of all, she expects to be the center of attention. In that, she is seldom disappointed.

One morning, I see an ad in the Tribune about a special puppet show in town. I know the children will love it, so I call for tickets. I tell Heather about it when she comes over later in the day.

I whisper, not wanting the children to hear, even though they're all in another room. "They'll just love it. But I want to keep it a surprise."

"Oh, Evie, we won't be able to make it."

"Why not?"

She hesitates, and looks away. "The kids will be with Joshua that weekend."

"What?" I rarely scream, but this time my voice echoes through the kitchen. "What are you talking about? You are going to let that pervert see the children?"

"Be quiet. They'll hear you."

I lower my voice, but I'm boiling inside. "How could you, Heather? I know the judge would have ruled against him."

"Yes, he probably would have. But I met with Joshua and his new wife at their apartment yesterday. We made a deal."

"A deal? These are your children, not pieces of property. How can you hand them over so casually? I thought you cared about them."

"I do. You know that."

"Heather, whatever else you are, you have always been a good mother. Tell me what is going on."

She turns away. "I lied."

"You lied? About what?"

"Joshua didn't attack me. I made it up."

I feel faint.

"I had to. I needed something to keep him quiet. I was afraid his lawyer would find out about my job at the Lion's Den and about Bryan spending the night at my place. If that had come out in court, I might have lost the kids."

"You've let that boyfriend of yours spend the night at the apartment when the children are there?"

"Yes, a few times. I have needs, too."

"Get out."

"If I leave now, you will never see the kids again."

"Don't give me that, Heather. I am sick of all your threats. I have always given in to you because of the children. I sat in that court and testified against my own son because of your lies, and because I was afraid you wouldn't let me see the children. It has to stop. Now."

"Evie, I'm warning you."

"I'm warning you, Heather. Your parents have cut you off, and I am the last person you have on your side. If you want, we can keep being friends. I like you, most of the time. We've had a lot of fun together. But if you keep those children away from me, I will be the one to take you to court. And I can prove that I am better suited to raise those children than either you or Joshua. I'm sure you don't want that."

"No," she says softly, "I don't."

"I feel like kicking you out of my house for what you have done to my son. I won't. I had a part in it, too, because I believed you. And he did bring some of it on himself with his foolishness. But you had better watch yourself from now on. Remember, I can afford the best lawyer in Chicago."

"I know."

"Good." I smile. "Michael, Jeremy, Jenny, come in here. The cookies are done."

Michael comes first. "Is everything okay, Gramma?"

"Everything's fine, Michael. Now sit down, and I'll get you some milk to go with your cookies."

❧

In the morning, I call Brad.

"You were right. Heather lied about Joshua. She told me."

"I thought so. Now what are you going to do?"

"What can I do? Heather met with Joshua, and she has agreed to let him see the children twice a month. The issue has been settled."

"Are you going to talk to Joshua?"

"No, I don't think so. Not yet."

"Why not?"

"Because it was too easy for me to believe he did that to Heather."

Chris still doesn't know about the lie. I've known for some time now, but have just never found the right opportunity to tell him. It's not the type of conversation you want to bring up over dinner.

It comes out one evening while we're having a barbecue at Brad's house. Michael is practicing his soccer moves.

"Hey, big guy, you're getting to be pretty good."

"Yeah, I know. We have a game on Saturday. Guess what, Uncle Chris. My dad is coming to see me play."

Chris's face turns red. I can tell he's trying to stay calm. "Really? That's interesting."

"Yeah, I can't wait."

"Well, keep on practicing. I have to talk to your mom."

"Okay, Uncle Chris."

He grabs Heather's arm and drags her inside to the kitchen. I follow.

"What are you thinking? Joshua shouldn't be within ten miles of those kids, or you."

"I've dropped the restraining order, Chris. It was a lie."

"What are you saying?"

"Joshua didn't attack me. I made it up, to keep him from getting the kids."

Chris hasn't cursed since he found Jesus.

"You're telling me that you made it up? How in the hell could you do something like that?"

Melinda gasps. "Chris, settle down."

"Don't tell me when the hell to settle down. What is all this crap, Heather? What are you trying to pull?"

"I just wanted to keep the kids. That's all."

"Dammit, Heather, you don't know what you did." He slams

his fist on the counter, and stomps into another part of the house. I don't see him again for the rest of the evening.

"Heather," says Melinda, "Chris and Joshua were finally starting to like one another. Why would you say something like that if it wasn't true?"

"I did what I thought I had to do, Melinda. Now lay off."

Chris calls me a few days later. It's the first time I've spoken with him since he stormed out of the kitchen.

"Hi Mom. I think we need to talk."

"Don't worry." I laugh. "I won't think anything less of you because you cursed a little. And I won't tell anyone at the Bible college about it."

"This is serious. We need to talk about Joshua."

"Chris, if you want to keep trying to convert him, go ahead. Just leave me out of your holy wars."

"That's not it. When I was testifying at the custody hearing, Joshua's lawyer accused me of being biased against him because he's a Muslim. I responded that my own religious beliefs require me to be truthful. And I didn't lie. Not exactly. But I didn't tell the full truth, because I was convinced Joshua shouldn't have the children. Now I'm not sure what to think."

"No, you didn't lie. You told the truth as you knew it then. I have spent many nights thinking about my testimony, and not because I'm worried about my soul. I said some terrible things about your brother, because I believed Heather."

"Do you remember when we were kids? Joshua and I fought constantly. It started with the time I dared him to climb up on the roof."

"You dared him? I didn't know that. You told me you tried to stop him."

He clears his throat. "I know. That was before my conversion. Anyway, I didn't think he'd be dumb enough to do it. As soon as they took off his cast, he beat me up for it. We haven't stopped fighting since then, except for that one time, when he came to my house and we actually talked and listened to one another. I didn't want to testify against him, but I felt I had no choice. I thought I was doing what was best for the children."

"We both wanted what was best for them. What about the holy wars? Are still worried about his soul?"

"Of course. He's wrong, and he needs to come back to the church. The question is, how can I take care of my brother's soul if I don't treat him like my brother?"

"Don't get theological on me, Chris. I am glad you care about your brother. It used to tear me up the way you boys fought."

"I'm sorry for all that, Mom. I hope my kids never give me trouble."

"I don't think you'll have any problems with Ruthie, but you had better keep an eye on Isaiah. That boy has a mischievous look."

"He's already keeping me on my toes."

"What do you plan to do to 'treat Joshua like your brother'? Have you called him?"

"Not yet. I don't know what to say."

Neither do I.

Our feelings about Heather have changed too. It takes Chris a month to be able to stay in the same room with her. Melinda is the peacemaker. She invites Heather to our Fourth of July celebration at their house and concentrates all day on maintaining peace and harmony in the family.

Heather and I continue to see each other, at least once a week, but it's different now. Without the children, there would be no reason for me to see her again.

I have tried to understand why she did it. Later, she tells me what really happened between Joshua and her, and how she felt rejected by him. Would I have done the same to Sam? Maybe. If I had thought it would keep him away from Cynthia? Probably. Still, she told such a terrible lie about my son. The fruit of my womb. I know now that I have to choose Joshua.

I feel guilty about the way we've all treated him. The way I've treated him. He has made many mistakes, but he does seem to be getting his life in order now. I think it is time to bring him back into the family.

I called him a few times last week, but all I got was the answering machine. I left a message the first two times, asking him to call me. So far, though, he hasn't responded. I wouldn't blame him for not wanting to talk to me.

～

It's a Sunday night. I'm watching television. I had quite a bit of work to do this past week, and it looks like it won't ease up next week. The television helps me relax. I'm becoming involved in a crime drama when the doorbell rings.

It's Joshua and . . . what is the name of that girl he married?

"Hi, Mom. How are you?"

"Hello, Joshua. I'm fine."

"These are for you." He hands me a beautiful bouquet of daisies.

"Thank you." I wonder if he knows they're my favorite.

"Can we come in?"

"Oh, of course, come on in. I'm sorry. I had a long week at work, and I've been sitting here thinking about a report I have to get out tomorrow. Come in, please."

"Hello, Mrs. Adams."

"Hello." What is her name? It's something unusual.

"Mom, we just came back from Moline. Aisha's father died last week."

Aisha, that's it.

"Oh yes, I was so sorry to hear about that. Heather told me, a couple of days ago. How old was he?"

"Fifty-six."

"He was still fairly young. What a shame. Your mother must be heartbroken."

"Yes, she is."

"Please, give her my condolences."

"I will, thank you."

I turn off the television. "Why don't you two sit over there, on the couch."

We all sit down and look at one another. What else is there to say?

"Um, Mom, I had the chance to spend some time with Dr. Evans, Aisha's father, before he died. I've only known him since last November, but he was like a father to me. The only Dad I've ever had."

I hope he doesn't start talking about Sam. Some of our earliest arguments started with Sam. It was my fault, he said, he didn't have a father.

"The point is, when Dr. Evans died, I realized how important we are to one another. All of us. We thought Dr. Evans would be around for a long time yet. We spent the last few days letting him know much he meant to us.

"These last few days, I've been thinking about you. I know I've given you a hard time. And I'm sorry, Mom. I'm sorry for all the times I hurt you or made you worry. I came, we came, because I want us to be close. I know, now, that life is so short. We can't waste it by arguing, or ignoring one another."

Is this Joshua? The boy who pushed me? The man who walked out on his children? The one who, in my mind, could have attacked Heather?

"Thank you, Joshua. I don't know what to say."

"Please, just say that you'll forgive me. That's all I need from you."

I look into his eyes. I haven't seen that look since he was a little boy and I caught him jumping on the furniture. It has been so long.

"Mom?"

"I don't know. All these years, I have had to put up with the trouble you brought me. Whether it was emergency meetings with teachers, or your shotgun marriage to Heather, you have brought me so much grief. And it didn't stop when you became a Muslim. You came here, with the strange clothes and the beard, and bragged about how much you had changed. But then you left us again. And you took Heather to court. And, I just don't know."

"And you believed Heather's lie about me."

"What was I supposed to think? I could imagine you doing that to her because you have always been so self-centered. I have never been able to imagine you coming here to ask for my forgiveness. And, to tell you the truth, I don't know if I'm ready."

He leans forward and puts his head in his hands. I'm still not used to the quieter Joshua. A few years ago, he would have been in a rage by now.

"Mrs. Adams, I have known Joshua for a little over a year. He has always been kind and loving toward me. I know about the old, wild Joshua, but he's different now."

"Do you know about the time he was with Heather?"

"Yes, I do. And when I found out, I was very hurt and angry. But I love him, and I know he loves me, so eventually I was able to forgive him. Since then, he has been a wonderful husband. He held my father's hand in the hospital, and he has always been by my side. I know he will be a terrific father to our baby."

"Another baby? He already has three children he barely sees." I look at her closely. "You don't look pregnant."

"That's because we waited until after we were married. I'm not due until March. Joshua is different now. Look, Mrs. Adams, we don't know each other, but I have to ask you something. My parents took Joshua in with open arms. My father was always very protective of me, but he allowed Joshua to marry me and become part of our family. If my parents could accept him, why can't you?"

Why? Because he has hurt me a thousand times. Because he has embarrassed me in front of my friends. Because he is different, and I have never understood him. Because if he hadn't been born, Sam wouldn't have left me.

No, that's not it. He was only a baby. I can't blame him for what Sam did. Can I? Have I?

"It's complicated. We have so many years of conflict between us. I think it's too late to start over."

"It's not too late, Mom. It's only too late when we're dead. And none of us knows how long we have."

He gets up. Will he throw something? Or grab Aisha and leave, slamming the door behind him?

He hugs me. And I remember that time in the office, before the lie came between us. That time in the office, we were almost there. But I believed the lie for so long. It's hard to know now what is true.

I feel his tears on my neck.

"Mom, please forgive me. I'm sorry for everything. Please, Mom."

Before I know it, I'm hugging him back. My baby boy. My Joshua.

"Let me look at you, Joshua." He pulls away. "On the day you were born, you looked at me straight in the eye. There was a connection between us. On that day, I thought we would always be inseparable. Look at me again."

Over the years, I have seen many things in those eyes. I've seen guilt, anger, even hate. Until today, I haven't seen the sweet, innocent eyes of my newborn son. Until now.

"I forgive you. I love you, Joshua." *Even when I hated you, I loved you.*

We hold each other for a long time. He has been lost to me for so many years. I finally have my son back.

～

I forgave Joshua. Now I have to ask him to forgive me.

Joshua and Aisha are coming here for dinner tonight. I want to get to know her better. She seems like such a sweet girl. I'll have to remember to tell her to call me Evie.

I have been thinking, these last few days, about when Sam left. I realize, now, that his betrayal was the single most significant event of my life. In the early days, I even talked about my life that way. Before Sam left. After Sam left. I haven't done that for a long time, but the feeling remains. I have never completely gotten over the pain.

Before Sam left, I was contented. Or would resigned be a better word? We had our problems, but who didn't? I thought I could make him change. I was determined to make our marriage work.

After Sam left, I was angry and bitter. He had rejected me. And Joshua, my poor baby. I took much of my anger out on him. I never hit him, not even later when, perhaps, I should have. But there were many days when I did not want to touch him. And he knew it.

When they come here tonight, I will ask for his forgiveness. Only then, I think, can we truly move on.

I wait until after we are finished eating. During dinner, Aisha has been telling me about her teaching assignment. She has already started gathering supplies to decorate her classroom, and she has many ideas to help the children become excited about learning. I know she will be an excellent teacher.

When we're finished eating, she helps me clear the table. Then she starts to do the dishes.

"Oh, no, Aisha, please don't. I want you to relax."

"It's no problem at all, Mrs. Adams. I'll be done in a few minutes."

"First of all, I want you to call me Evie. We're family now. I'm sorry it took me so long to welcome you."

She turns off the water, wipes her hands, and hugs me. "That's okay. Thank you, Evie." She turns back to the sink.

"Not now, Aisha. I need to talk with Joshua and you. Please. Come sit down."

I look at Joshua and reach for his hand.

"A few days ago, you came here and asked for my forgiveness. Now it's my turn. Will you forgive me, Joshua?"

"Of course, Mom. Why do you even ask?"

"I have been unfair to you. Believing the lie was part of it, but it goes much deeper than that. I realize now that I've always blamed you for Sam leaving us. These last few days, I have thought hard about all those times when you were small and I wasn't there for you. Please forgive me, Joshua."

"I already have forgiven you, Mom. I knew you blamed me, and I was angry about that for a long time. But with the help of some special people," he looks at Aisha, and smiles, "I came to realize that my anger was preventing me from growing up. Sam made his choices, and all of us were hurt by what he did. But life really is too short. We have to learn how to move on."

I reach over and touch his face. "I'm proud of you, Joshua. You really are a man."

He comes closer and kisses me softly on the forehead. I think I can get used to the beard.

We had such a nice evening.

He tells me they will be renting a house. They've found one with five bedrooms in Lincolnwood. There will be enough room for all of Aisha's family, with an extra room for the children when they come. He's concerned about Aisha's mother being alone. And by living together, he says, they can take care of each other. I think it is a lovely idea.

Aisha is a different kind of girl. The kind who wouldn't have given Joshua a second look when he was in high school. The kind I always hoped he would bring home.

Their baby will have two parents who love one another. Like Kyle, Ruthie, and Isaiah, he'll know the security of a happy home. Michael, Jeremy, and Jennifer will never have that.

Brad, Chris, and Joshua didn't have that, either. Sam never loved me. I wish I had understood that sooner. Before I let him walk all over me. Before I brought my three children into the world.

If I could go back in time, I know now what I would change. I would be careful to marry someone who could love me for a lifetime. I am so happy all of my sons have finally found that kind of love.

Joshua came by the office yesterday morning to take me out for lunch. We had such a nice talk, just the two of us. First, he told me more about the days and months when he was gone and I didn't see him at all. For the first time, I learned about Abdul-Qadir and all he has done for Joshua. Now I understand what he meant, that day after he came back from Pakistan. He was almost ready to be a man, but I didn't see it then. He still keeps in touch with Abdul-Qadir, and he hopes to take Aisha and their child to

Pakistan to meet him and his family one day.

He has so many ideas, so many plans. He told me all about the house, and his college classes, and his job, and his time with his children, and the new baby. He also told me a little about Islam. It's been years since I've thought about religion, but I sat there and listened politely. It still seems a little strange to me, but I can see it has given him peace.

Before we parted, he told me he wants to tackle life, not just live it.

That would explain a lot about Joshua.

❧

It is a Saturday in the middle of July. Michael's team won their game this morning. After the game, we all go over to Joshua's house for the barbecue.

This is no ordinary barbecue, he's told me. It's a tradition started by Aisha's father. He sounds like a wonderful person. I wish I had met him. I should have gone to the wedding.

I know now that Joshua and Aisha truly have forgiven me. In the last several months, we have been able to repair our relationship. Now, it's almost as if we have always been close. But I will always remember. I almost lost the chance to know my youngest son, and share in his life.

They let me be there in the room when the baby was born. Sharon was there too, of course. It must have been difficult for her to see her daughter in so much pain. Aisha was brave, though, as I knew she would be. I was so proud of Joshua. He massaged Aisha and fed her ice chips, while whispering words of love and encouragement. I have six other grandchildren, but it was such a special moment when Jamal finally entered the world, kicking and screaming.

This morning, Joshua brought the children to the soccer game. They spend Friday nights with him now. He was there on the sidelines, screaming like crazy and handing out balloons. He tied a blue balloon to the baby's car seat.

Heather arrived at the game with Bryan. Joshua knows who

he is. They nodded at one another and turned back to the game. Heather and Bryan were practically inseparable. I know she wants to marry him, but I don't think he's that serious about her. She has decided to let Joshua and Aisha have the children every weekend now. I think it's because she wants to spend more time with Bryan. I hope she can get her life together, too. She is studying art at the college, and Aisha helped her get a job with the university. I'm glad she's not working at that awful place any longer. I just hope she won't throw her life away on the wrong man again.

Joshua is in the kitchen now, making potato salad. I peek in through the back door to see him moving around and mixing ingredients like an expert. The last thing I thought I'd ever see is Joshua in a kitchen.

Umar is in the backyard, grilling up some chicken and hamburgers. I have enjoyed getting to know him these last several months. I can tell he has a great deal of inner strength. Joshua tells me he learned how to be strong from his father. I wish I had known how important a father can be in the life of a boy.

Umar's new wife, Safa, stands close to him. They've only been married for about two months now, and she's still a little quiet around us, but she seems to be very pleasant.

Joshua told me that her brother brought her to live with him in Chicago after her first husband was killed in a convenience store robbery. Safa and her first husband came to this country several years ago from Bangladesh. They had one daughter, Raheema, who is about two years older than Jennifer. Right now, the two girls are chasing each other around the yard.

There is a wonderful aroma coming from the barbecue grill. "Umar, your barbecued chicken is the best I have ever tasted. What is your secret?"

He smiles, and winks at Safa. "Well, Evie, if I told you, it wouldn't be a secret, would it?"

I laugh. "Safa, your husband is an interesting man."

"Yes. I know." She smiles shyly and looks up into his eyes.

I'm starting to feel out of place, so I quietly slip away. They don't seem to notice.

In all the time I've known Umar, something about him has bothered me. He seems so familiar. It's not so much the way he looks, but his voice. I'm certain I have heard that voice before, long before I actually met him. But I simply cannot place it. The odd thing is, Brad, Chris, and Heather have all said the same thing. I mentioned this to Umar once, but he just smiled and changed the subject.

Brad and Beth couldn't make it to the game, but they said they would come for the barbecue. They should be here soon.

Chris and Melinda came. Everything was fine until halftime. Then Chris and Joshua started up again. It happens every time. All they do is discuss religion. I think each of them knows it will never end. They are both so stubborn, and so solid in their faiths, but they both keep trying, just the same.

Now Chris is going over to talk with Umar. Umar has refused to get involved in the holy wars. They do share a common interest, though, in social causes. They will probably stand there, drinking their root beer, until the hamburgers are done, trying to find a way to end hunger or help troubled youth. Their approaches are different, but their philosophies are surprisingly very similar.

It's getting hot outside. I go into the family room to rest a minute. Aisha is in here, nursing the baby.

Jennifer bounces into the room and stops to look at the baby. Ruthie and Raheema are close behind. "That's my baby brother," says Jennifer. She pats his arm and bounces away.

She is still the princess. I wonder how she'll feel if Joshua and Aisha ever have a girl.

The baby is finished nursing now. He's lying on Aisha's lap, cooing. "That's our precious little boy. Yes he is." Aisha talks to him gently and plays with his wiggling toes.

"Can I have him, Aisha?"

"Sure you can, Evie. There you go."

He is a beautiful baby. He has Joshua's hair and Aisha's rich brown complexion. Also her smile. And there's a little dimple in his chin.

Jamilah Kolocotronis

"He's getting so big. He must be a good eater."

"Yes, he is. I think I'll start him on cereal soon."

"I remember starting Joshua on cereal at this age. He was a good eater, too. Are you a good eater like your daddy? Are you?"

When Joshua was this age, I thought Sam and I had a chance to save our marriage. I still had a husband, and I still paid attention to my baby.

I look into the eyes of my grandson, who looks so much like my baby boy of long ago.

"How's our little Jamal? How's Gramma's baby boy? You're getting so big. I'll have to start reading to you soon." He babbles and grabs hold of my finger.

I have to admit I was concerned when Joshua first told me he planned to marry someone of a different race. But Aisha is such a lovely girl. During this past year, I've come to know Aisha's family as well. They are very good people. Now I am proud to call them my friends.

I was also worried about having biracial grandchildren, but Jamal truly is a beautiful baby. When I look into his dark eyes, I don't see a mixed race child. I see my grandson, whom I love.

My old prejudices were part of my old life, which is slowly slipping away from me. I have felt better about everything since the day I asked Joshua for forgiveness, because that was the day I finally got over Sam. For twenty-five years I carried the hurt around with me, and that hurt overwhelmed me. Now I am finally free, and it feels so good. I almost feel sorry for Sam. He's missing out on his children and grandchildren. I suppose that is his punishment for the pain he caused.

I carry the baby into the kitchen, where Joshua is mixing the potato salad. He stops to grin at his son. "Assalaamu alaikum, big guy." Jamal babbles and reaches for his father, grabbing hold of his beard. Joshua takes the baby from me and flies him around the room like an airplane before returning him safely to my arms. Jamal laughs. Joshua mixes the potato salad and makes funny faces for his son.

Joshua has always loved his children. I know that now. But he rarely played with Michael, Jeremy, and Jennifer when they were small. He was almost always on edge. I know he's trying to make up for his lost years with them now. Just as I'm trying to make up for my lost years with him.

Frisky rubs against my leg. I step away. I still don't like animals, but I am trying to get used to Frisky. I should have let Joshua keep that kitten. It might have made a difference.

Sharon is taking the pies out of the oven. She looks over at the baby and grins. "There's our little Jamal. How are you, sweetie pie?"

"They're done?"

"It looks like it. They smell delicious. I want your recipe for that apple pie. It tastes so good."

"How about if I give that to you when Umar gives me the recipe for his marinade?"

"You'll never get that from him, Mom. That's a special recipe he learned from The Doc." Joshua finishes the potato salad and carries it out the back door.

"Then I guess I'll have to wait for Jamal to tell me. You'll tell Gramma, won't you, little guy?" The pies are cooling. Sharon and I sit at the kitchen table. She pours the lemonade.

"Thank you. Joshua has told me so much about Dr. Evans. I know he also calls him Dad. You and your husband gave something to Joshua that Sam and I couldn't. You showed him the love of a real family. And I have never told you how grateful I am to you for that."

"I've been very happy to have Joshua in our family, especially since Jim died. In those first few days, when the rest of us were overcome by our grief, it was Joshua who helped us get through it. You might almost say he rescued us."

"I have seen such a change in my son. I think your husband was one of the main reasons for that. He must have been a special man."

"He was, very special. I wish he could be here to see them. He would have loved this, seeing the way the kids are managing things now. Tony carrying on his tradition. And our little Jamal. I still miss him so much. Every single day."

I wonder how it feels to have loved someone that way.

"It's been just about a year now, hasn't it?"

"Yes. It was a year ago last week. I went back to visit his grave a few days ago. It's so hard, still, knowing that he's there, and that I'll never be able to see him or hold him again. But I did talk to him. I like to believe he heard me, just like he heard us all after his surgery when he was lying there so still. I know he wouldn't leave me all alone." She wipes her eye. "There are still days when I don't know how to go on living without him. He's been my strength all these years." She puts down her lemonade and stares into space. Tears run slowly down her cheeks.

I offer her a napkin and pat her hand. "I think you've been very strong."

She wipes away the tears. "I don't have much choice, do I? I need the kids, but the kids need me, too. Especially Marcus. He's still so young."

"How is Marcus now? I know he's had a hard time adjusting."

"His grades started to come up again by the end of the year. His attitude is improving, too. He wanted to go back to visit the grave on Father's Day. We all went. We gave Marcus his own private time to talk to him. And afterwards we went up to Sunset Park. After that, he seemed a little calmer.

"I couldn't believe it when he started talking back. A couple of times he even screamed at me." She shakes her head. "I sent him to a counselor, but I think what has helped him the most throughout the year is the time he's spent with Tony and Joshua. They've been here to take him aside and talk with him when he gets upset, and several times they've taken him on outings, just the three of them. They're trying so hard to fill Jim's shoes." She smiles a little. "They are quite a team."

"Yes, they certainly are. I was so proud of Joshua when he worked with Tony to get this house. I think it's wonderful, the way you all live together and help one another."

"It is. Especially now that I have my new daughter-in-law, and little Raheema. Did you know that Michael and Jeremy share a room with Marcus now, so that Jennifer and Raheema can be together? Marcus enjoys being with the boys, and he loves being the big brother for a change. I still miss Moline sometimes, but I can go back to visit as often as I want. It's good to live here with my kids. And our baby Jamal. He's so cute, yes he is." Jamal smiles and coos.

"What about your nursing career? Have you thought about going back?"

"I took a leave of absence from my job in Moline, but I could never go back there. I worked at the hospital where Jim died, and the memories are still too painful. Angela wants to teach at least one more year, so I've agreed to stay home and take care of Jamal while she teaches." She pauses. "I always loved my work, but Jim's death made it so much more personal. Eventually, I would like to work again somewhere in the health care field. But not yet. We'll see."

"When you are ready you could talk to Beth. I'm sure you could get a job at the hospital where she works."

"Yes, that would be nice. But not yet."

We've finished our lemonade. I take the baby back to Aisha and help Sharon carry the pies outside. Brad and Beth are here. Kyle and Isaiah are chasing Jeremy. They all end up in a pile, giggling.

Aisha follows us out with the baby. She exchanges smiles with Joshua before going over to talk with Beth and Melinda. Beth and Melinda got together and hosted a baby shower for Aisha in January, and they are always happy to offer advice to the new mother. They've also shared some of Kyle and Isaiah's hand-me-downs. Aisha and Melinda have their own version of the holy wars, but it is much more subdued. They are genuinely interested in learning from one another.

Brad, Chris, and Joshua have been playing soccer with Michael and Marcus. They've stopped now. My two oldest sons are sitting on the grass, breathing hard and sweating. Brad laughs. "I guess we can't keep up with the young guys anymore."

"Speak for yourself, old man," says Joshua. He goes out and runs around with the boys for a few more minutes, until he ends up sitting next to his brothers, panting.

"Who's old now?" says Chris.

Michael and Marcus keep the game going while my "old men" recover. "Give me a few minutes, guys," Joshua yells. "Looking good, Michael. Way to block, Marcus."

During this past year, I've watched Joshua interact with Marcus. Marcus is fifteen now. When Joshua was that age, he was completely out of control.

I was there once when Marcus yelled at his mother. I was shocked, because he seemed like such a nice young man. She had told him to turn off the video game and go upstairs to do his homework. When he refused, she told him he had to do well in high school, so his father would be proud of him. He threw down the controls and shouted that it didn't matter what he did because his father was dead. I think he was crying. I know Sharon was.

Joshua went over to Marcus and hugged him. Then they went into another room, and I suppose they talked. I saw Marcus again before I left their house that night. He didn't look happy, but he was calm. And I heard Joshua whisper to him, "She's your mother, man. You have to take care of her." He kept talking to him, softly, gently, until finally Marcus went over and gave his mother an awkward hug. I was amazed. I'm still amazed. My wild child is now the responsible man, trying to keep another child from becoming wild.

I'm still deep in thought when Joshua comes over to the food table, where I'm standing, and grabs three root beers from the ice chest. "Can I get you something to drink, Mom? Some root beer, maybe?"

"No, I'm fine. Thank you, Joshua."

I am fine. I never thought I would feel this fine again, not since the day Sam left.

As the day goes on, more friends and family arrive for the barbecue. Some of Aisha's relatives have come from Moline. I met most of them last Thanksgiving. Joshua and Umar prepared the meal last year, the turkey and all the fixings. Joshua told Aisha to sit down and relax while they did the work. He really does love her.

Dr. Evans's sisters are here, too. I think Sharon and Arlene are especially close. Arlene has come to see Sharon many times since she moved to Chicago, and once she even stopped by my house for a visit. If she is anything like her brother, I can tell why everyone loved "The Doc."

Fawad, Zainab, and their four children come by for some chicken and apple pie. Fawad says he has to get back to the restaurant soon, but he sits and visits for a while. He's the one who gave Joshua a chance to prove himself, on the same day I turned my son away. I recommend his restaurant to all my friends, but I will never be able to repay the debt I owe him.

Mahmoud and Halima are here now, too, with their little girl. Halima goes over to talk with my daughters-in-law, while Mahmoud joins my sons. I asked Joshua, several months ago, why he went to stay with Mahmoud after he left Heather. It hurt when he said that Mahmoud was the only one who would take him in. But it was the truth.

Ismail, Tariq, and Bilal have just arrived in Ismail's little red compact. The first time Joshua told me about the "guys at the house" who taught him about Islam, I pictured them as shadowy terrorists who were stealing my son's soul. When Jamal was born, I finally met them. I know, now, that they didn't destroy my son, they saved him.

Ismail always surprises me. One minute he'll be carrying on an adult conversation and the next minute he'll be running around with the children. Joshua's told me that Ismail has helped him through many rough spots.

And here I am. I never expected to be attending a barbecue with a United Nations of family and friends. But here I am.

I should have known Joshua. He always had too much energy for normal, everyday life. For so many years, he didn't know what direction to go in, and I didn't know how to show him.

I think, sometimes, about all those wasted years. I should have just let Joshua be Joshua, and loved him for who he was. I am so glad it is not too late.

Epilogue

When Jennifer Adams was thirteen years old her father sat down to have a talk with her.

"Jennifer, your brother tells me that you've been meeting a boy when you go to the movies with your friends."

"Jeremy is such a weasel. He should mind his own business."

"You have to be careful, Jennifer. You're too young to get mixed up with boys. You don't know what you're getting yourself into."

"If you and Aisha had your way, I would never be allowed to get near a boy."

"That's right. Not until you're old enough to get married."

"But I have the right to live my own life. I don't want to be a Muslim. I want to have some fun. Besides, didn't you used to go out with girls when you were my age?"

Joshua's face turned red. Jennifer laughed.

"Where did you hear that?"

"Kyle told me. He heard Uncle Brad and Aunt Beth talking about how wild you were when you were young. Did you really smoke weed? I can't imagine you being that cool."

Joshua sighed deeply. The echoes never end.

Printed in the United States
51898LVS00002BA/1-51